Slow Dancing

by

Joan Elizabeth Lloyd

Carroll & Graf Publishers, Inc.
New York

First Carroll & Graf edition 1997

Carroll & Graf Publishers, Inc.
260 Fifth Avenue
New York, NY 10001

Lloyd, Joan Elizabeth.
Slow dancing / by Joan Elizabeth Lloyd. — 1st Carroll & Graf ed.
p. cm.
ISBN 0-7867-0436-5 (trade paper)
I. Title.
PS3562.L72S58 1997 97-4260
813'.54—dc21 CIP

Manufactured in the United States of America

Slow Dancing

Other books by Joan Elizabeth Lloyd available from Carroll & Graf:

Black Satin
The Pleasures of JessicaLynn

Slow Dancing

Chapter 1

"Maggie mine," Paul Crowley's voice echoed through the phone, "please marry me."

Maggie Sullivan's laughter warmed the miles of wire between them. "Paul, you're so sweet and you know I love you, but be real." She spread her voluminous purple silk robe out on the wide satin-covered bed and pressed the phone against her ear.

"I am being real. Marry me. Or, if not, let's run away together. We'll find an island with no one there but the two of us. We'll live on fish and mangos."

Maggie pictured Paul's deep brown hair and could almost feel its softness. He was in his midthirties and had a body that told everyone he worked out and prided himself on his physique. "Lord, after a bad day that's such a tempting offer." Maggie tangled her fingers in her black curls. As she twirled one strand around her index finger, she remembered when her hair had been that color without the help of her stylist. "But sweet, you're who you are and I'm what I am."

"That doesn't matter, Maggie mine. Let's forget all that and do what makes us happy for a change."

"Paul, we've been over and over this. I'm a prostitute. A hooker. Very high priced," she added, tucking the phone between her ear and her shoulder and leaning back against her collection of primary-colored pillows. She flipped one Mondrian-print curtain from in front of the air conditioner with her toe so the fan blew more cold air in her direction. "But still a hooker. And you're a banker. Very straight."

"I don't care. I just want you." She heard his sigh.

"And what about our ages. I'll begin to collect Social Security just about the time you reach forty."

"Sweet thing," he moaned. "We were just born at the wrong time. Anyway, what difference do a few years make?"

"What are you wearing, Paul?" Maggie purred, stretching her long, shapely legs and crossing her ankles. She spread the sides of the robe and looked at her body beneath it. Still slender, with muscular thighs from working out daily, and full breasts that sagged only a bit.

"What difference does that make?"

"I just opened my robe and underneath it I'm wearing a lilac teddy. It's a smooth satiny material and I'm running my palms up and down my side right now." Maggie's hands were, indeed, rubbing the slick material.

"Oh, sweet thing," Paul groaned.

"I had my nails done today, you know," Maggie said, gazing at her hands. "They're extra long and bright red now. The color's from a series called Romance. This shade is called Slow Dancing. Like we do when we're together. That's why I chose it. Now I'm running my nails over the front of my thigh. It feels really good."

Maggie could hear Paul drag air into his lungs. "The inside of my thigh is so soft, but I'm making bright red marks with my nails." She smiled. "Talking like this always makes me hot. I wish you were here." Paul was on a business trip and was calling Maggie in New York from his hotel room in Denver.

"I do too. But . . ."

"What are you wearing?"

"Jeans and a blue shirt."

"Take them off, baby. Please." She could hear his resigned sigh. Again she had deflected the conversation. Maggie could hear the rustling of Paul moving around his room.

"I'm pulling off my jeans and shirt even as we speak. You always do this. I propose and you reject me in the nicest way possible." There was a pause, then Paul said, "Now I'm only wearing my shorts."

"What color are they? I want to be able to picture you."

"Black. With a white waistband." Paul's voice was ragged.

"Is your cock big and hard?"

"Oh, Maggie," Paul groaned. "Why do you do this to me?"

Her smile broadened. "Because I love to make you hot. It's one of the things I do best and enjoy most. Now tell me. Is it hard?"

"Yes," he groaned.

"Do you want to touch it while we talk?"

Silence.

"Tell me, Paul. Do you want to touch it? Tell Maggie."

"Yes," he whispered.

"Wrap your fingers around it and I'll slip my fingers under the crotch of this teddy and rub all those spots you know I love. Come on, baby, do it for me." After a moment she continued, "Are you touching your cock through your tight black shorts? Does it feel good? Sort of muffled through the fabric?"

"Yes."

"I'm sliding my fingers over my slit. I'm very wet." Her fingertips danced over her skin as she pulled the thin strip of fabric aside and explored her wetness. "Ummm," she purred, "it feels so good. And I love knowing that you're touching yourself, too." She stroked her clit with her index finger, listening to Paul's heavy breaths. "Yes, baby. Do it to your hard prick while I rub myself." There was a long silence during which the only sound was rapid breathing. "Do you know what I'm going to do?" Maggie asked, opening the drawer of her bedside table.

"What?" His voice was raspy and hoarse.

"I'm getting that big dildo, you know the one, the really big one that fills my pussy almost as well as your cock does." She pulled a large, flesh-colored penis from the drawer. "I'm going to rub it over my pussy while you slide your hand under the cotton of your shorts and hold your naked cock in your hand." She rubbed the artificial cock over her wet skin. "Ooh, that's cold. I'm going to push it inside. Hold your beautiful prick while I fill myself. We can pretend that you're here beside me."

Maggie heard Paul moan softly and she pushed the dildo into her cunt. "So full," she whispered. "So full of your hard shaft." She rubbed her clit faster as she moved the dildo inside her body. "I'm so close. Are you close, too?"

"Yes. Oh, yes, sweet thing."

"I'm going to come soon," she purred. "Come with me. Soon. Soon." She felt her climax building, flowing up through her, curling her toes and arching her back. "Yes," she cried as the heat flooded her body. "Yes." She could feel the clutching movements of her muscles against the artificial phallus as waves of pleasure engulfed her. "Yes."

"Yes," Paul called. "Right now."

For a while the only sound through the phone lines was panting and a few low moans. Then Maggie slowly withdrew the dildo from her body, reveling in the soft relaxation that always followed a good, hard climax. "That was so good," she said, her heartbeat slowing. "Not as good as having you here, of course."

"Oh, shit, sweet thing. I got goo all over the bedspread."

Maggie giggled. "It probably isn't the first time. It will wash. Just leave the chambermaid an extra-big tip."

"It never ceases to amaze me how easily you do that to me."

"That's what I'm good for. I love giving you pleasure, but," she said, not allowing him to interrupt, "that's not what you build a marriage on. Good sex is wonderful, but it's not enough."

"Oh, Maggie mine, it's not just good sex. We have great times together."

"I've got to go now, Paul. Call me when you get back."

"I will. Good night, and please think about marrying me."

"Good night, Paul." Maggie placed the receiver on its cradle and sighed. Maybe if I'd found someone like Paul twenty years ago, she thought, but things are as things are. She rubbed the heel of her hand up and down her breastbone trying to ease the sudden feeling of pressure. But I'm truly happy, she thought. I have regrets as everyone who is human does, but I enjoy making love and I'm well paid for it. And why not?

Maggie took a hot shower then climbed into her wide bed, already wondering what Carl would enjoy the following evening. Carl had the most creative mind. Maybe she'd use the handcuffs and spreader bar. She fell asleep, unconsciously rubbing her breastbone.

Maggie was totally confused. She was standing in a large room, wearing now a soft, flowing white garment. "What the hell . . ."

"Not exactly," a voice said through the heavy white mist that covered the ground and swirled about her waist as Maggie took a step forward.

"What's all this?" Maggie asked, her arched eyebrows almost meeting the middle. This is a very strange dream, she thought.

"You like the mist?" the woman's voice continued. "We had it added a few months ago. Gives the place a bit of atmosphere, don't you think?"

Unable to make out the speaker, Maggie took another couple of steps forward. "Real nice," she said dryly. This is the most bizarre dream I've had in a long time, she thought.

"It's not a dream, Margaret Mary."

"Lord, I haven't been called Margaret Mary since grammar school."

"That's right. Forgive me," the voice said, sounding genuinely sorry. "Maggie. Right?"

"Yes. Maggie. I hate to ask the obvious, but where am I?"

"That's a bit hard to explain," the voice continued. It was soft, melodious, and somehow soothing.

Maggie thought she should be afraid, but somehow she wasn't. Maybe she should be angry at whoever was playing a joke on her. But instinctively she knew it was no trick. A dream, she told herself again. This is all just a dream.

"No," another, sharper, voice said. "It's not a dream. We're quite real. Well, not real exactly."

"Lucy," the soft voice said, "let me do this. You'll just confuse Margaret Mary unnecessarily. Sorry. I mean Maggie."

"According to the record, she's Margaret Mary Sullivan. We should call her by her true name."

"Don't pout, dear," the soft voice said. "Let's just get this done, shall we?"

"You know I hate it when you take over," Lucy said.

"I know you do, but when you do the introductions, you tend to get pushy and scare people to death, so to speak."

Maggie took another few steps and was finally able to make out the shapes of two women seated at a long table. "Maggie, my dear," the soft voice said, "do sit down."

The speaker was a blonde, with shoulder-length hair that waved softly around her ears. She was extremely attractive with a perfect, heart-shaped face, tiny, sloping nose, and beautiful lips. Her most arresting feature was her eyes, sky blue and fathomless, making Maggie suddenly picture calm seas or featureless blue skies. Those eyes should look cold and distant, Maggie thought, but they gazed almost lovingly at Maggie and made her feel warm, somehow. The woman motioned Maggie to a folding chair at the table, her long graceful fingers almost hidden beneath the sleeve of the diaphanous white gown she wore.

"Yes, yes, sit. Please." The harsher voice came from a dark-haired, dark-eyed woman, dressed in a tight black scoop-necked top that showed off her deep cleavage to its greatest advantage. She wore heavy makeup that accentuated the slight catlike tilt to her deep-set eyes. Her eyes, like her tablemate's, were her most amazing feature, so dark brown they were almost black, with long curling lashes and magnificently arched black brows. As Maggie looked into this dark woman's eyes, she fleetingly pictured a deep, bottomless well. "I'm Lucy," the dark woman said.

"She already knows that," the woman in white said gently but firmly to her neighbor. Then she turned to Maggie. "And I'm Angela."

Maggie took a seat at the table, and crossed her legs in a businesslike fashion. "How do you do. Now, if it's not too much trouble, would one of you two ladies tell me what this is all about?"

"Yes, yes," the one called Lucy said. "You see, you've presented us with a considerable problem."

"I'm afraid Lucy's right," Angela said. "A considerable problem." She checked the computer monitor at her elbow, pressed a few keys and continued. "Most people are easy. One or two keystrokes, a peek at their history and the decision's made. Actually, we're going to introduce a system whereby the computer actually makes most of the decisions. Very straightforward. Usually."

Maggie looked at the two women, so different, yet unconsciously mimicking each other's motions. Patience, she told herself. I will understand this eventually.

"You, on the other hand," Lucy said, clicking a few keys on her own console, "are a real dilemma."

"I'm really sorry about that," Maggie said, having no idea what was going on but willing herself to play along with this dream or hallucination or whatever it was.

"No, dear," Angela said, "it's not a hallucination either."

"No, no, of course not." Lucy turned to Angela. "I told you that the mist might be misunderstood. But no, you had to add it. 'Gives the place an ethereal air,' you said." Lucy grumbled, "Now you see? It just adds to the natural confusion."

"It might help if you'd begin," Maggie said, "by telling me where we are. That might end some of the confusion."

"That's a bit hard to explain right off," Angela said.

"Well, why don't you try," Maggie snapped, beginning to get a bit impatient despite all her best efforts.

"You won't believe it," Angela continued, shaking her head.

"Just get on with it, Angela," Lucy snapped. "Oh, never mind. Look, honey," she said, staring at Maggie, "you're dead."

"I'm what?" Maggie shrieked, jumping up from her seat.

"Lucy, don't do that," Angela said. "It just scares people unnecessarily. You have to break these things to them gently. How many times have I told you?"

"If you had it your way," Lucy said, "we'd be here for hours, breaking the news so gently that I'd starve."

"Ladies!" Maggie yelled. "Could you please stop arguing and just tell me what's going on."

"Of course, dear," Angela said. "Now sit back down and try to open your mind to new experiences."

Maggie dropped into the chair, her wobbly legs suddenly unable to hold her weight.

"Actually," Angela said, "although she said it crudely, Lucy is right. You are dead. You died quietly in your sleep of a massive heart attack."

Maggie tried to grasp what she was being told. "I did what?"

"It's always hardest to understand," Angela continued, "when you've had no warning. The chronically ill. They understand. They've been expecting it. But you. You appeared to be in perfect health."

"But your coronary arteries," Lucy said. "Shot. Too many french fries and rare steaks." She gazed at the ceiling. "Actually, right now, a thick sirloin with a baked stuffed potato. . . ."

"Dead?" Maggie whispered, unable to make any louder sound come out of her mouth. "I'm dead? Really, truly forever dead?"

"I'm afraid so, dear," Angela said. "Remember that pain right here?" She pointed to her breastbone. "Just before you went to bed that night?"

Numbly, Maggie nodded.

"Well," Lucy said, then snapped her fingers loudly. "That was the beginning of the end."

"But," Angela said, "being dead is not bad. Really."

"Dead," Maggie muttered. "And what is this place?"

"We call it the computer room. It's kind of a decision station," Angela said. "You know, up or down." She motioned with her thumb.

"You mean heaven, hell, that sort of thing?"

"Exactly," Lucy said.

"I'm finding all this a bit hard to believe," Maggie said.

"I can understand that," Angela said. "But I think we can convince you." Angela stood up and turned her back to Maggie. Two glittering white wings extended from her shoulderblades through an opening in her gown. "Angela, angel, you get it. Right?" The wings quivered and Angela rose about five feet, then gracefully settled back down.

Lucy stood up and turned. The tight black catsuit had a small opening just above her buttocks, through which a long sinuous black tail extended. "Lucy, Lucifer. Okay?" She extended her index finger and a narrow shaft of flame shot out, then, as quickly, was extinguished.

"Shit," Maggie hissed.

"Don't curse," Angela said.

"Let her say what she wants," Lucy snapped. "After all, it's her life, or death, as it were."

Slowly, Maggie was starting to accept the unacceptable. "Does everyone come through here? And what happens now? Do I meet someone like Mr. Jordan in that movie with Warren Beatty?"

"Ah, yes, *Heaven Can Wait*. That movie has led to more misunderstandings than anything in the last fifty years," Lucy said. "People expect some kindly old gentleman, a mixture of God, Santa Claus, and James Mason. Nope. No one like that. Just us."

"Actually," Angela said, "very few people get to see us at all." She clicked a few keys on her computer keyboard, then continued. "It's usually very easy. People die and the decision's already made. Good, bad, up, down. It's usually pretty straightforward."

"But, as we told you before," Lucy said, "you are a problem."

"Really," Maggie said dryly, staring at the two women clicking away at their terminals.

"We have a decision to make here that will affect you for all eternity," the women said in unison. "Heaven," Angela said. "Or hell," Lucy added.

"And what's it like," Maggie asked, looking into Lucy's deep black eyes, "down there? Is it like the movies, all fire and brimstone?"

"Nah," Lucy said, "actually it's been air-conditioned. The staff couldn't bear the heat any longer. It's not pleasant, however. Everyone has tedious tasks to perform, like the rock up the side of the mountain thing or cleaning up after the trolls or collating a thousand copies of my daily, hundred-page report.

"Or reading it," Angela said dryly.

Lucy glared at her, "Yes, lots of hard work and constant, blaring rock music." She rubbed the back of her neck. "And recently, we've added some rap. But you have the evenings off and the food's not half bad. Very hot, of course, vindalu curry and four-alarm chili at every meal." Lucy hesitated, then added, "What I wouldn't give for a steak, medium rare." She shook her head and grew silent.

"I see." Maggie turned to Angela expectantly.

"Oh, heaven's wonderful," she said, beaming beatifically. "There's sensational organ and harp music all the time, and we have little to do but relax on fluffy clouds and think wonderful thoughts. There is a constant supply of ambrosia to eat and nectar to drink and wonderful intellectual people to talk to." She sighed. "Ah, the talks we've had about the meaning of life and the future of mankind."

Maggie thought that hell sounded much more like her type

of place, but she hesitated to say so in front of Angela. There was a lot at stake here. She waited for the two silent women to continue, but when long minutes passed, Maggie brought them back to the present. "And I'm a problem for you."

"Yes, yes, of course you are," Lucy said, her head snapping back to her console. "You're a prostitute, a hooker. You have sex with men for money. And you're unrepentant."

"I guess that's true," Maggie admitted. "I don't apologize for what I do." Suddenly a bit uneasy, she said, "Does that mean . . ." She made a thumbs-down signal with her right hand.

"It should," Lucy said. "It certainly should."

"But," Angela jumped in, "you're a truly nice person. Kind, considerate, loving. We checked your record." She turned the monitor on her computer toward Maggie and clicked a few more keys. "Remember Jake? It was just a month or so before you, er, died."

On the screen, Maggie could see a view of her apartment. Jake. She remembered that evening well as the scene played out.

The doorbell rang. Maggie rose gracefully from her chair, slid the crossword puzzle she had been working on under the seat cushion, straightened her simple yellow tennis sweater and rubbed her hands down the thighs of her jeans. "Coming," she called. She crossed the large living room and opened the door. "You must be Jake," she said, careful not to touch the young man who stood awkwardly before her. "Please come in."

She backed up and motioned for Jake to come inside, but the young man didn't budge. She looked him over quickly, noting his carefully combed sandy-brown hair and his gray tweed sport jacket and black slacks. She knew from his father that he was seventeen, but at that moment he looked about twelve, with large ears and skin deeply scarred from childhood acne. She tried not to smile at the nervous twining and retwining of his fingers and his deer-in-the-headlights expression. There had been so many similar young men over the years and most of them had looked like Jake.

"You don't look like . . ." Jake swallowed hard, his eyes uneasily flicking from her face to her breasts. "I mean . . . You look nice. I don't mean . . ."

"Jake," Maggie said, "I know exactly what you mean. Come inside. I promise it will be just fine." She reached for his arm, but he entered the lavish apartment without the need for her to touch him.

Jake stopped, standing restlessly in the center of the room. "This is really nice," he said, looking anywhere but at her.

"Thanks. I've collected lots of treasures over the years. I enjoy having things around me that have special memories." She crossed to a small white linen-and-lace butterfly that seemed to have settled in the corner of a framed photo of an old European village. "There's a town in Belgium called Bruges. It looks like it hasn't changed in four hundred years." Jake walked over and looked over her shoulder, and she sensed his effort not to let any part of his body touch hers. "Wonderful old buildings," she said softly, "churches that were old before our country ever thought about George Washington. I was there about six, no, seven years ago. They cater to tourists, of course, but the city is an old center for lace making and they still make some." She ran the tip of her finger over the butterfly's white lace wings.

"That's real nice," Jake said, tangling and untangling his fingers.

"And this," she said, pointing to a smoothly carved statuette of a seal perched on a rock, "is a soapstone carving that I got in Anchorage a few years ago." She picked up the six-inch-high stone piece and placed it in Jake's hand. "I liked the shape, but what sold me was the way it felt in my hand the first time I held it." She stroked the back of the seal. "Cool and so soft," she said as Jake imitated her movement without actually touching her hand. She took the seal from him and replaced it on the mantel.

"Come on, Jake, let's sit down. We can talk for a while. About anything you like." Deliberately, she sat in a chair rather than on the long sofa. She watched Jake's face relax as he sat on the end of the sofa nearest her chair, keeping his knees from touching hers. "Would you like a drink?" Maggie asked. "I have soda, wine, beer, whatever you might like."

"Could I have a beer?" he asked, then cleared his throat.

"Sure. I have Bud, Miller, Miller light, and Sam Adams." She grinned. "I sound like a waitress. Actually, to be honest, I did wait on tables many years ago."

"What are you having?" Jake said.

"I thought I'd have a Sam Adams," Maggie said.

Jake smiled tentatively. "Okay. Me too."

Maggie walked into the kitchen of the large Madison Avenue apartment, knowing that Jake was watching her retreating ass, which was barely contained in the tight jeans she wore. Not bad for a broad on the far side of fifty, she thought as she opened two beers. She placed them on a tray, pulled two mugs out of the freezer, balanced the tray on her palm and returned to the living room. "See," she grinned, holding the tray at shoulder level. "I used to be very good at this." She twirled the tray, set it down on the coffee table and deftly poured two beers.

She handed Jake his drink, took a swallow of hers and resettled in her chair. She smiled as Jake took several large gulps of the cold liquid. "Gee," he said, "this is nice."

"Tell me about you," Maggie said. "Your father tells me you're at Yale."

For the next fifteen minutes, as Jake visibly relaxed, they talked about Jake's classes, his plans for the future, his social life at school. When they had finished their first round, Maggie went into the kitchen for two more beers. "I guess I don't date much," Jake admitted as Maggie reentered the living room, the two fresh bottles on the tray, along with a large bowl of popcorn. "I'm not very good-looking either." He ran a finger over his chin and through a few deep pits on his jawline.

"You'll never be Paul Newman," Maggie said softly, putting the tray on the coffee table. She prided herself on never lying to anyone. "But you do have his eyes." Jake's eyes were sky blue, deeply set, with long sandy lashes.

"I do?" Jake said. Then ducked his chin and quickly added, "Don't bullshit me."

"I'm not," Maggie said, keeping her voice soft. "You've got beautiful eyes." She moved to sit beside him on the sofa. "Would you like some popcorn?" She picked a piece from the bowl and held it in front of her mouth. "It's very garlicky so I won't have any if you're not going to."

Jake reached out to take a piece of popcorn, but Maggie held the one in her hand out for him. "Here, take this one," she said.

He reached for it, taking it from her while barely skimming his fingertips over hers. He popped the piece of corn into his mouth. "This is really good," he said, reaching for a handful.

"Aren't you going to return the favor?" Maggie asked, raising one eyebrow. "You took my popcorn . . ."

Slowly he took a piece of popcorn from the bowl and held it out to her. She leaned over and took it from his fingertips with her teeth, nipping his index finger lightly. She watched him pull his hand back as though burned. "Do you know," she said, swallowing, "that I met your father through a few of his friends when he was in college?"

"You're kidding. That was a hundred years ago."

"I was in business even then, back in the dark ages. I fought dinosaurs with one hand while keeping track of my customers on clay tablets."

Jake looked sheepish. "I'm sorry."

Maggie laughed, no trace of scorn, only rich warm enjoyment. "Don't be. I know it seems like centuries, and maybe it was. But I did meet your father kind of like this."

"He never told me how he knew you. I guess I thought he met you after Mom died."

"He hadn't even met your mom when I first knew him. A few of his fraternity brothers were, let's just say, friends of mine. They dared him to visit me, even paid his way." Maggie sat back on the sofa and rested her head on the back.

She kicked off her shoes and, at her glance, Jake did the same. She ran her long fingers through her tight black curls. "My hair was naturally this color back then," she remembered. "He was so cute. Scared to death, like you are now."

"I'm not scared," Jake protested.

"It's all right to be nervous," Maggie said. "I was living in a small apartment in Greenwich Village and he came to my place that first evening." She giggled. "He spilled an entire bottle of Scotch on my sofa, as I recall."

Jake laughed. "He did?"

"He offered to pour us each a drink, but his hands shook so much that he couldn't get the top off the bottle. He twisted one last time, the top came off in his hand and, of course, the bottle was upside down. It took weeks to get the smell out of the upholstery."

"I can't picture my dad as a nervous teenager."

"No one can picture others having the same fears, the same feelings of inadequacy they have. I remember a certain rock star who, well let's just say, couldn't get it up."

"Who?"

"I never reveal any of the secrets I learn," Maggie said. "But, if these walls could talk. . . ."

"What did he do?" Jake asked, his eyes widening. "The rock star, I mean."

"We sat and talked. Once he was comfortable with the fact I didn't want anything from him, that he could do what he chose, he relaxed." Maggie giggled. "We actually played spin the bottle. Then we made love. Several times, as I remember.'

"And my dad?"

"Uh, uh. No tales about anyone like that. How would you feel if I told him about you?"

Jake flinched. "Okay. Point made."

"Is it warm in here?" Maggie asked, pulling her sweater off over her head. She smiled as she felt Jake gaze at her erect nipples, clearly visible through her white stretch tank top. "Why don't you take off your jacket?"

Maggie didn't move while Jake removed his sport jacket,

his eyes never leaving her ample breasts. Without lifting her head from the back of the sofa, she turned to Jake. "You know what I'd like to do? How about some slow dancing." She sat up and leaned forward, giving Jake a good view of her large breasts and deep cleavage. She reached for the remote control on the coffee table and pressed a button. As Michael Bolton's voice filled the room, Maggie stood up and held her hands out to Jake. "Come on. Dance with me."

Hesitantly, Jake stood up and walked around the coffee table. "I don't dance much."

"That's really too bad," Maggie said as she moved into Jake's arms, keeping space between them. "I love slow dancing. It's like making love to music."

Jake placed one arm gingerly around Maggie's waist and held her hand with the other. He slowly shifted his weight from one foot to the other.

"Relax," Maggie said, leading him, helping him to move more gracefully. "You're doing fine." She pressed her body closer, so the tips of her nipples brushed his shirtfront. She felt him shiver, his hands trembling. She hummed along with the music, slowly moving closer until her mouth was against his ear, her chest pressed fully against his. His excitement was evident against her lower body. "This is so nice," she said into his ear.

"Ummm," he purred, moving his feet with increasing sureness. "This *is* nice."

"And we're in no hurry," Maggie whispered. As the songs changed, the two moved around the living room, locked in each other's arms. She could feel his growing hunger and nursed it until she knew the time had come. "Would you like to kiss me?" she whispered, leaning away from Jake's body.

Unable to answer, Jake pressed his mouth hard against Maggie's.

"Soft," she murmured as she cupped her hands against his cheeks and pulled back slightly, gentling the kiss, her feet still moving in time to the music. Her lips whispering against his, Maggie said, "Kissing and dancing. So good. So slow and soft." She could feel his heavy breathing against her mouth and she kissed his cheek gently. She murmured soft nonsense words, kissed his face and ran the tip of her tongue over the skin of which he was so self-conscious. He tried to pull away, but her hands and the pressure of her body held him immobile.

Without breaking contact with his mouth, Maggie slid her hands between them, unbuttoned his shirt and pulled it off of his shoulders. His chest was hairless and surprisingly smooth as she slid her palms over his skin. "I know you would like to feel my breasts against your body." In one swift motion, she pulled her tank top over her head and, as they continued to dance, she rubbed her nipples over his skin. Minutes later, when she knew he was ready, she took his hands and placed them on her ribs. Her palms covering his, she guided his hands up her sides, to her breasts. "Yes," she purred. "Hold them, feel them. Yes. Like that."

His eyes watched his hands as his fingers played with her nipples, his breathing ragged, his feet still moving to the music. Maggie helped him, showing him where she wanted to be touched, how she liked to be pinched gently but firmly. Then she placed one finger under his chin and raised his face. She held his gaze and said, softly, "We will be a lot more comfortable in the other room."

Both naked to the waist, the two walked into Maggie's bedroom, Michael Bolton's voice following them through the apartment. The bedroom was large, dominated by a king-size bed covered with a soft off-white satin spread and a dozen pillows in bright reds, blues, and violets. The thick carpet was white, covered by an area rug of a bright geometric design in the same colors. There were two white leather side chairs with matching hassocks and a lounge chair with a chrome frame and black leather webbing. Jake's eyes widened. "I know," Maggie said, her arm around Jake's naked waist, "it's a bit flashy. But it makes me happy."

Jake turned to face the older woman. He tangled his fingers in her black curls. "You're quite something," he said. "And not what I expected at all." He pressed his lips to hers, now more sure in his motions. "I want you." He reached down and started to unzip his pants.

"Let me," Maggie said, running her fingernails down his chest and moving his hands aside. She deftly unfastened his pants and, in one motion, pulled down both his slacks and his shorts until he stood naked except for his socks. She knelt and pulled them off, her eyes level with the stiff, hard erection that stuck straight out from Jake's groin. She resisted the urge to take his hard cock into her mouth, knowing that their first time together should be plain vanilla. There would be time later to introduce Jake to the dozens of other pleasures she enjoyed.

"Would you like to undress me, or should I do it?" she asked.

Jake grinned and held his trembling hands in front of him. "I think you'd better."

Quickly she pulled off her jeans, panties and socks and led Jake to the bed. She stretched out on the spread and patted the space next to her. "Come here, darling. Let's try slow dancing this way." He lay beside her and she placed the soles of her feet against his insteps. Slowly she slid their feet over the satin spread, keeping the rhythm they had established in the living room. "Slow dancing isn't just for standing up." She wrapped one arm around him and took his hand with the other, holding him just as if they were dancing. She moved against him until the length of her body was against the length of his. Quickly she took a condom from the bedtable drawer and deftly unrolled it over Jake's throbbing cock. Then she maneuvered so her body was beneath his, her legs spread, the tip of his erection against the soaked folds of her entrance. "Yes?" she whispered. "Do you want me?"

"Oh, yes," he moaned.

"Then you know what to do."

He pushed his hips forward, sliding his cock deep inside Maggie's body. Maggie cupped his buttocks and held him still for a moment, then moved, still in the rhythm of the music. "Yes, sweet," she purred. "Dance with me. Do it. Make it feel so good."

It was only moments until Jake came, his hips pounding against Maggie's. "Oh, Maggie," he bellowed. "Oh, yes." He collapsed against her, then rolled onto one side, his cock sliding limply from her body. "Oh," he groaned, clutching her against him. "Too fast."

"Now comes the first lesson," she said, taking his hand and guiding it to her wet pussy. "You came, but I didn't. I need you to help me, to give me the same pleasure you just got."

Suddenly tense, he said, "I don't know how."

"Of course you don't," Maggie said. "How could you unless someone showed you?" She held one of Jake's fingers and rubbed it over her swollen clit. "This is where most of a woman's pleasure comes from. Rub like this." She showed him and found he was a fast learner. "Yes," she said, "like that." As she arched her back, she said, "Put two fingers of your other hand inside me. It will feel so good for me and you will feel what it's like when a woman comes."

Jake inserted his index and middle finger into Maggie's cunt and slowly stretched her hungry flesh. "Don't stop rubbing right here," she said, reminding his fingers where she got the most pleasure. "Yes," she purred. "And I like it if you suck my tit, too."

With his mouth on her nipple, his fingers filling her and his other hand rubbing her clit, Maggie could feel the familiar tightness start deep in her belly. "Yes," she said, "like that. Oh, baby, don't stop." The heat grew and filled her lower body until it exploded. "Feel what my body does when it comes," she cried. "Feel it. Share it." Waves of muscular spasms clenched at Jake's fingers.

"I've never felt anything like that," he said, his voice filled with wonder. "It makes me so hot. Can I fuck you again?"

"Of course," Maggie said, barely able to talk through the waves of pleasure. She felt him withdraw his fingers, put on a fresh condom and slide into her again. Still coming, the waves of orgasm engulfed both of them as Jake climaxed again.

Later, as they dressed, Jake said, "I never knew."

"I know, and that's what I love about doing this. I can introduce someone as sweet as you to a joy that will continue for the rest of your life. There's a lot more, too."

"I know. Can I see you again?"

"Of course," Maggie said. "Call and we'll make another date. And we can work out finances then."

"Thanks, Maggie," Jake said. "I never dreamed that this evening would be this wonderful and so," he winked, "educational. When he first approached me about this, I thought my dad was nuts."

"Give him my love," Maggie said as she guided Jake to the door.

"I will." Jake kissed her good-bye and grinned as she closed the door behind him.

"You see," Lucy said, looking up from her computer terminal. "You're a nice person. I hate that."

"But, you also have sex with married men for money," Angela said sadly.

"But I never do it without first suggesting that the men discuss things with their wives," Maggie said. "Men don't realize that their wives might be just as interested in some fun and games as they are." Maggie had little use for timid women who didn't understand the pleasures of lovemaking.

"I know that," Angela said. "But remember this evening? It was just last winter."

As Maggie stared, the monitor showed the face of Gerry O'Malley. A sales representative for a computer software firm, Gerry had been recommended to her by an old friend. She recalled their first evening together and how she had tried to convince him to share his fantasies with his wife. Adamantly refusing, Gerry and Maggie had made love in his hotel room, then arranged to meet there the following Wednesday. "I want something special," he had said, his hands clenched tightly, his fingers twined. "Dress up. Would you wear white . . . ?"

Chapter 2

Maggie had dressed in a white knit dress, short enough to show off her long, well-shaped legs and low cut enough to highlight the shadowed valley between her breasts. She added light gray thigh-high stockings, held up by elastic lace at the tops, and gold strappy sandals with four-inch heels. Long gold earrings that brushed her shoulders and a heavy gold necklace completed her outfit. She was not overly made up and her lipstick was soft pink.

Dressed in gray slacks and a light blue shirt, Gerry opened the door to his hotel room and stared, his face flushed. "You look wonderful," he said to Maggie. Gerry was medium height with thick brown hair with a hint of gray at the temples. Clean shaven, his jaw was tightly clenched and he stood filling the doorway.

Maggie smiled. "May I come in?" she asked, her voice soft and melodious.

Almost stumbling, Gerry backed away from the door. "I, uh, ordered some champagne," he said.

"Good. We both need to relax," Maggie said, patting Gerry on the arm. "It will all be fine. Really."

Almost bonelessly, Gerry dropped onto the sofa in the sitting room of the two-room suite. "I know."

With a practiced hand Maggie opened the champagne bottle and half-filled two flutes from the tray. "Here," she said, handing Gerry a glass, "sip this."

Gerry emptied the glass. "I guess it shows," he said. "That I'm really nervous. About this, I mean."

Maggie laughed. "It does show. But what are you so nervous about? We were together last week and it was very pleasurable."

"I want something different from what we did last week."

"That's fine with me. What would give you pleasure?"

Gerry took his wallet out of his back pocket and withdrew ten fifty-dollar bills. "I understand that I can pay extra for something special." He counted out four more fifties and handed all seven hundred dollars to Maggie. "I want to have you completely in my power. I want to feed you a potent sex drug. I mean," he hesitated, "I mean that I want to be able to do everything to you and have you beg for more." Maggie could see his throat muscles work as he swallowed hard.

"You do remember my rules. No real drugs and if you decide you want to have sexual intercourse, you will use a condom."

"Of course. I remember everything you told me last week and I will abide by your rules. No problem."

"And I get no pleasure from serious pain, so whips and things like that are not for me."

"I understand."

Maggie looked up at Gerry from beneath her long lashes. She smiled. "How will you give me this drug, or have you done that already?"

Gerry hesitated, then grinned and said, "Yes. Yes. I did give it to you already. It was in the champagne."

"Is that why I'm feeling so warm?" Maggie said, slipping into the role Gerry wanted her to play.

"It certainly is."

Maggie stretched out on the sofa and fanned herself with her hand. "I'm so hot, baby. So hot."

"Yes, you certainly are. Maybe you'd better take off your dress."

"Oh, yes," Maggie said, standing up and turning her back to Gerry. "Would you help me unzip? I seem to be all thumbs. I can't seem to make my hands work right."

Maggie could feel Gerry's cold fingers on her back as he fumbled with the zipper. As he slid the zipper down, Maggie began to move her hips. "I don't know what's wrong with me," she said, her voice low and breathy. "I can't seem to stand still." She wiggled out of her dress, let it fall around her feet and stepped out of it. Maggie had selected a pale pink satin bra and matching bikini panties. Although her age couldn't help but show, her frequent aerobic classes kept her figure tight. She rubbed her palms over the tips of her breasts. "God, I can't stand this. I'm so . . . I don't know."

Gerry stared at Maggie's breasts which more than filled the small cups of her bra. "Are you uncomfortable?" he asked with mock innocence.

"I don't know," Maggie answered, undulating her hips and rubbing her nipples. She watched Garry's eyes, and from the gleam surmised that the fantasy was playing out to his satisfaction. "I just want something."

"I know exactly what you want and only I can give it to you."

"Please. Do it. Help me. I'm so hot."

"I know. You're hot all over, aren't you. Especially between your legs. Hot and itchy. Do you need to rub yourself?"

"Oh, yes," Maggie moaned.

When Maggie's fingertips started to slide under the elastic of her panties, Gerry pulled it back. "Well, you can't. Not yet. Not until I give you permission. Do you understand?"

"Yes. But . . ."

"No buts. You are mine to command and I say you may not have any relief yet."

Maggie played the game. "Please. Don't make me suffer like this. I need to rub and touch and stroke myself. I need to make myself come."

"I will let you when you've been a good girl and done your chores."

"What chores?"

"First you must undress me."

"Oh, yes. May I undress you very slowly? May I kiss and touch you, caress you and make you as hot as I am?"

Gerry spread his arms wide, wordlessly indicating she could begin. Maggie closed the distance between them and pressed the length of her body against his. Sinuously she rubbed her chest and thighs against his as she licked his lips. Then she unbuttoned his shirt, licking his chest as she exposed it. Slowly she pulled the tails from the waistband of his slacks, rubbing her pelvis against his erection as she did so. With her entire body pressed against his, she worked the shirt down over his arms and tossed it on a chair. Her hard nipples pressed against the fabric of her bra and she sensuously rubbed them across his lightly furred chest. "Oh, baby," she purred as she moved around behind him, constantly rubbing her body against his side, his arm, his back, stroking his skin with her satin-covered breasts and mound.

She moved completely around him until she was again in front of him. She knelt at his feet and put her fingers on his belt buckle. She gazed up at him, a silent question in her eyes.

"Say please," Gerry said.

"Oh, please. Let me." Slowly she pulled the end of his belt through the loops and unfastened the buckle. With fumbling fingers she unbuttoned and unzipped his fly. "Oh, baby," she purred. "You're not wearing anything underneath." Careful not to touch his large, fully erect cock, she pulled his slacks down and, at her signal, he stepped out of them.

"Are you hot enough to suck my cock?" Gerry asked.

"I don't have to be hot to want to suck such a beautiful cock," Maggie said, sensing these were the right words at the right time. She looked up at him. "Please. May I?"

Gerry wrapped one hand around his erect penis and aimed it at her mouth. His grin said that this was progressing exactly the way he had imagined.

"Do you have to touch it?" Maggie asked. "I want to hold it and suck it myself."

"Even better," Gerry said, his mouth open and his breathing quick.

Still kneeling at Gerry's feet, Maggie placed one finger on the tip of his cock and rubbed the tiny drop of pre-come around the head. "I want to taste you." She flicked the tip of Gerry's cock with the end of her tongue and watched him shiver. Afraid his knees would buckle, she said, "I would like to go into the bedroom, if that's all right with you."

"Yes," Gerry said, breathless. "Of course." Quickly they moved into the other room and Gerry stretched out on the bed on his back. "Now," he said, "continue what you were doing."

Maggie spread his legs, then climbed onto the bed and crouched between his thighs. "Right here," she said, wrapping her hand around the hard staff that stuck straight up into the air. "And right here." She licked the tip, then, making a tight ring with her lips, she sucked him into her mouth.

She looked toward his face and saw that his eyes were closed. "Look at me," she said, "and watch me suck your cock." She watched his eyes open and the glazed expression as he looked at her head, bobbing on his cock.

"Good," he moaned. "Good." It took only moments until he shot his come into Maggie's mouth. "Good," he yelled. "So good."

Maggie fingered his balls until he was completely drained.

Not even thinking about the fact that Maggie was unsatisfied, Gerry disappeared into the bathroom and Maggie heard the sound of the shower. "That was wonderful," he called from the bathroom. "I need to get cleaned up now." His tone was dismissive, so, with a sigh, Maggie dressed, wandered into the living room and poured herself another glass of champagne. It was far from the first time she had been asked to perform oral sex on a man who believed that it was such an onerous task that his wife wouldn't want to satisfy his hunger for fellatio. Nibbling on some of the peanuts from the champagne tray, she gathered Gerry's clothes and walked back into the bedroom. "I will leave now, unless there's something else you want." She folded his slacks and shirt and put them on the foot of the bed. She put his wallet on the dresser.

"No. That was fantastic."

Maggie counted out four of the fifty-dollar bills he had given her and put them on the dresser with his wallet. "It was wonderful for me, too," she said. "You know, oral sex isn't a chore at all. I really enjoy it."

"I guess your kind does."

Stung, but understanding, Maggie left the suite.

As the scene faded, Angela said, "See what I mean? He was a married man and you did what you did for money. That's adultery and it's a sin."

"Oh, lighten up, Angela," Lucy said, clicking the keys on her terminal. "Get real. It's done all the time. Sex is fun stuff and everyone should have his or her share."

"Yes. I suppose you're right to a point. I do take this sin thing a bit too seriously. But that still leaves us with a problem." She turned to Maggie. "You."

"Okay. So what does that mean exactly?" Maggie asked.

"Well," Lucy said, "I've talked Angela into giving you a way to help us make the decision. A task for you to do. Like the labors of Hercules and all that."

"Yes, Lucy did come up with an idea. We have someone for you to teach about sex. Someone who's so ignorant, it's shameful even to me."

Maggie grinned. "Teach some guy about sex? That's what I do best and enjoy the most."

"That's not exactly what we had in mind," Lucy said. "It's not a guy, it's a girl."

"I have to teach a girl about sex? A little girl?"

"A grown woman. Actually, she's thirty-one," Angela

said. "And she's never had a good experience in bed. A few bad experiences since high school and no real boyfriends."

"Is she a nun? A total dog? Come on. Give me a break here."

"Actually," Lucy said, "she's a nice woman, which makes me dislike her from the start."

"She's sweet," Angela continued, "and she cared for her dying mother for eight years. During the final two, Barbara moved into her mother's house and tended to her almost nonstop. She had a nurse come in during the day while she was at work, but Barbara was with her mother almost every other minute."

"What does she do?"

"She's a secretary to a big-time lawyer type," Lucy said, "and she's half in love with him. But during all the time she lived with her mother, she had no time to consider dating. Now that Mom's no longer around, she has no clue where to start, and no self-confidence at all."

"And why do you two care?" Maggie asked.

"Well, actually it was her mother who got us interested," Lucy said. "She came through here about six months ago and asked us for help before we told her where she was to go." Lucy and Angela looked at each other and made the thumbs-up signal. "She was a good and caring woman and regretted what she had put her daughter through. Ugh. Self-sacrifice. I hate that, too." Lucy made a face.

"Anyway," Angela said, "we haven't done anything about it until now, but this seemed to be a great opportunity to put you to work to help us decide about which way you go, and do something for that nice mother, too."

"And," Maggie said, "put off the decision about me."

Lucy grinned. "And there is that as well."

"Okay," Maggie said. "If that's the only way to get a bit more time to play, it's okay with me. Do I get powers?"

"Powers?"

"Yeah. Like Michael Landon on *Highway to Heaven*. Remember, he had the *stuff*."

"The *stuff*? Oh, yes, I remember, Angela. He did little magic things. Tossed bad people into swimming pools and made flowers bloom for nice folks."

"I do remember." Angela sighed. "I always loved that show. Sent that nice Mr. Landon straight upstairs when he came through."

"Sorry but no *stuff*, Maggie. Only Barbara, that's her name by the way, only Barbara will be able to see and hear you. You can appear to her and converse with her when the two of you are alone. In public, she'll be able to see you, but no one else will."

"As to powers," Angela said, "I think not, although if we see that you're getting into trouble we may, and I emphasize *may*, help you out."

"This is sink or swim for you, girl," Lucy said. "If you succeed and help Barbara become a sexually whole person, you'll get to go up there." She raised her eyes heavenward.

"But," Angela said, "if you louse this up, it's . . ." She aimed her thumb at the floor and Lucy grinned.

"I'm not so sure where I want to be or, for that matter where I belong." Maggie sighed. "Okay. Tell me more about this hardship case of mine."

Angela and Lucy looked at each other, then Angela began. "She's not a hardship case. She's a very nice woman who has just gone through some difficult times."

"I know. Her mother and all." Maggie tapped her foot on the soft floor. "So what's her problem. Men?"

"I guess that's the heart of it."

"Is she still in mourning for her mother?" Maggie asked. "That will make my job much harder, you know."

"She's not really in mourning," Angela said. "Her mother's death, when it finally came, was a blessing. It had been a long and very rough time."

"She lives in Westchester County," Lucy continued, "in the house that used to belong to her mother. Her father died when she was only four."

"No brothers or sisters?" Maggie asked.

"No. And no other close relatives either."

"How do I meet her?"

Lucy's fingers clacked the computer keys. She swiveled the monitor so Maggie could see. Slowly the picture crystallized. Maggie watched the image of a plain-looking woman materialize. "That's Barbara," Lucy said, "right now." There was momentary sound, but Lucy tapped what must have been a mute button.

Maggie looked at the screen. A nondescript-looking woman sat beside a desk, typing furiously on a laptop computer as the hunky-looking man behind the desk talked. She saw him pick up the phone on his desk, press the receiver against his ear and swivel his chair so his back was toward the woman, who continued to work on the laptop.

Maggie watched Barbara tuck an errant strand of her shoulder-length medium-brown hair behind one ear while her boss talked on. "Look at that woman," Maggie said. "She's not even wearing makeup. And that blouse . . ." Barbara was wearing an orangy-yellow blouse and a brown tweed skirt. "It's so wrong for her coloring. And sensible shoes, no doubt. Who's the guy?"

"That's Steve Gordon, one of the partners of Gordon, Watson, Kelly and Wise." Angela gazed at the screen. "He's rich, bright, successful, and very eligible. And as I said, she's crazy about him."

Maggie watched Steve hang up the phone and turn back toward Barbara. He opened a desk drawer, propped his feet on it and began to talk. Lucy tapped the button and the three women could hear the sound.

"That was Lisa," the man said. "Make me a reservation for eight o'clock tonight at Enrico's and send her a dozen roses. No, on second thought, make it just an arrangement."

"Of course," Barbara said. Maggie caught the heat of the woman's gaze as she looked at her boss, while he seemed oblivious.

"Well, that's your job, for starters," Lucy said, tapping the mute button again. "First a physical makeover, then the rest."

"Yes," Angela said. "I think she should end up with that gorgeous Mr. Gordon. I can see it. A large house in the country, kids, horses, dogs . . ."

"Actually," Maggie said, "he reminds me of Arnie Becker on *LA Law*. A real ladies' man and just a bit sleazy."

"Yeah," Lucy said, "me too. But Barbara really likes him."

"She would," Maggie said, rolling her eyes.

"Well, I think he's perfect," Angela said.

"Does it have to end up with them together for me to succeed?" Maggie asked, thinking that Arnie was all wrong for Barbara.

"Oh, no, of course not," Lucy said. "Actually, I think she should get out, see the world, maybe end up like you did."

"Free will," Angela said. "That's what we advocate here. Her life is her choice. It's just that she has no real choices now. We want to grant her mother's request and see what happens."

"Do you think you're ready for the task?" Lucy asked.

"I guess so." Maggie shrugged her shoulders. What choice did she have? This was kind of like the Mad Tea Party in *Alice in Wonderland*, but her options were few. And, of course, this project did buy time for her back on earth. Wondering how long she could stretch this out, she uncrossed her legs and waited for the magical zap to transport her to meet Barbara.

"Well?" Angela said, raising an eyebrow.

"I'm waiting for the magic," Maggie answered.

Lucy motioned in the direction from which Maggie had entered the room. "The elevator's that way. Just press the ground-floor button."

"Oh," Maggie said, standing up. She looked down at her diaphanous white gown. "And do I get clothes? This is a bit overly dramatic, don't you think? I'll scare poor Barbara to death."

"Hmmm", Lucy said. "You're right. We'll see to it that there are proper clothes in the waiting room on the ground floor. It's on the right just this side of the front door. Change, then go out the door and you'll be just where you should be."

Maggie nodded, then turned toward the door. "Good luck," Angela and Lucy said in unison.

"Thanks," Maggie said over her shoulder. "I guess."

As the computer room door closed behind Maggie, Lucy held out her hand to Angela. "It's a bet?"

Angela took the proffered hand. "I firmly believe that Barbara will end up settled and happy in six months. Mrs. Steven Gordon. It has a nice ring to it, doesn't it."

"And I believe that once she discovers sex, there'll be no stopping her. Whoever invented it, it's the strongest drive we have, thank Lucifer. She'll get into no end of trouble and she'll love it. I'll bet on it."

"You know, people would never believe that you want anyone to be happy. You're supposed to represent misery, suffering, and hardship, and here you are betting on happiness of one sort or another."

"I know. But happiness isn't all it's cracked up to be either."

In the room on the ground floor, Maggie found a pair of well-washed jeans, a soft light gray turtleneck sweater along with underwear, socks, and slightly worn running shoes. She dressed, leaving the almost-transparent white gown on a hook behind the door. Then she left the room and walked across what appeared to be a marble lobby toward the revolving door. When she pushed the brass handle, the door turned and she exited on the other side, right into what she somehow knew was Barbara Enright's bedroom. Fortunately, Barbara wasn't in it at the time. Maggie could hear sounds from the kitchen below. "God," she muttered, recognizing the unmistakable sound of a food processor, "I'll bet she cooks, too." She shook her head, then crossed to the large walk-in closet, pulled the door open and flipped on the light.

Oh, Lord, she thought, riffling through a collection of slightly dowdy dresses, blouses, and suits. Way in the back, she found a soft chiffon dress in shades of blue. She lifted the hanger from the rod and held the dress at arm's length. It was slightly out of style, but beautiful nonetheless. "Now this is more like it," she said, putting the dress back where she had found it. "There's hope yet."

Suddenly she realized that she had been moving things and feeling things just like she had when she'd been alive. Phew. Been alive. That sounds awful. I don't feel dead. Actually, she thought, pinching her arm, I don't feel any differently than I did yesterday. She looked at the darkened window. It must be evening now, she thought, but I thought it was morning when I was with the gruesome twosome up there and I was on the phone with Paul last evening, I guess.

She looked at Barbara's bedside table and spotted the clock. "Five-thirty and it's pitch dark," she said aloud. "But it should still be light. It's midsummer." She crossed to the window and looked out. There were small areas of snow on the ground and the stars shone brightly in a blue-black sky. "I guess time doesn't work for the girls the way it works here on earth." She thought about Lucy and Angela and marveled at how sanguine she had become about something so impossible. "I feel like a character in a play and soon the curtain will go down or we'll break for a commercial and all this will all make sense." She shrugged again. "Oh, well." She crossed to the door and started down the stairs. "Better get this over with."

Dressed in a baggy sweat suit, Barbara Enright scooped the butter-and-garlic mix from the food processor and carefully spread it on the slices of French bread she had laid out on the cutting board. Meticulously she covered the bread to the edges so it would toast properly under the broiler. As she finished the second slice, she reached out and almost without looking swirled a spoon through the small pot of simmering marinara sauce. She popped the bread in the oven, then lifted a strand of spaghetti with the clawlike device and snipped off about an inch. She popped the piece in her mouth and chewed thoughtfully. Still just a bit too firm, she thought, remembering when she had to get it almost mushy so her mother could chew it.

As she mused, she realized that her mother's death didn't hurt anymore. With almost seven months gone by, she could remember the wonderful life her mother had led before the pain.

Barbara tucked a strand of hair behind her ear, stirred the sauce and checked on the bread. She pulled one of her mother's good Límoges plates from the closet, poured a Coke and set herself a place on the large kitchen table. With perfect timing born of years of cooking for herself and her mother, Barbara removed the bread from the oven, drained and served the spaghetti and poured sauce over the top. She flipped on the TV on the counter and watched *I Love Lucy* fade in from the darkness.

"Some red wine would really go better with that."

Barbara jumped and tipped over her chair at the sound of the voice behind her. With one hand reaching for the phone, her fingers ready to dial 911, she turned slowly. "Who the hell . . ."

"It's okay," the jeans-clad figure said. "It's really okay. I'm Maggie and we're going to be spending quite a bit of time together for a while."

"Get out before I call the police," Barbara said, trying to make her quavering voice sufficiently forceful.

"Don't do that or you'll look like a fool," Maggie said, crossing the kitchen and leaning over the pot on the stove. "Nice sauce. I always loved a good marinara sauce." She lifted a strand of spaghetti and dangled it over he mouth. Nipping off the bottom, she said, "Vermicelli. And properly al dente. Not many people know how to cook pasta correctly."

Barbara stood, mouth slightly open, with her hand on the phone. For some reason she couldn't quite fathom, she hadn't lifted the receiver yet.

"I know," Maggie said, picking up a slice of garlic bread, "this is something of a shock, but believe me, it's taking me a little while to adjust, too." She took a large bite and chewed thoughtfully. "You know, I don't even know whether I can eat." She swallowed. "I guess I can, but I'm not very hungry." She pulled out the chair opposite Barbara's and sat down. "Wouldn't you know it. I can probably eat what I want and not gain weight, but I'm not hungry."

"Would . . ." Barbara cleared her throat and tried again. "Would you kindly tell me what the hell you're doing here?"

"I'm not here to hurt you," Maggie said, swallowing the chewed mouthful. "But before I try to explain, you'd really better sit down."

Barbara thought she should be afraid, but she was more baffled than frightened. This woman had arrived in her kitchen unannounced and had made herself totally at home. She shook her head, righted her chair and dropped into it. The woman had, Barbara admitted, warm, honest eyes that looked directly at you when she spoke and an open, friendly smile. Wasn't that what made con artists so hard to resist? "Okay. Tell me what you're doing here. And if you're a salesman with a very peculiar way of getting my attention, I'm not buying."

"I'm not selling anything," Maggie said, "but if I were, you'd be buying. I've actually come to change your life."

"Out," Barbara said. "Get out. I don't know how you got in here with your 'I'm not selling anything' sales pitch, but if you don't leave I *will* call the cops." She reached over and moved the phone from the counter to the table beside her right hand. "Now get out."

"Hmm. How to explain? Let me begin by introducing myself. My name's Maggie Sullivan and I'm dead." She reached over and flipped off the TV.

Her mind whirling, Barbara reran all the six P.M. sales pitches she'd heard over the years. It had gotten so she didn't answer her phone between the time she got home from work and eight P.M. *Hi*, they all started, *my name is Maggie*. She'd heard them on the phone hundreds of times. She glared. "Sure. And your next line is 'And how are you this evening, Ms. Enright,' " she parroted as the last words of Maggie's speech penetrated, " 'and I'm calling on behalf of . . .' You're *what*?" Had she heard correctly?

"I'm afraid you'll find this hard to believe, but I'm dead."

"Sure and I'm Minnie Mouse."

"You're not Minnie Mouse, but I *am* dead." Maggie hesitated. "How can I convince you? You know, I'm really new to this and I don't know what I can and can't do." She reached for the bread knife that Barbara had used earlier. "I hate this, but I think it just might work. I mean a dead person shouldn't be able to feel pain and I shouldn't bleed. Right?" To test the first part, Maggie pinched herself in the arm. Hard. "Well, I didn't feel that." She picked up the knife and held it poised over the index finger of her empty hand. "Do I really have to prove this to you? It may not be pleasant if I'm wrong."

Barbara raised one eyebrow. "This is certainly the most original pitch I've ever seen. I can't wait to see how you'll get yourself out of this." Strange, Barbara thought, but I actually rather like this ridiculous woman.

"Okay then," Maggie said. "Here goes." She took the knife and drew it slowly across the pad of her finger. "Amazing," she said. "I really didn't feel that at all." She held the finger toward Barbara. "See? No blood. And you can see I made a really deep cut."

Barbara could see that there was a deep cut across Maggie's finger that wasn't bleeding. "What's the gimmick? Are you selling artificial limbs? And why would that interest me?"

"Cut me some slack, will you?" Maggie said, putting the knife aside. "I'm really dead." She stood up. "Have you got any wine? I find I need something to fortify myself."

Barbara motioned toward a lower cabinet, and when Maggie opened the door she saw a reasonably well-stocked wine rack. "I guess it will have to be red since white wine should really be chilled." She pulled out a Chianti classico. "Corkscrew?" Numbly Barbara motioned to a drawer. While Maggie quickly removed the cork from the bottle, Barbara walked into the living room and returned with two glasses. Maggie quickly half filled the glasses and raised hers in silent toast.

As Barbara watched, Maggie took a sip, swished it around her mouth and swallowed. "Not bad, but a bit harsh. It really could have breathed for an hour or two, but it's okay." She waved at Barbara's glass. "Drink."

Barbara took a sip and swallowed. "I'm not much for wine, but my mom used to enjoy a glass with dinner." She put her glass down and took her seat. Maggie took a few more sips, then again sat opposite Barbara. "You know," Maggie said, "I don't even know whether I will have to pee as the evening progresses or whether this just goes into the ether somewhere. I have no blood, so I can't get tipsy. I wonder."

Without thinking, Barbara took another swallow. "Okay. You've been here fifteen minutes and I still have no idea why."

"I'm here for you. God, that sounds like a line from a bad sci-fi drama. Actually, I'm here because of your mother."

Barbara bristled. "What does my mother have to do with this? She died a while ago."

"I know. About seven months ago to be precise. And after she died, she asked a favor of two women I know. She wants you to be happy. Get out in the world. Date. Fuck. You know."

"I don't know anything like that at all and I'll thank you to leave my mother out of this."

"But she's an integral part of it." Maggie reached out to pat the back of Barbara's hand, but the younger woman pulled away. "Let me explain." Briefly Maggie told Barbara about her heart attack and how she had suddenly found herself in the Mad Tea Party with Lucy and Angela. "They can't decide whether I'm to go . . ." Maggie made a thumbs-up with one hand and a thumbs-down with the other. "So they gave me a project. You."

"I don't for a moment believe any of this," Barbara said, drinking more of her wine, "but why me?"

"I told you before," Maggie explained. "It was your mother. On her way through, she asked the girls to help you out." Maggie's head tipped to one side and she gazed into space. "Actually, I don't quite understand how your mother ended up in the computer room. Acçording to Angela and Lucy, the interview process is only for the undecideds. Your mother's goodness seems to have left the girls little choice. Maybe it was a special request of some kind." She refocused on Barbara. "Anyway, I'm now here for you."

"Your reference to the Mad Tea Party is accurate. I still don't believe you."

"Well, that's neither here nor there, actually. I assume you want to get out more. Date. I saw the way you looked at your boss this afternoon."

Barbara's head snapped up. "How the hell do you know how I looked at my boss earlier?"

"The girls have a monitor and they can tune in on people. We watched you at work today so I would know who you were."

"This gets crazier and crazier," Barbara said. "Do you mean that they could be watching us right now?"

"Probably not. With the millions of people they have to check on as people come through for approval, I doubt whether they have time for idle peeping."

Barbara shivered. "It gives me the creeps nonetheless." She found she was actually playing along with this fantasy. Or was it a fantasy? "So you're supposed to give me a makeover. What's this going to cost me?"

"Nothing. And it's more than a makeover, it's a whole change of attitude. According to your mother, you're . . . How can I best say this? You're a bit of a prude."

"Nonsense. I'm just selective. Just because I don't let every Tom, Dick, and Harry into my bedroom doesn't make me a prude. Not in the least."

"Selectivity is good, Babs, but it's not life."

A handsome face suddenly flashed through Barbara's mind and her patience snapped. "Don't call me Babs. I hate it."

"All right. Don't get huffy."

"I'm sorry. I just really hate Babs. Anyway, you were telling me about my makeover."

Maggie sipped her wine. "Well, as I understand my job here, I'm supposed to teach you about yourself and sex and men and dating and all that. In the end, you're supposed to get out more, go dancing, make love."

Barbara toyed with her fork. "And what makes you such an expert?"

"I am, or was, a . . . Again how to put this. I was an expert at making men happy. Let's just say I did it professionally."

The fork dropped out of Barbara's hand. "You were a hooker!"

"I prefer call girl. Very highly priced, I might add."

"But you look like you could be my mother."

Maggie winced. "Ouch. That hurt." She walked into the hallway outside the kitchen and looked at herself in the ornate mirror that hung just inside the entrance. She studied her face for a moment, then returned to the table and sat down. "I don't look that bad, despite my current circumstances, I'll have you know." She paused. "But I guess I am almost old enough to be your mother."

"So why would some man . . . ?" Barbara suddenly realized that without being totally insulting she had no way to finish the sentence.

"Why would some man want to make love with me? Because I know how to make men happy, how to fulfill their fantasies, how to make them feel strong or weak, brave or pitiful, whatever they want. I'm damn good at what I do and I have a client list as long as your arm."

"What do you . . . I mean, *did* you charge?"

"I was worth the five hundred a night that men paid me."

"Five hundred dollars? For one night?" Barbara's mouth literally hung open.

"Not the whole night, of course." Maggie ran her long fingers through her hair and fluffed it out at the sides. "And more if they want something special."

"I don't want to know about that part," Barbara said. "Look, I don't pretend to understand any of this, but I really don't need your help. I'm happy just the way I am." In response to Maggie's raised eyebrow, Barbara continued. "Really. My life is just what I want it to be. And I'm just the way I want to be."

"Sure," Maggie said, her voice dripping with sarcasm. "Listen. You've heard enough for one evening. You really need to take a day to digest all this. Let me run along now so you can think about what we've said." Maggie paused, then asked, "By the way, what day is it?"

"It's Tuesday," Barbara said, her head spinning. She was sitting in her kitchen having a conversation with a dead prostitute. She certainly did need some time to digest this. But she didn't need any help with her life. None. Absolutely not.

"What date? What year?"

"It's Tuesday, March 4, 1996. What did you think?"

"I'm totally disoriented. This bouncing from time to time. The last date I remember was July 18, 1995." Pain flashed across Maggie's face as she recalled Paul Crowley and their phone conversation that last evening. I wonder how he felt when he found out about me. "And where are we? It looks like New York, but everything wonderful looks like New York to me."

"We're about twenty miles north of the city, in Fleetwood."

"I know the town well." Paul lived in Bronxville, the next town up. With a sigh, she emptied her wineglass and shook off her negative feelings. "I'm not sure how this time thing will work, but I think I can manage to be here, same time tomorrow."

"I don't want to seem rude, but I don't want you to come back. Just go away and leave me alone."

"Sorry, but I can't. I have a job and my ultimate future depends on doing it well. And remember, this is what your mother wanted."

"I'm sure my mother didn't want some whore giving me makeup tips," Barbara snapped. Then her head dropped into her hands. "I'm sorry. That was uncalled for."

"Yes, it was. But I am what I am. I am—I was—a woman

who made men happy for money. I did my job well, and got a lot of pleasure myself as well. And I was highly paid for my talents."

"I'm sorry. But this whole thing is so ridiculous."

"Just think about it. Consider what you have to gain. Think about looking appealing to your boss and having him ask you out. Dream about what your third or seventh date could be like. Think about all this and I'll see you tomorrow." Maggie crossed the room and walked into the hall.

Suddenly the house was silent. Having not heard the front door open, Barbara got up to be sure this crazy woman wasn't lurking somewhere waiting to pounce or something. "Maggie? Where are you?" She searched the house, but Maggie was nowhere to be found.

Chapter 3

Later that evening, Barbara lay on her bed, the romance novel she had been trying to read now discarded beside her. It had been foolish, she realized, to even try to think about anything besides the weird visit she had had with the ghost of a sort of motherly, utterly charming prostitute. Images had whirled in her brain as she had tossed her uneaten dinner in the trash and methodically washed the dishes and cleaned the kitchen.

She considered what Maggie had said. Her life wasn't dull, it was just predictable. She went to work five mornings a week, arriving in White Plains, barring car trouble, at almost exactly eight o'clock each morning. Gordon, Watson, Kelly and Wise was a small but elite firm, run by Mark Watson and John Kelly, two aging lawyers, and Steve Gordon, the thirty-five-year-old sexy-looking lawyer for whom Barbara worked. Barbara brought her half-sandwich and salad with her each day and ate her lunch at her desk. Steve Gordon Junior, son of one of the founding partners, wasn't overly dependent on her so Barbara usually left at four-thirty and was home before five.

Most weekends she did odd jobs around her two-story raised ranch. In the summer she mowed the lawn, in the winter she shoveled the driveway. Her kitchen and bathroom floors were clean enough to eat off of, and at the first sign of mildew she attacked her tub and shower with cleansers and brushes. She was an active member of her local church and could be counted to cook and bake for every benefit, chaperone the youth events and join parishioners in holiday visits to local nursing homes.

My life's not dull. It isn't. But when was the last time she had been out on a date? Carl Tyndell's face flashed again through her brain. He was the last, she realized, and that was . . . She counted on her fingers. Let's see. Mom got really sick and moved in two years ago and it was a few months before that. Maybe more than a few months. Phew. Had it really been more than three years since she had had a date? Well, after that last debacle, it was just as well. Anyway, she was happy. Wasn't she?

She thought about Steve. He was almost six feet tall with piercing blue eyes and just enough gray at his temples to be distinguished and sexy. He had a strong jaw, and large hands with slender fingers and well-sculptured nails. Frequently Barbara would find herself watching his hands as he signed the correspondence she typed for him.

Was Maggie right? Barbara sighed and popped an M&M into her mouth from the open bag on her bedside table.

She slept little that night and, the next day since Steve was in court, she typed, arranged and organized several important briefs, two wills and a few mortgage documents. Without too much thought, she opened Steve's mail, dealt with the items she could handle herself and arranged the others in folders on his desk. She answered the phone, made and confirmed several appointments for her boss and gave him his messages and took copious notes about his responses each time he called in. She nibbled on her American cheese sandwich and salad at lunch and left the office at four thirty-five.

As she drove home, she realized that, although she had thought about her life and the things Maggie had said most of the day, she had made her decision the previous evening. If this whole thing wasn't an elaborate hoax or some kind of boredom-induced hallucination, she would go along with Maggie, at least for the moment.

When Maggie had walked out of Barbara's kitchen the previous evening she suddenly found herself back inside the revolving door. She pushed her way to the other side and stepped out, only to find herself walking back through Barbara's kitchen door.

"I didn't know whether you'd really be here," Barbara said as Maggie entered the kitchen.

"This is really disorienting," Maggie said, rubbing her forehead. The kitchen was different, with two plates on the table, each with hamburger on a toasted bun, mixed vegetables, and rice. "When am I?"

"That's an interesting takeoff on the typical question. It's almost six-fifteen. I wasn't sure you'd be back."

"Did we meet last evening or just a few minutes ago?"

"We met yesterday." Barbara sat at one end of the table and pointed to the second place setting. "I cooked some dinner for you, but I remember you told me you didn't get hungry. I can put it away and eat it for lunch tomorrow if you don't want it."

"This is all new to me, too," Maggie admitted. "I don't know exactly what I do and what I don't." She sat down and sniffed, enjoying the slightly charcoal smell of the grilled burger in front of her.

"Is this the first time you've helped someone?"

Maggie nodded ruefully. "I'm not like Michael Landon in *Highway to Heaven*. This isn't my job, you know. It's just a test to see where I go."

"I love *Highway to Heaven*. Michael Landon is so adorable."

Maggie raised an eyebrow. "Well, it's good to know you notice things like that." She picked up the burger and took a bite. "Delicious."

"Thanks. I did all the cooking for my mother and me until she died. Good wine and good food were her only pleasures toward the end, and I did what I could to make special things for her."

"Well," Maggie said, her mouth full, "this is really wonderful."

Barbara found herself delighted that Maggie liked her cooking. "What does an angel do all day? I mean, what did you do today?"

"I'm certainly not an angel as anyone who knew me in my old profession can tell you. That's the problem that puts me here with you. And for me, there was no today. I walked out of your kitchen and just walked back in." She blinked, then took another bite of her burger. "I guess I'll get used to it. Tell me what's been happening in the world since I left. Did the O.J. Simpson trial ever end?"

For the next hour Barbara caught Maggie up on what had occurred in the last eight months. Strangely, Barbara realized as she poured coffee for each of them, she had completely accepted the fact that Maggie was dead. She also realized that she hadn't enjoyed an evening this much in a long time.

"I think it's time we got down to business" Maggie said as she sipped her coffee. "I'm here to see that you get out, date, have some fun."

Barbara stretched her legs beneath the table and sighed. "It won't work. I am what I am."

"Do I hear self-pity? A bit of 'poor little me?' "

Barbara sat upright. "Not at all. It's just that you can't make something out of nothing."

"All right, let's get serious here. Do you have a full-length mirror somewhere?"

"I guess." Together the two women walked upstairs and into the guest bedroom. It was a simply decorated room with a flowered quilt, matching drapes, and a simple dresser. The room looked and smelled unused. Maggie walked behind

Barbara and together they stood in front of the long mirror that hung on the closet door.

"Now, look at you," Maggie said, looking at Barbara's reflection over her shoulder. Barbara was wearing a pair of nondescript gray sweat pants and an oversize matching sweat shirt. "You look like you've just come from a rag-pickers' convention."

"But this is just for comfort," Barbara protested.

"Comfort is one thing but dressing in sacks is another." Maggie grabbed a handful of the back of the shirt and pulled. The fabric stretched more tightly across Barbara's chest. "There's a body under this," she said. "Nice tits." She pulled the pants in at the seat. "And you've got nice hips, a small waist. Yes, there's actually a shape under all this material."

Barbara looked, but remained unconvinced.

"Look at your face," Maggie said, grabbing a fistful of hair and pulling it back, away from Barbara's face. "Nice eyes. Actually, *great* eyes. Good cheekbones, good shape. A definite nose, but not too much, and nicely shaped lips. Your skin's not great, but nothing that a decent foundation wouldn't cure." She released Barbara's hair and the two women stood, gazing into the mirror. "There's really a lot of potential. We just need makeup, a good hair stylist, and a new wardrobe."

"I don't need a new wardrobe," Barbara said, almost stomping toward her own room. She crossed to her closet, opened the door and flipped on the light. "Just look. There are lots of really nice clothes in here."

"Nice for a dowdy moderately shapeless old maid, but not for you. You need high shades, sapphire and emerald, deep claret and purple. Oh, you'd look sensational in eggplant."

"I have all the clothes I need."

"But not the ones you want. You seem to want to slide through life virtually unnoticed. Nonsense. Make a statement. Be a real person."

"I am a real person."

Maggie made a rude noise. "In attitude, you rate a D and

in self-esteem you get an F. In looks, I'll give you a 'needs improvement.' And with the improvement will come a change in attitude as well. Are you game?"

Barbara dropped onto her bed. "I don't know, Maggie. Part of me wants to be adventurous, stick out in a crowd, have men notice me. But the rest is terrified. It's such a risk."

Maggie sat beside Barbara and put her arm loosely around the younger woman's shoulders. "Why is it a risk?" she asked softly.

"It just is."

"Think about the worst thing that could happen if you walked into a room in a bright red dress with black stockings and black high heels, with golden highlights in your hair and a 'here I am, come and get me' expression on your face. What's the worst thing?"

To her surprise Barbara burst into tears. Helpless, Maggie handed her a handful of tissues and, with her arms around Barbara's shoulders, let her cry it all out. It took fifteen minutes for Barbara to get calm enough for Maggie to attempt to talk to her again. "You have to tell me what's eating you."

Barbara wiped her face and shook her head.

"I can ask Lucy and she'll find out with that computer system of hers." Maggie explained Lucy's ability to replay events in her life at will. She had no idea whether she could even get to Lucy or whether Lucy could bring up bits of Barbara's past, but she thought it was a decent bluff.

"Oh, no. That would be too humiliating."

"Well, then, let me get us each a glass of wine and then you tell me what it is that frightens you so much. Where's the rest of the bottle we were drinking last evening?"

"In the closet next to the refrigerator, and the glasses are in the hutch in the living room."

"Lord. Unless I was entertaining I left dishes in the sink for days and in my drainer even longer. Okay. You think about how you're going to tell me the ugly details while I fetch for us." Maggie left the room.

Barbara listened to Maggie's footsteps on the stairs and

slumped onto her back. Maybe I can just run away. Maybe I can tell her to go to hell. Maybe I can slit my wrists. She sighed. Maybe it will feel good to tell someone about Carl and Walt. But maybe Maggie would just give up on her if she did. Didn't that serve her purpose anyway, make Maggie go away? Too soon, Maggie returned and thrust a glass of wine into her hand.

"Drink this like it's medicine," Maggie said, brandishing the bottle and her glass in the other. "There's enough here for another half-glass for each of us."

Staying flat on her back on the bed, Barbara awkwardly emptied the glass, then held it out for Maggie to refill. Maggie emptied the bottle into Barbara's glass, then stretched out beside her on the bed. Softly she said, "Tell me about him."

"How did you know it was a him?"

Maggie chuckled. "When a woman has an ego that has been smashed as flat as yours it's always a man—or a woman. And from the way you gazed at that boss of yours yesterday, I assumed the asshole who flattened your self-esteem was a man."

"Oh, yes," Barbara said. "Carl Tyndell was definitely a man, and I guess an asshole, too."

"That's the attitude." Maggie stared at the ceiling, giving Barbara time to decide where to begin.

"I met Carl at a party. It was about four years ago and I had just had my twenty-seventh birthday. Notice I didn't say I celebrated, because, for some unknown reason, that birthday hit me very hard."

As she set the scene for Maggie, Barbara could almost see the room, hear the incessant babble of suburban conversation, smell the cold cuts on the dining-room table. A couple she knew slightly from her church had given the party to introduce some new neighbors. She had put her coat on the bed in the master bedroom and as she walked back down the stairs she saw a sensational-looking man talking in low whispers to Walt McCrory, a neighborhood bachelor whom she had dated a few times a few months earlier. The two men laughed loudly, then the stranger worked his way through the crowd and engaged her in conversation.

"I should have suspected something was up the way Walt leered at me," Barbara said.

"You and this Walt didn't part on good terms, I gather."

"We went out for a few weeks. We had dinner a few times, then one warm evening he invited me back to his place to check out his new above-the-ground pool. One thing led to another, but obviously not fast enough for Walt. After I told him I didn't want to be groped, he called me a cold bitch, incapable of giving a man a decent wet dream much less a hard-on."

"So he presumably talked this Carl person into picking you up."

"I guess that's true, but I was so naive that I didn't make the connection until much later."

"We never do," Maggie said sadly.

"Anyway, Carl and I made dinner plans for a few days later. We had a wonderful meal and a few too many drinks. He was attentive and seemed interested in everything I had to say. His eyes were so deep brown as to be almost black. His hair was also dark brown and he had nice hands. I'm a sucker for men with great hands."

"Me too." Maggie smiled, thinking about how many men's hands had touched her over the years.

"After dinner, Carl suggested a drive along the Hudson. We used my car, parked in a darkened area he knew about and kissed like teenagers. One thing led to another and suddenly my blouse was off and my bra was open. His mouth was on me and he was whispering, 'Babs, sweetie, oh, Babs.' Suddenly Walt pulled the car door open and snapped a flash picture of me, naked from the waist up.

" 'You win, Carl baby,' Walt said. 'I can't deny it when I have the proof and a great shot of Babs' tits right here.' I watched the picture spit out of the front of the camera and slowly appear before my eyes."

"Win what?" Maggie asked, annoyed by the pain inflicted

by something that to those two probably amounted to nothing more than a prank.

"They had made a bet that Carl couldn't get my upper body exposed on the first date. Right there in the car Walt counted out a hundred dollars and handed it to Carl. Walt said that he didn't think anyone could get the ice bitch out of her clothes in under six months. They laughed, pounded each other on the back, then the two of them walked to Walt's car, and took off."

"Oh."

"Yes, oh."

"Well that wasn't the end of the world, was it?"

Barbara just stared at the ceiling. "I never told anyone about that night and, I guess, Walt never did either. I spent the next few weeks waiting for the picture or the story to circulate, but for some unknown reason, nothing happened."

"Did you ever see them again?"

"I never saw Carl again. He must have been 'imported talent.' " She said the phrase with a sneer. "I see Walt once in a while, but he's not a church type and I stick almost completely to church gatherings."

"Safe stuff. No risk of anyone getting sexual." Maggie took Barbara's hand. "Wouldn't you like to get him back sometime?"

Barbara smiled. "I'd love to, but there's no hope of that."

"I wouldn't be so sure. It just gives us another reason to make you over and get you some experience." She paused. "Are you a virgin?"

Barbara sat upright. "What a question."

"Well . . ."

"No. I've had relationships." She slumped back down onto her back. "But not recently."

"And Steve? Wouldn't you like him to notice you?"

"Of course."

"So you'll let me help you? For your mom and Steve and maybe even Walt and Carl."

Barbara sighed. She wanted to let Maggie help. It was all

so bizarre but it was a chance to get some of the things she wanted. It might be her only chance. "I guess."

"Good," Maggie said. "First, call in sick tomorrow and we'll get your hair done, get someone to help you with your makeup and see what we can do about some clothes for you. I need to know something that's a bit embarrassing. Is money a problem? I'm a bit short of funds, you realize."

Barbara laughed out loud for the first time since Maggie had appeared the previous evening. "No. My job pays well and I don't spend much. I'm not Saks Fifth Avenue-well off, but we could certainly go to the mall and dent my credit card."

"Great."

"You know, it sounds like fun."

"It does, doesn't it."

"Will you be able to be here? I mean how do you just appear and disappear the way you do?"

Maggie thought, then answered, "I don't know how." She told Barbara about the revolving door. "I seem to be able to set some kind of clock, so I just come out of the door here at the right time."

"Do you have powers? Like moving stuff with your mind or walking through walls?"

"I don't think so, but Lucy and Angela seem to be in charge of that. They said I'd have what I needed when I needed it, so I'll just have to trust them." She stood up. "I've got to be going now." She cocked her head to one side. "I don't know how I know that, but I do." She walked toward the bedroom door, then turned. "Tomorrow. Nin-ish."

Barbara raised her hand and waved as Maggie walked through the bedroom door and vanished.

Barbara's dreams were troubled for the first part of the night. She was in the car with Walt and Carl, but the car was really the gaping jaws of a giant mythical beast and, as the two men jumped out, the jaws began to close on her naked, immobile body. Then she was walking down the aisle in church dressed in a bridal gown, with her mother holding her arm, ready to give her away to the man who stood beside the priest, his back turned to her. When she reached his side, he turned, but he had no face. She looked down and saw that he was a tuxedoed store mannequin with two poles holding him up where his legs should have been.

The following morning, Barbara called her office and told the woman who answered the phone that she had urgent personal business and wouldn't be in the office until the following day. She dressed in a man-tailored shirt and jeans, white socks and sneakers, grabbed a denim jacket and bounced down to the kitchen. Bounced, she thought, was a good word for the way she felt. Light. Elastic. Good!

She made a pot of strong coffee and toasted a bagel. She sat at the table munching and thinking about the day's activities. "Good morning," Maggie said from the doorway.

"Hi, Maggie," Barbara responded. "Coffee?"

"I guess. This time warp thing I'm in is still very confusing. It seems like only a moment ago I left you last evening."

"Nice outfit," Barbara said.

Maggie looked down, puzzled. "I didn't change clothes," she whispered. Last evening she had had on an outfit similar to the clothes Barbara was wearing this morning. But now Maggie was wearing a pair of wide-legged black rayon pants and a soft gray silk blouse. "Very disconcerting," she mumbled.

Barbara poured Maggie a mug of coffee and set it down beside a pitcher of milk and the sugar bowl. "Maggie," she asked as her friend dropped into a chair. "How did you become a . . . I mean . . . ?"

"Hooker?"

"Yeah. Well. . . ."

"You mean how did a nice girl like me end up entertaining men for money."

"You can't blame me for being curious."

Maggie grinned. "Of course not. And let's get this settled right now. I've said it before. I am proud of what I do, er

. . . did. I had my own rules and I stuck by them at all times. My customers and I had fun. We were careful and honest."

"It's just difficult for me to believe in the hooker with the heart of gold. It's so clichéd."

"Heart of gold. I like that. I like that a lot. Anyway, you asked how I got started in my business. It began with my first divorce."

"You were married?" Barbara said, her eyes wide.

"Twice, but this is my story to tell. Anyway, Chuck and I married right out of high school in 1955 and stayed together for six years. The split was amicable. We just had nothing in common anymore. No kids, we both worked, our sex life was dull, dull, dull. He married again by the way, to a nice, mousey woman who seemed to make him happy. But that's another story.

"As a divorcee, I slept around. That was a very loose time, before AIDS, very into me first. I found that I loved sex. I enjoyed pleasing the men I was with and I had fun learning how to do it. I was still just beginning to learn about fantasy when I met Bob. He had a wonderfully creative mind and taught me about all sorts of new things in the bedroom. When he suggested we get married, I thought I'd found my ultimate sex partner and in order to keep us together, I said yes."

"He sounds like a wonderful lover."

"He was and he taught me to be a giving, creative partner."

"But . . ."

"But I couldn't stand him outside of the bedroom. He and I were exact opposites. He was a neat freak, I'm a bit of a slob. He liked his meals at specific times, all organized, I like to scrounge for myself. You get it. So, after two fantastic years in the bedroom and two awful years everywhere else, we split, too. That was 1974, and it seems like forever ago. I was intensely glad when he left, but I was horny as hell. All the time. The one good thing about marriage is that you can usually have all the sex you want."

"That sounds terrible."

"It was for me. I still worked, of course. I was manager of the computer input department at a regional bank. I had very good people skills, as my boss called them, but I was bored. Bored, lonely and horny at home and bored, stressed, and frustrated at work. Not much of a life."

Barbara patted the back of Maggie's hand, well able to sympathize with the older woman.

"One evening I just couldn't bear to go home to that empty apartment so I stopped at a bar near work. I'd been sitting at the bar for about an hour, feeling sorry for myself, when a cute-looking guy sat down on the stool next to mine." Maggie closed her eyes and a smile changed her expression from despair to enjoyment as she remembered that evening. "I remember. I called myself Margaret at that time."

"Hi," the man said. "My name's Frank."

Maggie looked up, ready to brush the man off with a clever remark. But as she took in his charming smile, she changed her mind. "Hi. I'm Margaret."

"Glad to meet you, Margaret. I come in here whenever I'm in town but I've never seen you before."

"I've never been in here before," Maggie said.

Frank placed his elbow on the bar and leaned his chin on his hand, studying Maggie's face. "You know," he said after a moment, "you don't look like a Margaret."

Maggie sipped her white wine, unwilling to make any overt gestures of friendliness toward this stranger who was in the process of picking her up in a bar. "And how would a Margaret look?"

"Oh, let's see. Margaret is very serious. Tight bun. Thick glasses. Sensible shoes."

Maggie thought about that and realized that, in the months since she and Bob had gone their separate ways, she had become just what Frank pictured. No, she thought, I won't be that person. I'm only thirty-three. She took a large swallow of her wine and sat up a bit straighter. "Okay. I guess I can't be that kind of Margaret. What would you call me?"

"Well, Margie is young, pert, and too cute to be believed, so that's not you. And Peggy is an Irish lass with red hair and freckles."

"Okay. Neither of those sound like me. So who am I?"

"You look like a Maggie. Nice-looking. Interesting and interested. Open to new experiences."

"What a line you've got," Maggie said, realizing that, whether it was a line or not, this man had made her feel younger than she had in years. She lowered her chin and looked up at Frank through her lashes. "And I must say I like it."

Frank grinned. "Me too. And it usually works."

Maggie laughed. "You admit that it's a line? How original."

"The line's original, too," he said. "And you're the first woman who's picked up on it so quickly." He tried and almost succeeded in looking like a small boy with his hand in the cookie jar. It helped that he had medium brown hair naturally streaked with blond, wide blue eyes, and a fantastic mouth.

They talked for an hour, then went to a nearby French restaurant and shared a sumptuous meal which included a bottle of fine Chardonnay and a glass of sweet, golden dessert wine. She learned that Frank was divorced, in town from Dallas for a week for his firm's quarterly department meetings and that he was charming and sexy and determined to get her into his bed. As he dropped his credit card onto the check, he took Maggie's hand. As he held it across the table, his index finger scratched little patterns in her palm. "We could be good together," he purred.

She had to admit to herself that she was turned on. But this was a man who had picked her up, not someone she worked with or who had been introduced to her by friends. He was only in town for a short time. She couldn't even delude herself into thinking this was the beginning of a long-term relationship. But she wanted to go to bed with him nonetheless. "How can you be so sure?" she said.

"I can be very sure. I can see it in your eyes, your body,

the way you smile, the way you can't quite sit still. You want this as much as I do. How do you like your sex?"

"Excuse me?"

"You heard me. How do you like your sex? Long and slow, with lots of kissing and stroking? Hard and fast, like the pair of animals we are? Standing up with your back pressed against the wall and your legs locked around my waist? In the shower under torrents of hot water? Tell me and I'll make it that way for you."

Maggie shrugged. She couldn't tell him how she liked her sex because she loved it all ways. "You tell me," she hedged. "How do you like it?"

"Oh, Maggie, I think I'd like it every way with you." He lifted her hand and nipped at her fingertips.

"No," she said, more seriously. "Tell me. How would you like to make love with me? Create the fantasy and let's see how we mesh."

"You're serious. You want me to tell you." When Maggie merely nodded, Frank said, "I see you slowly removing your clothes while I watch. I watch you reveal your body to me, one small piece at a time."

Silently Maggie reached up and unbuttoned the top two buttons on her blouse and parted the sides so the valley between her breasts was visible.

"Shit, baby. I'm hard as stone already."

Maggie raised an eyebrow but remained silent.

"Okay. I see you in your bra and panties." He looked around the tablecloth at Maggie's shoes. "Yes. Black high heels. I like that. You're not wearing pantyhose, are you?"

"I won't be," she said, contemplating a quick trip to the ladies' room. She watched the flush rise on Frank's face. She was turning him on. What a trip.

"You're walking toward me, then unzipping my pants."

Maggie was very turned on and more than a little drunk. Without changing her expression, she slipped one foot out of her shoe and stretched her foot across the space between them and rested her stocking-covered toes against the swelling in his crotch.

His startled look, followed by a shift of position to place her foot more firmly against his zipper, told Maggie exactly what she was doing to him. "Shit, baby, let's get out of here," he moaned.

"The waiter hasn't brought your credit card back," Maggie said, feigning an innocent expression. She wiggled her toes in his lap. "As I remember, I was unzipping your pants. Tell me more. I want to know exactly how you see this evening we're going to have."

She watched Frank take a deep breath. "I can't think when you do that."

Again she silently raised an eyebrow. She was in charge now, quite deliberately turning Frank on, a man she had met only three hours before.

His voice uneven, he continued. "You were unzipping my pants and taking out my cock. It's so hard it sticks up like a flagpole. You're wrapping your hand around it and licking your lips."

Maggie slowly ran the tip of her tongue across her upper lip. "Like this?"

At that moment, the waiter returned with Frank's charge slip, which he signed with an obviously shaking hand. As he wrote, Maggie moved her toes in his lap. As the waiter took the restaurant copy, Maggie asked, "Could I have just a bit more coffee?"

"Certainly, madame."

"But, Maggie, I thought we were going to my room." He was almost whining.

"We will. But I need just a bit more coffee and you haven't finished your story. I was holding your cock, as I recall. Squeezing it as it sticks up through the opening in your pants. Let's see, I'm wearing a black lace bra, bikini panties, and my high black shoes. Right?" Bob had taught her about the power of a well-set erotic scene and he had marveled at her ability to use words to turn him on. Now she was using all her skill to turn Frank on. And it was working better than she could have imagined.

Frank was again lost in his fantasy. "Right," he whispered.

"And I'll bet you want me to take your cock into my mouth and suck you."

"Oh, yes," he groaned as the waiter refilled Maggie's coffee cup. Without removing her hand from his, or her foot from his lap, she poured cream into her cup and stirred.

When he didn't continue, she said, "You want me to touch the tip of your cock with my lips, kiss it, lick it, make it wet." She deliberately slowed the cadence of her speech. "Then I can slowly suck it into my mouth. Very slowly. Pulling it deeper and deeper into that hot, wet cave."

Frank's eyes closed, obviously lost in the fantasy.

"Now I pull back, but I keep sucking so your cock pulls out so slowly. Down and up, my mouth is driving you crazy." She remembered a trick Bob had taught her. "But I wrap my fingers around the base of your cock so you can't come as I keep on sucking. I don't want you to come yet, baby."

"But I want to come."

"Not until we're both ready. So now I pull my panties off and rub myself. I'm very wet, you know. I let you lick my finger so you can taste me. Do I taste good?"

"Oh, yes."

"Good. Now I pull off your pants, but I leave your shirt on. It's very sexy for me to see you all dressed in your business shirt and tie while I slowly put a cold, lubricated condom over your cock. It feels tight, like it's hugging you. Now I push you down onto the bed, straddle your waist and use the tip of your slippery cock to play with myself." She looked at his closed eyes. "Can you see me?"

"Yes," he said, his voice harsh and almost inaudible.

"Let me take off my bra so you can watch my breasts as I play with your cock. I'm rubbing my clit now. It's hard and you can even feel it against your cock. And I'm so wet. Your hips are moving, trying to push your cock inside. Shall I let you?"

"Please."

"Yes, I will. I lower myself onto you, pulling you deep inside. You fill me up so well, baby. I raise up and drop, over and over, fucking you so good. Do you want to come now? I'm almost ready." With his eyes closed, Frank groaned. Maggie rubbed her foot along the length of his cock under the tablecloth.

"I'm almost ready. Almost. Wait for me, baby." Maggie was so turned on by her description of Frank's fantasy that if she reached under the table and touched herself, she would come. But she didn't.

"Yes, baby," she said. "I'm coming now. You can feel my pussy squeezing your cock. Come with me."

"Yes," Frank groaned. Then his eyes flew open. "No." He pushed Maggie's foot from his lap. "Not here."

"No. Not here," Maggie said. "But I need a trip to the ladies' room first." To remove her pantyhose. When she returned, Frank was waiting for her with her coat in his hands. "My hotel is just around the corner."

Maggie slipped her arms into the sleeves. "Good," she said. "I find I'm in a bit of a hurry."

"Are you sure you're not a professional at this? No offense."

"No offense taken. And no, I'm not a pro."

"Well, you should be. I've been with my share of professional entertainers and no one holds a candle to you."

As they walked out of the restaurant, Maggie asked, "You've been with call girls?"

"Sure. Sometimes the company provides entertainment for the out-of-town reps. And not one of them could come close to the way you turn me on. That little story back there . . ." He wrapped his arm around her shoulder. "Holy shit."

"I enjoy turning men on. I dated a lot before I met Bob, and then he taught me about fantasy and lots of variations on straight sex. I love it all."

"You should get paid for it."

"How much do call girls make?"

"The classy ones like you make hundreds a night."

"Hundreds of dollars?" Maggie gasped.

They turned the corner and approached Frank's hotel. "Sure. I know a few people and I could introduce you."

"Hmmm."

Maggie looked at Barbara. "The evening went exactly like the fantasy we had created." She took a drink from her coffee cup. "And he introduced me to someone who introduced me to someone else and, as they say, the rest is history."

"Wow."

"Yes. Wow. And I entertained men for twenty years."

"Did you ever have any bad experiences? You read about hookers getting beaten up and stuff."

"I had one or two men who didn't get the message when I told them to knock it off, but I know how to defend myself and I seldom take chances. All the men I entertain, er . . . entertained—it's so hard for me to think of myself in the past tense. The men I entertained were all recommended, lonely business types who just wanted someone to have some fun with. You know, do the things they wouldn't do with their wives."

"Like?"

"Mostly oral sex and anal sex. Some were into power fantasies, both giving and receiving and a few were into pain."

"You mean like whips?"

"I slapped a few men on the ass, but I never did whips because I can't get pleasure out of that. Heavy pain is such a turn-off for me that I made it clear I wouldn't play those games. But most other things were as exciting for me as they were for the men I was with."

"That's amazing."

Maggie looked at her watch. "It's getting late. Get your pocketbook and your credit cards and we're off to shop."

Barbara stood up. "I can't wait."

Chapter 4

"Now this doesn't mean I'm going to jump into someone's bed so fast," Barbara said under her breath as they walked into the Galleria Mall in White Plains. "You can't make a silk purse and all that."

"Let's first get you dressed and looking like the attractive woman you are," Maggie said. As they walked, the few shoppers they saw walked around Barbara but seemed unaware that Maggie was there. "You know," Maggie said, turning to stare at a woman with a stroller who had just missed bumping into her, "I don't think anyone can see me."

"But I can see you just fine," Barbara said.

They walked passed a large clothing store and paused in front of a mirrored section of wall. "I can see us both," Barbara said as Maggie dodged to avoid a mother pushing a blue-and-white stroller.

"It's really weird," Maggie said. "I'm here. I can see me." She rubbed her arms. "I can feel me, hear me. You can, too. But to judge by the people walking by, I don't exist."

"But you do exist," Barbara said.

"Mommy," a little girl said as she passed, "why is that woman talking to herself?"

"Let's go, darling," the mother said, hustling the tot off. "It's not nice to talk about . . ."

As the woman's voice faded, Maggie said, "We better be careful. People will think you're nuts."

As they strolled around the mall, getting the lay of the land, Barbara was careful not to speak to Maggie where anyone might overhear. Together the two women stopped periodically so Maggie could show Barbara outfits and shoes that would fit her new image. With Maggie steering, the two walked toward a hair salon called Expert Tresses. "We really should start with your hair."

"I like my hair," Barbara said, reflexively tucking a strand behind her ear. "It's easy and comfortable."

Maggie raised an eyebrow. "Easy and comfortable. Two of the most awful adjectives I can think of." She stopped and turned Barbara to face her. She peered at a section of hair just above her right temple. "What's this? The roots are white here."

"I was hoping we could overlook that. It's a white streak. My mother used to call it a witch's mark."

"You dye it?"

"My mother started doing that for me when I was a kid. It's just dyed to match the rest of my hair."

"It's sexy as hell. I want you to get someone to style this mop," Maggie said, staring at Barbara's soft, medium-brown hair. "And get the dye out of that section."

"But it's unlucky and creepy. I won't."

"Barbara, baby. It's unique and beautiful and it looks great. Your mother was a wonderful lady, but in this one instance, she was wrong. Please. Cooperate. Try this."

"No."

"Look," Maggie said, guiding Barbara into a small alcove. "Do this for me and for this project. Let someone do your hair. My way. Then give it one week. If you don't like it, you can dye it back. Okay? Please. I have a job to do here."

When Barbara hesitated, Maggie continued. "And get your nails done, too."

"But . . ."

Maggie put a hand in the small of Barbara's back and pushed, aiming her toward Expert Tresses. Since the salon was almost empty, three women walked toward her as she walked in. "May we help you?"

"I need a haircut," Barbara said.

"You want it styled," Maggie said, knowing that no one else could hear.

"I want it styled."

One of the women looked her over. "My name's Candy and I think you're mine this morning. Come on over here." The pink-smocked woman led Barbara to a chair at one side of the studio.

"I have a streak right here," Barbara said, fingering a section of hair as Candy covered Barbara's clothes with a plastic apron.

"Yes, I see," Candy said. "Why do you dye it?"

"It's a witch's mark."

"And it's so kinky." Candy lifted a strand of her long blond hair from her temple. "It wouldn't look as good on me," she said. She returned her attention to Barbara. "But on you . . ."

"Well . . ."

As they started to talk about styles, Maggie said, "She sounds like she knows what she's talking about, so let her do whatever she wants. I'll be back." Over her shoulder, she called, "And don't forget the nails."

Maggie left the salon and walked purposefully back to the mirrored section of wall. With people unable to see her, Maggie stood staring at herself. Since no one could hear her, she talked aloud to herself. "It's been six months since I, whatever, and my hair hasn't grown nor does it need to be colored." She looked down. "My nails are perfect and I don't look any older." She walked close to the mirror and stared at her skin. "No new lines. No signs of age. Nothing."

"And you won't age," a voice she recognized as Angela's

said. "You'll just continue as you were on the day you died. That's one of the advantages of an assignment like this."

"Have you done this kind of thing often?" Maggie asked.

"Not really, but it does happen occasionally," Lucy said. "How's it going?"

"Don't you know?"

"Not really," Angela said. "We don't have the time to watch what's happening. We just drop in from time to time."

"Could Barbara hear you if she were here?"

"No," Angela continued. "Only you can hear us, and see us if it becomes necessary. But creating corporeal images on earth is very energy inefficient and in most cases unnecessary."

"How do you like Barbara?" Lucy asked.

"Actually, she's really nice. But mousy. She's got zero self-confidence. Even with a good hairstyle and attractive clothes, she's not going to be a beauty."

"You're not a Miss America candidate yourself," Lucy said.

"Oh now, Lucy," Angela said, "that's unkind."

"Look you two," Maggie said, "I know I'm not gorgeous, but I'm attractive. I use what I've got and I've never wanted for companions, paid and unpaid."

"That's the first lesson your friend Barbara has to learn," Angela said. "It's the gleam in the eye not the meat on the bones that makes a woman sexy."

"Listen, we've got other fish to fry, as it were," Lucy said. "Go pick Barbara up. She's waiting for you."

"But it's only been about five minutes," Maggie protested.

"You already know that time has little meaning in your existence," Angela said. "Go pick her up."

Her head now empty of voices, Maggie walked back to Expert Tresses and, sure enough, Barbara had just finished signing the charge slip. Maggie looked her friend over. The white streak was now prominent in Barbara's slightly darkened, carefully cut brown hair. Styled so it fell just at her shoulders, her hair curled up at the ends and moved gracefully as Barbara moved. She looked at Maggie and shrugged.

"You look just great," Maggie said. "What an improvement. And you've got makeup on."

Barbara stuffed the charge-card receipt into her wallet and walked out of the salon. "It's hard remembering not to talk to you where anyone might hear."

"Sorry."

"Candy gave me a few tips about foundation and eye makeup so I bought a few things and she and another woman helped me put this stuff on. Does it look okay?"

Maggie studied Barbara's light taupe shadow, soft brown liner, blush, and lipstick. "You really look nice. You'll need more for evenings, of course, but for day wear, it's just great."

Barbara stopped at the same mirrored section of the wall. "You really think so? It's so obvious. I look made up."

"You look like you took some time to enhance your looks. That's great. You don't always have to look like you got up late for work."

"I don't . . ."

"You do most of the time. There's nothing wrong with taking a little time to look good."

"It's vain."

"It's just good sense. Vanity in large doses is bad. Feeling good about the way you look is good. Let's see what we can do now about your wardrobe."

"After lunch. I'm starving."

"We just had breakfast."

Barbara looked at her watch. "That was almost five hours ago and I, for one, am famished."

In the food court, Barbara bought a corned beef sandwich with fries and a pickle. With her plate in one hand and a 7Up in the other, she found a small table off to one side of the seating area. She sat with her back to the other shoppers so she could talk to Maggie without everyone thinking she was nuts. As they talked, Maggie occasionally picked up a french fry and nibbled on it. Barbara wondered what others would see if they looked. Would a french fry just lift up into the air, then disappear?

The two women then spent the afternoon doing serious damage to Barbara's credit card. They bought several soft bright-colored silk blouses and two skirts, considerably shorter than Barbara had been used to. "You have great legs," Maggie said several times. "Show them off. You want to catch the eye of that boss of yours, don't you?"

Unable to argue without seeming like a nut, Barbara went along. In a shoe boutique, Maggie bullied Barbara into purchasing a pair of black, two-and-a-half-inch high opera pumps and a pair of knee-high brown butter-soft suede boots with stiletto heels.

As they started for the parking lot of the mall, Maggie spotted a Victoria's Secret store. "Let's go in," she said.

"I have underwear," Barbara said.

"I'll bet not the right kind."

Barbara had just about given up arguing so together the two women entered the store. Maggie all but dragged her friend to a display of lacy bra and panty sets. Both the bra and the panty were mostly net with flowers embroidered in strategic places. "Get the black one, the white one, and the light blue."

"But, Maggie," Barbara said, "they're so slutty."

A saleswoman whirled around. "Yes," she said, "can I help you? I'm sorry I didn't hear your last question."

"I wasn't talking to you."

The saleswoman looked around, then shrugged. "Those lace sets are on sale," she said. "It's buy two and get the third for a dollar."

"The black, the white, and the light blue," Maggie said, knowing she couldn't be heard by anyone but Barbara. "And don't argue. You know you want them and you don't ever have to wear them. Just indulge me."

"Okay," Barbara said, looking at the pleasant saleswoman. "I'll take the light blue and the white."

"A third set will only cost a dollar more."

Maggie tapped her foot and arched an eyebrow.

"Okay," Barbara agreed. "I guess I'll take the black as well."

"Good choice," the woman said. "And the size?"

"It's been a long time since I bought undies. Maybe I better try them on." She selected bras in three different sizes.

"Certainly," the woman said and showed Barbara to the fitting room.

In the tiny room, Barbara pulled off her shirt and bra and put the new white one on. Maggie appeared in the corner of the mirrored room and let out a low whistle. "You've got a great body, you know."

Barbara turned sideways, raised her rib cage and sucked in her tummy. "I could have if I never breathed again." When she relaxed, her belly bulged a bit and her diaphragm protruded.

"You've got a very nice figure," Maggie said. "And those bits of stuff you're wearing do wonders."

Barbara looked at the white lace bra she wore. She really didn't look half bad, she had to admit. The flowers woven into the fabric were designed so that leaves and blossoms covered her nipples but the rest was almost transparent.

"Very sexy," Maggie said. "Yes, very nice. I think your boss would approve."

Barbara blushed. "He will never see me like this," she said, replacing the silk with her serviceable cotton undies.

"He will if you want him to. He'll notice you and he'd be a fool not to be impressed. You will go into the office tomorrow a different woman."

Barbara smiled.

The following morning, Barbara showered and, when she returned to her bedroom, Maggie was sitting on her bed. "Wear that new cornflower blue blouse with the black skirt. And the light-blue bra and panties."

As Barbara reached for her traditional underwear, she asked, "What difference does it make what I wear underneath?"

"If you feel sexy under your clothes, it affects the way you behave. I want you to spend the day knowing that your breasts are being held by that wonderful erotic fabric."

"But . . ."

"Do what I ask, Barbara," Maggie said. "Trust me. You want him to notice you, don't you?"

"Well, yes."

"Good. So do it my way, just this once."

Barbara sighed and dressed as Maggie had suggested. After a quick breakfast, Barbara put on her coat. "Will you be at work with me today?"

"No," Maggie answered. "I'll see you here tonight and you can tell me all about it."

Barbara arrived at work at two minutes before eight, got her coffee and settled down to work. Her boss was in court that morning and wasn't due in until after lunch. Except for a quick trip to the ladies' room, Barbara stayed huddled at her desk all morning. The people who passed by noticed her new hairstyle and makeup and several commented cheerfully on how lovely she looked. One woman complimented her on the silver streak in her hair and a young male associate actually winked at her, something that had never happened before.

Throughout her almost solitary morning, she occasionally forgot her makeover, but then she would look down at her hands typing or dialing the phone and her nicely shaped nails, polished in a medium pink, reminded her again. Maybe Steve would notice her, like in one of those romantic movies. "Oh my goodness, Barbara," he would say, "I never realized." She smiled at the thought, then shook her head and got back to work.

As she usually did, Barbara ate lunch at her desk, then returned to work, her eyes glued on the screen of her word processor. At one-thirty, she jumped as her intercom buzzer sounded. She picked up the phone and her boss said, without preamble, "Barbara, I hope you finished the Sanderson documents. Mr. and Mrs. Sanderson are due here at two for the closing." Barbara realized that she had been so engrossed in hiding her new look that she hadn't even heard Steve come in.

She prided herself on her efficiency and always had documents completed long before they were needed. "Of course, Mr. Gordon, I've got them whenever you're ready."

"I wondered with that day off you took yesterday. Bring them in here, will you?"

"Ccrtainly, Mr. Gordon." Barbara stood up, carefully arranged her black wool skirt and straightened the collar on her periwinkle blouse. As she walked into her boss's office, he was bent over, rifling through his briefcase which lay open on the floor beside his desk. "Damn," he swore, "I can't find a thing in here. Barbara, help me, will you?"

"What are you looking for?" Barbara asked, putting the documents she held on his desk.

"The Norton file. I had it just before lunch."

Barbara crouched, exposing a long expanse of thigh and began to systematically go through the contents of Mr. Gordon's briefcase. "It's right here," she said, quickly locating the missing file. As she looked up, she saw Mr. Gordon staring at her.

"What have you done with yourself?" he asked.

"I just got a few new things."

"And had your hair done, and got new makeup. Stand up."

Barbara stood, trying not the back up under his intense scrutiny. She watched his eyes travel from her hair to her heels and back up, several times. Then he released a long, low wolf whistle. "Not bad."

"Thank you, sir," Barbara said, straightening her shoulders. "I just felt I could use a lift."

"Well, you certainly got a lift." He stared for another full minute, then cleared his throat. "Okay. I see you have the Sanderson closing documents. I think everything should be in order. I have some notes from court this morning that need to be typed up."

Barbara sat in the small chair across from Steve Gordon's desk, smoothed her skirt and crossed her legs. As she arranged her computer on her lap, she caught Mr. Gordon staring at her knees. She sat, waiting for him to begin. "Mr. Gordon, I'm ready whenever you are."

"You know we've been together for how long? Almost two years?"

"Actually, it's almost six years."

"Well, don't you think it's about time you started calling me Steve?"

Totally taken aback, Barbara said, "I guess so, Mr. Gordon. I mean Steve."

"Good." He hesitated, then opened the folder in his hand. "I had a call from Mrs. Norton this morning. Take this down . . ."

At four-thirty, Barbara cleared the top of her desk, locked her laptop in her drawer and got her coat. As she was about to leave, Steve came out of his office. "Good night, Barbara," he said cheerfully. "And by the way, that silver patch of hair is very, well, very attractive. Have a nice evening. Got a date?"

"No, sir, I mean Steve. No date."

Steve put his arm around her waist and guided her toward the elevator. "Well then, maybe there will be time for me some evening."

Unable to breathe, Barbara merely nodded as the elevator doors opened.

"Well, have a nice evening."

"And he suggested that we might have dinner sometime," Barbara told Maggie several hours later. It was all Maggie could do not to swear when Barbara mentioned the whistle. He reminds me more and more of Arnie Becker, she thought.

"He looked at me," Barbara continued, unaware of Maggie's reaction. "I mean, really looked. He thought I looked good."

"Well, you do look good. Did work go well, too?"

"Sure. We did the Sanderson closing. I had caught a few minor errors and fixed them before they became problems. I also checked on the title insurance for him."

"What would he do without you?" Maggie said dryly.

"You're not happy for me, Maggie," Barbara said. "I don't understand."

"Sorry. I'm the one who helped you with the makeover and all and I'm glad you're pleased. It's just I have a basic dislike for men who only notice women when they're attractive."

"Oh, Maggie," Barbara said, sipping a glass of Chardonnay while she sautéed chicken and vegetables. Since Maggie's arrival, she was beginning to develop a taste for wine with dinner. "That's not really true. He always knew I was there. He just, well, you know. He's got other things on his mind."

Maggie patted Barbara on the shoulder. "I do know, baby. And maybe he'll ask you out. Is that what you want?"

"Oh, that would be wonderful. Dinner, maybe a little dancing."

"Ah, yes. Slow dancing. A wonderful way to make love standing up."

"You know, I never thought of it that way, but you're right. Making love standing up." Barbara placed the chicken mixture on two plates and sat across from her friend. In only two days it had become comfortable to have Maggie around. She had a friend.

"Do you like making love?" Maggie asked, anxious to move Barbara along to phase two of her makeover.

"It's not like it is in the novels I like to read, but the few times I did it it was tolerable."

"Tolerable. What a terrible way to think about making love. No bells? No stars? The earth didn't move?"

"That doesn't happen to people like me. That's for glitzy novels and X-rated movies."

"It can happen, and it does, and it should."

Barbara sipped her wine, her curiosity aroused. "Did the earth move for you?"

"You mean did I climax?"

Blushing slightly, Barbara nodded.

"No, not every time I made love. It takes a bit of effort and consideration on the part of both partners for orgasm to occur. But I did more often than not. I found that my men friends liked it when I came even though they were paying me to be sure *they* climaxed."

"But you only discovered good sex after your divorce."

"That's true and a bit sad. I regret that Chuck and I never found out what good sex was all about."

"Do you and he still see each other? I mean, did you? Does he know what you do, er . . . did?"

"Boy, tenses are a problem, aren't they. Anyway, no, I don't see Chuck anymore. He and his new wife moved to the West Coast many years ago. We had no kids, no ties, not much in common except a lot of history, and reminiscing wears thin very quickly."

"Can I ask you a question?"

"Sure." Maggie watched Barbara sip her wine as if searching for the right words. "Look, Barbara," Maggie said, "you can ask anything you want. I may choose not to answer, but please, we're friends and this is a really strange situation."

"As a, . . . let's say woman of the evening, you had to do all kinds of things with your customers. Is all that kinky stuff really fun?"

"You mean like oral sex and bondage?"

Barbara merely nodded.

"There are a thousand things people enjoy in the bedroom. Some enjoy plain straight sex, missionary position. Some enjoy telling stories in the dark, tying a partner up, spanking, anal sex. There are probably as many variations as you can dream of. Most I enjoy, a few I don't. But that's true with all things. I love almost all foods, but I hate liver and lima beans."

Barbara laughed. "What sex-type things don't you enjoy?"

"I already told you that I don't find pain pleasurable." Maggie thought a minute, then continued. "That's about all."

"Pain? That's sick."

"No, it's not. Listen, I hate to sound preachy, but I think this is very important. Anything that two consenting adults get pleasure from is none of anyone else's business and isn't sick. As long as both partners know it's important to say no if anything feels the least bit wrong, anything else is okay."

"I guess. How did you discover which things you enjoyed and which you didn't?"

"Trial and error. Lots of trial," Maggie grinned, "and a few errors."

"Errors?"

"Sure. I got myself into a few situations where I had to give someone his money back."

"Were they mad?"

"Not really. There was one guy from the Midwest. I won't go into details, but he wanted me to hurt him. Knowing that it would please him, I tried to do what he wanted, but I couldn't. However, I had a friend who was more into the pain side of pleasure than I was so I called her. He put on his clothes and hustled over to her house. He was so grateful that he called me the next day. He told me it had been everything he had ever fantasized about."

"No accounting for taste, is there?"

"No. And you may find as time passes that there are things you enjoy that you never dreamed of."

Barbara looked startled. "I'm not interested in kinky stuff. I don't mean to put you down, it's just that I'm not that type of person."

"You have no idea what type of person you are. I'll bet you have no real idea of what gives you pleasure."

"Of course I do." Barbara got a dreamy look in her eyes.

"You want romance, slow dancing, kissing and hugging. Long, slow sex with gentle penetration and a long rest period afterward."

"Sure. Why not?"

"No reason. But there's much more to good fucking than that."

"Fucking. Such a terrible word. It's so animal."

"That's what we are, animals. And human beings enjoy a good fucking as much as the average animal does. You know when you think of it, sex is a really awkward and embarrassing thing to do. It violates any feelings of personal space you might have, you get into lots of not-too-comfortable positions, and it's really messy."

"I never thought about it that way."

"So in order to create offspring, God, or Mother Nature, or evolution had to give the animals some reward for doing this ridiculous stuff. So that's where the pleasure comes in. I read somewhere that animals will go through much more maze-running and the like for sexual gratification than for any other reward."

"It's really pleasurable, isn't it?"

"It really is. I doubt you've ever experienced an orgasm."

"Of course I have."

Maggie raised an eyebrow and Barbara looked down and sipped her wine. "There's no shame in not having climaxed. It takes time and an understanding of your own body. You're not born knowing, you have to learn. Do you know where you like to be touched? What makes you hungry for more?"

Barbara continued to stare into her wineglass.

Maggie reached into her pocket and found the audiotape she had somehow known would be there. She pulled it out and stared at the label. "I don't understand how this got into my pocket, but there's a lot about my assignment I don't quite get yet. This is one tape in a series that a friend of mine made. He creates sensational erotica and has a soft, sexy voice, so he found this unique way to package his stories." She put the tape into Barbara's hand. "I'm going to give you an assignment."

Barbara looked up and giggled. "Homework?"

"Sort of. You must have a tape player." When Barbara nodded, Maggie continued. "I want you to fill the bathtub with nice warm water and play this tape. Just play it. If you're tempted to follow the instructions you'll be given, do it. No one will be watching, no one judging. Just you. Will you do that for me?" When her friend hesitated, Maggie said, "Please?"

"If it's important to you and your assignment."

"It is."

"Okay."

"Good." Maggie patted the back of Barbara's hand. "And find a new bar of soap, one you've never used of a different brand than your usual. You'll understand eventually. And I'll see you tomorrow evening."

Before Barbara could react, Maggie strode through the kitchen door and was gone.

An hour later, Barbara tidied up the kitchen and ran herself a bath. She had always loved the huge tub in the master bathroom. It was deep enough to fully cover her body almost to her shoulders. "This is pretty silly," Barbara said out loud as she plugged in an old cassette player she had recovered from the back of her closet. But if it was important to Maggie, it was important to her, she realized. In two short days she had gone from incredulity and scorn to friendship. She rummaged in the back of the bathroom closet and found a new bar of soap, then pressed the cassette machine's play button and stepped into the steamy water.

Music filled the bathroom, music with a quiet yet pulsing beat and a soft, slightly mournful clarinet and a baritone saxophone. The sounds that filled the room felt like soft summer nights with the sky filled with stars. Barbara thought of couples in open-topped cars staring down at city lights from darkened lover's overlooks. She rolled a small towel and placed it at the back of her neck and stretched out. She sighed deeply and relaxed.

"Are you all relaxed?" a soft, sensuous man's voice asked as the music faded slightly. "That's very good." Barbara started to sit up. "No, don't move," the voice said. "Just lie back and relax. Let the music fill you, create dreams, fantasies. Let it evoke pictures of teenagers in parked cars."

How did that man know what she was thinking? Barbara wondered. The music swelled again, and for several minutes the voice was silent. Then the music faded slightly and the voice returned.

"I hope you're naked, lying in a tub of warm water. The naked female body is such a wonder. It's so beautiful."

Yeah, right, Barbara thought. For all he knows, I'm a dog, a hundred pounds overweight with droopy boobs and three stomachs.

"Don't think like that. All female bodies are beautiful regardless of the way they actually look. Breasts are soft, firm, large or small. Nipples are chocolate brown or dark pink. Skin is deep ebony or almost transparent white. God, I love a woman's breasts. And your bellies are concave, with prominent hipbones, or full and round. I love to feel the pulse in a woman's throat and know how it speeds up when she listens to me tell her how beautiful she is. Can you feel your pulse? Find it by stroking your throat. Go ahead. No one's watching."

Without really thinking, Barbara slid a wet finger up her neck and felt her pulsebeat.

"That's your life flowing throughout your body. You can feel it all over, in your wrist, in your foot, at your temple, in your groin. If I tell you that I want you to imagine me touching your breasts, does your pulse speed up? I love that I can do that for you."

Barbara felt her pulse. No silly man's voice was going to make her pulse beat faster. But it did.

"I want you to make your hands all soapy. Please, for me. Feel the soap, so smooth and slippery. Rub your hands over the bar, touching its contours. Close your eyes and just feel the soap as your hands caress it."

Barbara took the soap from the holder and rubbed it. She was strangely aware of the slick surface.

> *"Take the soap and make a rich lather, then slowly rub it on your throat. Feel the difference between the hard surface of the cake of soap and the soft, warm skin of your body. Move your hands around. Feel your jaw, the back of your neck. Now caress your cheeks. How smooth and soft they are through the lather. Keep your eyes closed and just feel. Feel rough and smooth spots, places that are warm and those that are cool. If you have fingernails, use them to scratch your shoulders, just lightly."*

Barbara did, her eyes closed, her head resting against the towel on the rim of the tub.

> *"You need more lather, so rub the soap again. Can you smell the perfume? Does your soap smell like flowers or spice? Can you picture a field of summer blossoms or an Oriental harem? Maybe lemons or blackberries. Inhale deeply. Fill your lungs with the scent and imagine."*

As the music filled the room, Barbara breathed deeply and saw a Parisian boudoir with perfume bottles on a mirrored vanity. She vaguely remembered her mother buying her this soap many years before. She lay there seeing the boudoir. A woman sat at the vanity putting on makeup. She was dressed in a filmy negligee, waiting for her lover. Barbara opened her eyes. Now why had she created that scene? Waiting for her lover, indeed.

> *"I hope your eyes are still closed," the voice said softly. Barbara snapped her eyes shut. "I want you to feel other places on your body. Start with your breasts. Your soapy hands will feel so good on your soft flesh. I want you to use the pads of your fingers to stroke the*

flesh of your breasts, just around the outside. Press a bit and feel. Are your breasts full, or small and tight? As I told you, I like them all. Can you feel your ribs or is there deep softness? Please. I can't be there to feel your skin so you must do it for me."

Tentatively Barbara sat up slightly so the tops of her breasts were above the waterline. She slid her soapy fingers over the crests, then pressed her fingertips into the flesh. Deeply soft and pillowy, she thought.

"Find the areolas, just where the color changes, darkens. Open your eyes if you must, then close them again. Run one fingertip over the slight ridge there, all around. Keep swirling around that line. Can you feel your nipples tighten? No, not with your fingers, but feel it inside. Don't look, feel. Can you feel your nipples contract? Yes, I know they will."

They did.

"I wish I were there to touch your nipples. I would first swirl my fingers around the outside the way you are doing it. Then I wouldn't be able to resist sliding toward the tightened buds. I want to feel them but I can't, so you will have to do it for me. Touch. Squeeze. That's what I would do. I would squeeze those tight nipples. It's hard to feel it when you touch lightly so make yourself feel it. Do what you have to so that you know the touch of your fingers. Pinch, use your nails."

Barbara used her newly manicured nails to tweak the tips of her breasts. She felt it, tight, slightly painful yet very stimulating.

"I know you think this is strange and maybe you feel a bit guilty, but it's your body and you are entitled to touch it. It's God's creation and so beautiful. I know

also that you're noticing that you're not just feeling your fingers touching your breasts. You are also starting to become aware of the flesh between your legs. You're feeling full, maybe getting wet, not from your bath but from your excitement."

Barbara was aware of her groin. This is ridiculous, she thought, yanking herself from her dreamy state. It's dirty.

"I know you feel that what you're doing isn't what nice girls are supposed to do, but that's nonsense. Feeling sexual and sensual is wonderful. It is what I would want you to be experiencing if I were there. Relax. You and I are alone. No one will know, or care, what you're doing. You are just making your body feel good. What is wrong with that?"

Nothing, Barbara thought, taking a deep breath. Nothing at all. He's right. It is my body and I can touch it. That's why it was designed to feel good.

"I know you want to touch the flesh between your legs and that's so good. I get so much pleasure out of knowing I excite you. I know the water covers the parts of you that you want to touch, but you must make your hands soapy and slippery anyway. Do it for me since I can't caress you myself. Rub the soap while I tell you what I'd like to be doing if I were there."

Barbara picked up the soap and rubbed, closing her eyes as she did so.

"If I were there with you I would cup your beautiful breasts in my hands and lick the water off the tips with my rough tongue. I would suckle and lick, and maybe nip the erect tip from time to time with my sharp teeth. Can you feel me? I hope so. Don't touch yourself, just rub the soap and imagine my teeth and lips and tongue.

Imagine what they are doing and how they make you feel. Are you getting tight between your legs? Do you want to touch? That hunger is what I want you to feel. Think of how my fingers would feel touching your ribs, your sides, your belly. If you're ticklish, I can touch you so it feels good, yet not make you laugh. I don't want you to giggle right now, although laughter is wonderful. Do you want me to touch you?"

The erotic music and the man's voice filled Barbara's ears, penetrating to her soul. Yes, she admitted, she did want him to touch her.

"I can't touch you, you know, and that makes me so sad. But you can touch all those places I cannot. Rub your palm over your belly. Scratch the skin on your sides. Now the insides of your thighs. Rub, caress, stroke. It's your skin and it feels so good."

Barbara had never touched herself like this before and it was a bit embarrassing. But it felt good and she didn't really consider stopping.

"Move your fingers closer to the center of all that you need. You want to touch. Do you know how? Do you know what would feel good? Well, I do. It would feel good if you rubbed the wet, slippery place. Find that place and know the difference between the water and your own slippery juices. Feel that slick, slithery substance? Your body is making that to make it easier for me to penetrate you, but, of course, I cannot. But you can.

"Have you ever wondered what you feel like inside? Under the water, make sure your fingers have no soap left on them. Then slide one into your passage. Touch the slick walls, rub all the places you can and find out which feels the best. I would learn that if I were there. I would know when you moan or purr, when your hips

move to take me in more deeply, when you become wetter and more slippery. I would know the secrets of your pleasure, and you know them now, too. Run your fingers over the outside folds. Use the other hand if you like the feel of that finger inside you."

Barbara did have one finger inside her channel, in a place she had never touched before. It felt very good and she wanted more. She used the middle finger of her other hand to rub the deep crevices, moving from side to side, enjoying her own flesh.

"Have you found your clit? I would have by now. I would have rubbed up and down both sides, feeling the tight nub swell and reach for me. I would have put one finger on either side and rubbed. Oh, that does feel good, doesn't it. I can almost see your back arch, your eyes close, and your mouth open. Put a second finger inside your body to fill it up, and a third if that feels good. Rub your clit and all the places that feel as good."

Barbara was stroking her body, marveling at all the spots that gave her pleasure.

"If I were there, I would use my mouth now. No, it's not a bad thing. It's a beautiful experience. I would lick your clit, flick my tongue over the end, then wrap my lips around it and draw it into my mouth. Just a slight vacuum to suck it in and hold it while my tongue rubs the surface. Just don't stop what you're doing while I lick you."

Barbara filled her pussy with her fingers and rubbed her clit, feeling the pressure in her belly. This was dirty, but so good. She didn't want to stop, and she didn't. The words and the music and the rubbing and the fullness inside all drove her higher. She felt something build deep in her belly, then suddenly waves of ecstatic pleasure spasmed through her.

"Oh, yes, my wonderful girl," the voice said. "Make it feel so good."

Barbara continued as the clenching subsided.

"I will not talk anymore, but leave you to the music and to your pleasure," the voice said. "Until the next time."

"Oh," Barbara said, panting. "Oh."

Chapter 5

For the next several days, the tape was never far from Barbara's mind. She thought about that night in the tub and, with guilty pleasure, repeated the experience several times, twice while listening to the tape and, more recently, once while picturing Steve Gordon. That had happened at almost three in the morning when Barbara awakened from an erotic dream, a dream she couldn't remember but one that left her so excited that she had to reach beneath her nightgown and touch herself to relieve the tension. As she touched her body, now able to find the places that gave her pleasure, she thought about her boss, his slender hands with their long fingers and carefully trimmed nails. She could almost feel those hands on her body as she climaxed.

Maggie showed up at dinner time every two or three days and they talked about inconsequentials. Barbara was dying to ask questions about Maggie's life as a prostitute but never seemed to be able to work up the nerve.

One evening almost two weeks after Maggie's first visit,

Barbara said, "There's an office party tomorrow night. It's a celebration for a big case the firm won, and they've invited all of their clients, all of the staff and who knows who else. Steve, Mr. Gordon, told me that he's looking forward to seeing me there. I think he might be ready to ask me to dinner."

"That's great. Will you go if he asks you?"

"Sure. It makes my palms sweat just thinking about it."

"I'm sure it does." Maggie grinned and arched an eyebrow. "So. He makes you hot, does he?"

"Maggie!" Barbara said. "That's not it at all. He's a very nice man and I'd like to get to know him better. That's all." The thought of her middle-of-the-night fantasies made her blush slightly.

"Okay. I won't tease. But being hot, horny, and hungry isn't a crime. As a matter of fact, it's delightful. It's a high, frustrating but delicious." Maggie hesitated. "I've been meaning to ask, did you like that tape?"

Barbara blushed several shades darker. "I'll get it for you. I'm sorry. I forgot to return it and now I'm not too sure where I put it."

Maggie reached out and covered Barbara's hand with her own, calming the nervous fingers. "Don't. Just don't. You and I both know you're lying. That tape is meant to do exactly what it did. It woke you up to things about your body you didn't know. That's why I gave it to you and that's why you can keep it. Sensuality is a joy and, once awakened, well, let's just say that it's very difficult to get the genie back into the bottle."

Barbara sighed. She couldn't hide anything from Maggie. The woman was too perceptive. And anyway, there was so much that Barbara didn't know. "Maggie, you're right. This is silly. But it's very difficult, after thirty-one years on this earth to admit that I'm such a dunce about sex."

"How are you supposed to learn?" Maggie said. "All those articles in *Cosmo?* How to have an orgasm any hour of the day or night. How to lure the man of your dreams into your camper. The things about men that women don't want men to know they know. Oh, please. Give me a break."

Barbara laughed. "I read those," she said.

"And many of them have good information. But many others are pure crap. How to climax seven times in three hours. Everyone in those articles is a stud, male and female. Let's hear it for people who like to make love, climax once or twice and cuddle. Sex is so much more than how many times a man ejaculates or a woman has an orgasm."

"It is?"

"Oh, Lord, darling," Maggie said. "Sex isn't the destination, it's the journey. It's how you get to that wonderful level of excitement that allows both partners to soar together, then relax. Did you even think that if it weren't for orgasm and the calm afterward, we'd be chasing each other all the time and we'd never get anything else done. Orgasm is the final chord in the symphony, but it's the music before that counts."

"Oh" was all that Barbara could say.

"I don't mean to preach, but I just love making love."

"But isn't there one right man, one person, who knocks your socks off? One man with whom you'd like to climb into bed for the next hundred years? What about your husband?"

"When Chuck and I were married I thought it was forever and I settled down, worked, fucked, and enjoyed. But even then I used to imagine handsome men adoring me, licking and touching me. I wasn't quite clear on exactly what they would be doing, just doing kinky things to my quivering body."

"Really?" Barbara said, grinning.

"Sure. Chuck and I had a good relationship, but it wasn't enough for either of us. He found his SueAnn. She's probably a lovely girl, and because of her I was pushed out of the plain-vanilla nest I had been in, into the world of Heavenly Hash." Maggie grinned. "And let's hear it for all twenty-eight flavors."

"There's no one special? No one man who you ever

wished would take you away to a deserted cabin and keep you there forever?"

"Not really. I love the deserted cabin idea for a weekend, but one man? For life? I don't think so. Someone once said that if the plural of louse is lice, then the plural of spouse should be spice. I just happen to like lots of spice."

"Well, I'm not like you," Barbara said, somehow wondering whether what she was saying was entirely true. "I just want one man to love me and make a life with me."

"That's wonderful. Everyone should try to figure out what his or her dream is, then go for it. If that's what you want, then let's see what we can do to make it come true. Steve Gordon?"

Barbara's grin widened. "He could be the one."

"Why?" Maggie asked.

"Why?"

"Yes. What about him makes him the right one. I don't know him much at all. Tell me. Does he have a great sense of humor? Do you two share many common interests? Is he moody or more placid? Is he easy to be with?"

"Actually, I don't really know. I haven't spent much time with him. He's not too bad to work for. He understood about my mom and let me take time off when I needed it. And he depends on me to keep him going. I'm valuable to him."

"That's not a reason to make a life with someone. He has to be valuable to you as well."

"Of course he is," Barbara said. "He's wonderful."

"Okay, great." Maggie stood up. "What about this party? How dressed up is it?"

"It's cocktail dress."

"So. What are you going to wear? You want him to notice you, don't you?"

"I do. I mean, he does." Actually, he had noticed her the first few days after her dramatic makeover, but since then it had been business as usual. Several of the other men in the office seemed to pay more attention to her new persona than Steve did. One man had actually asked her to dinner, but she had politely refused, preferring to meet with Maggie and concentrate on Steve.

"All right then, let's decide what you should wear. I saw a dress in the back of your closet the first night I was here."

The two women went upstairs and Maggie quickly pulled out the dress. "How about this?"

"Oh, Maggie. I bought that as a favor to my mom. It was one of the last shopping trips we took together before she became bed-ridden. I've never even worn it."

"Why not?"

"It's so, I don't know, obvious." She took the hanger from Maggie. The halter shaped chiffon bodice was soft blue with a full skirt that shaded from the pale blue of the top to a deep royal at the hem. She pointed to the low-cut back. "You can't even wear a bra. I couldn't wear this."

"Try it on for me," Maggie asked. "Come on, what will it hurt. Only I will see you."

With a deep sigh, Barbara stripped off her clothes and slipped into the dress. She adjusted the wide medium-blue belt and fastened the rhinestone buckle. While she was doing that, Maggie was rummaging around on the floor of Barbara's closet. Suddenly there was a triumphant "Taa Daa" and Maggie tossed out a pair of strappy black patent-leather sandals. "Put those on."

Barbara did, then the two women looked at Barbara in the full-length mirror. Maggie stood behind her and pulled her hair into an upswept mass, with a few strands artfully caressing her neck and the white streak prominently displayed. "God, I wish I had hair like this," Maggie sighed. "Mine's so tight and curly, I had to keep it short all the time."

"That's not me," Barbara said, looking at the striking brunette who looked back at her. "That dress and hairstyle are meant for a beautiful woman. And I'm certainly not beautiful."

"Not classically beautiful, no," Maggie said. "But a woman who looks comfortable in her skin, and particularly one who has that gleam of sensuality that you will have if I have anything to say about it, is attractive. And you are."

"Oh, Maggie. I couldn't." Could I?

"You can if you want to."

"Do you really think so? Could I knock 'em dead? Could I really get Steve to notice me?"

Maggie grinned. "I know so and I think maybe you're beginning to also."

Barbara suddenly realized things about herself she hadn't understood until that moment. She wanted to be that woman she saw in the mirror. Like Cinderella. No, not like Cinderella, she corrected herself. I don't want to be someone else for just one night. She thought about her new hairstyle and her new clothes. She realized, as she looked at herself, that in this dress she stood up straighter, looked herself in the eye. And she glowed.

"Maybe just a little," Barbara said.

"Good. That's all I ask. Enjoy the party, and don't dance only with Prince Charming. Cindy missed a lot of other really great folks at that ball."

The party was being held in the King's Room of a local hotel. Almost two hundred people were expected. When Barbara arrived, there was a four-piece dance combo playing innocuous music. Uniformed waiters and waitresses circulated with hot and cold hors d'oeuvres, glasses of red and white wine, and flutes of champagne. There was also an open bar for those who enjoyed soft drinks or hard liquor.

Barbara stood off to one side trying to figure out how to join one of the groups of laughing people. She searched the crowd for Steve, but could not find his familiar tall, slender shape. I wonder whether he's bringing someone, she thought. She looked down at the yards of bright blue skirt and thought about the hour it had taken for Maggie to fix her makeup and choose her accessories. As she moved her head, Barbara felt the large rhinestone earrings brush against her neck. Why had she allowed Maggie to talk her into those chandeliers? Why the wide bracelet? Why not her plain gold chain around her neck and her gold studs in her ears? She'd certainly feel more comfortable.

For want of something to do, she took a glass of white wine from one waiter's tray and a salmon puff from another.

"You've changed your hair," a voice said behind her. "I like it."

She turned and recognized Jay Preston, an investigator whom the firm employed for divorce work and other secret projects. "Thank you, Mr. Preston. I'm surprised you noticed." I never noticed how cute he is, she thought, still scanning the room for her boss.

"I have noticed a lot about you in the past few weeks. And it's Jay."

"I don't know what to say," Barbara said. God, he was sexy. Not handsome, Barbara thought, but the gleam in his deep gray eyes was directed entirely at her. His hair was almost black with just the beginnings of silver at the temples. Because Barbara wore two-inch heels she was only an inch shorter than he was, but he seemed to tower over her, making her think of some desert chieftain holding a sweet young woman captive. Now where had that thought come from? Barbara wondered.

"Don't say anything," Jay said. "Just tell me, are you alone tonight?"

"If you mean did I bring a date, the answer is no."

"Bring a date. You don't have to be a detective to know that that phrase means you're not married or engaged. This must be my lucky night." He took her elbow, his fingers on her naked skin causing shivers up her spine.

"You are a bit too fast for me," she said.

"I'm sorry. I just don't believe in wasting time when I see something I want."

Barbara took a step back. "It feels like you're using up all the air in here," she said honestly, sipping her wine.

Jay didn't try to close the distance between them. "Tell me about you. What do you do when you're not being Steve Gordon's Ms. Everything?"

They stood and talked for about half an hour, and found out they shared an interest in old TV comedies and cooking and abhorred partisan politics and snow. "I tried skiing once," Jay said, "and, well, I guess it's not macho to admit that after I fell more times than I could count, I took off my skis and walked down the baby slope."

Barbara laughed. "I never even tried. I had a few friends who invited me to go with them several years ago. I got there, put on boots that hurt my feet, took off the boots and spent the day in the lodge drinking hot chocolate and eating chili."

"Not together, I hope," Jay said.

"Not together, but I think I gained two pounds that day. So much for exercise."

Jay gave her an appraising look from her hair to her feet. "Not a problem," he said. "You look just right to me."

"Barbara," a familiar voice said, "there you are. I've been looking for you."

"Hello, Steve," Barbara said. "You know Jay Preston."

Steve nodded. "Preston." He turned to Barbara and put a friendly arm around her waist. "I wanted you to meet Lisa." He reached out and draped his other arm around the shoulders of a strikingly gorgeous woman. "Lisa, this is Barbara."

The woman smiled warmly and reached out a hand. "It's so nice to meet you. Steve talks about you so much."

Weakly, Barbara extended a hand. "It's nice to meet you, too." He didn't tell me much about you, she thought, and there was obviously a lot to tell. Lisa was a knockout in a long silver sequined gown.

"This is so great," Steve said. "My two girls." He hugged them both. "Dinner will be served soon. Will you sit with us?"

Jay put his arm around Barbara's shoulders. "I think Barbara intended to eat with me." He looked at Barbara and smiled.

"Yes, Steve," she said quickly. "Jay and I were just in the middle of something, if you don't mind."

"Of course not," Steve said. "Come on, Lisa. I see some

people I want you to meet." The two walked away. As Barbara gazed after them, she felt a glass thrust into her hand.

"Have some champagne," Jay said. "It's good for what ails you."

"Does it show that much?" Barbara said, unable to pretend.

"Only to someone as perceptive as I am. And don't worry. I'm very good at cheering people up. I do limericks, bad jokes, and I promise not to sing while we dance."

"There's nothing between Steve and me, you know."

"I know. I do understand. And I'll leave you alone if you like. That business of sitting together at dinner was just for his benefit. Unless you'd like to."

Barbara turned from watching Steve and Lisa talk to one of the other partners and said, "I'd like that." She grinned and felt her shoulders relaxed. "This feels like a bad movie. Shunned by her boss, the heroine," she tapped her chest, "that's me, finally notices the handsome hero." She patted the lapel of Jay's tuxedo. "That's you. Then they fall madly in love and live happily ever after."

"Not *ever after,*" Jay said, covering her palm with his. "I'm not that type of guy. I live for the now, not for next year. But, my love, I could definitely fall in lust with you."

"Excuse me?"

"Let me lay my cards on the table. I find you very attractive and you fit one of my favorite fantasies."

"Oh I do, do I?"

"Yes. I know more about you than you might wish. You're in love with your boss, or at least you think you are. You're an innocent, inexperienced woman who hasn't learned her own power yet. And you do have power. You radiate with it. But you don't understand it. I want to teach you so you can have anything you want."

"What power are you talking about? You're confusing me. This is some kind of line you use with people like me and I don't think I like it."

"It's not strictly speaking a line, because it's entirely honest. And you say you don't like it, but I have my fingers on your pulse and it's pounding right now. This whole thing excites you and you don't quite know what to do about it. I won't press you for the moment."

The doors to the dining room opened and Jay took Barbara's glass and put it down on a nearby table. "Will you sit with me?"

Barbara thought about how much this man was like Maggie. He was a free thinker, dangerous, charming, and totally unsuitable with goals that were completely different from hers. But she *was* terribly excited. She hesitated only a moment, gazed at Steve and the knockout, then back at Jay. It's time, she told herself. As a matter of fact, I'm long overdue. "I'd like that," Barbara said, taking Jay's arm as they joined the stream of people walking toward the dining room.

During the almost three-hour dinner, Jay was a perfect gentleman. They talked, laughed, and argued, with each other and with the other couples at their table. Between courses, they danced to the music of the combo, but Jay kept a discreet distance between them. After coffee was served, the place began to empty out. Steve and Lisa stopped at their table to say good night and Barbara smiled and wished them a good evening. The pain of seeing her boss with Ms. Knockout on his arm had diminished considerably.

As the band began a slow song, Jay took her hand and once again led her to the small wooden dance floor, now crowded with the few other couples still left. Jay took her in his arms and held her against him and their feet moved reflexively to the music. His mouth beside her ear, Jay said, "I've tried to give you some time to think about me as a real person, not as a lecherous private eye, but now the evening is almost over and I might not see you again, except in the office. I want to tell you again that I'm in lust with you and I want you in my bed. I want to lay you out on the sheets and touch you and lick you. I want to make you want me so badly you beg me to take you. I want to want you so badly that I do." He pressed his hand in the small of her back, leaning the bulge in his trousers against her belly.

Barbara couldn't speak. She was barely able to think.

"I want to do strange, unusual, extremely pleasurable things with you, things that will make you blush and scream and cry out in joy. But nothing long term. I live for now. Nothing exclusive. I love women and I love making love to them."

"Again I'm speechless."

"Let's dance for a few more minutes, then I'll take you to your car. I want you to think about everything I've said and I will call you tomorrow night. I want you to say yes, but on realistic terms. Will you think about it?"

"Will I think about anything else?"

Jay's warm chuckle tickled her ear. "Good."

Half an hour later, Jay dropped Barbara at her car. "I'll call you tomorrow, but if you haven't decided, I'll call you the following evening. Take as much time as you like. And understand that I do take no for an answer and I won't pressure you, except to promise you that it will be wonderful."

It was fortunate that, since the hotel was only two blocks from the office, Barbara had driven this route every day for many years, for she drove in a total fog. She knew what Jay was asking. He wanted to have an affair with her. A "no commitment, no tomorrow" affair. No, she told herself, It was impossible.

But God, how she was turned on. She didn't know what strange, unusual things he had in mind, but she was so curious. She wasn't stupid. She knew about oral sex, bondage, all the kinky things she had read about in novels, and she was fascinated. Isn't that how the cobra entices its victims? Doesn't he fascinate them until he can bite?

But what is the downside to all this? That nice girls don't? Is that a realistic reason not to do something that might be so good? She was so confused.

She wasn't at all surprised to see Maggie sitting in her kitchen when she arrived home. "How was it?" she asked, then hesitated. "Something happened. Did you spend the evening with Steve? Did he ask you out? Tell me everything."

Barbara did, with little comment from Maggie. "And Jay

wants me to go to bed with him. No strings. No nothing. Just making love."

Momentarily Maggie thought about Angela's desires. "Get her married to that cute lawyer. Home, kids. . . ." If Maggie wanted to get to heaven, the best way was to do what Angela wanted, wasn't it? She should tell Barbara to reject Jay out of hand and concentrate on Steve. But she couldn't. Jay was right for Barbara now and what she wanted what was good for Barbara. "You have to do what you think is best," Maggie said. "But that's sometimes hard to sort out. I guess my philosophy would be, If it feels good and doesn't hurt anyone, do it."

"I keep thinking that going to bed with a man just for sex makes me a bad girl. What would my mother say?"

"From what I heard about your mother, both from you and from the girls . . ." She gazed at the ceiling, "I think she'd tell you to do what you want with none of the *good* and *bad* labels."

"I'm so confused."

"Sleep on it," Maggie said. "You don't have to decide tonight." As usual, to end the discussion, Maggie walked out the kitchen door and disappeared. Barbara went up to bed and, for the first time in her life, slept naked.

"I need to be honest with you, Jay," Barbara said into the phone the following evening. "I'm intrigued, but I'm scared to death, too. I don't know whether I want to have an affair with you that has no future. I wasn't brought up that way."

"Oh Barbara, you're wonderful. I completely understand. Look, how about this? Let me take you to dinner next Saturday. Just dinner. No commitment to do anything except enjoy each other's company."

"Well . . ." Barbara sat in the edge of her bed, playing with the hem of the pillowcase.

"We had fun together last evening and I'm not willing to let that go. Do you like Italian food? Not spaghetti, but real zuppe de peche, good osso buco with orzo. And they make the best tiramisù."

"Actually, I love Italian food." He's such a sweet man, she thought. And he seems to understand how I feel.

"As I remember, you told me you're a great cook, but let's let someone else do the cooking and we can get to know each other better. Please."

Barbara vacillated. She liked Jay a lot, but she wasn't ready for what he wanted, and she knew that hadn't changed. She didn't want a sleazy affair. Did she? "I did enjoy last evening a great deal." She took a deep breath. "All right. Just dinner."

"Great."

They made arrangements for Jay to pick Barbara up at her house the following Saturday evening.

"Maggie," Barbara said the following evening, "I'm really nervous about this dinner date."

"What are you afraid of exactly?"

Barbara sat at the dinner table, dirty dinner dishes spread around her, a cup of coffee cooling in her hand. "I've been trying to sort that out. I think I'm afraid that I'll be tempted to jump into bed with the guy. He's nice, warm, honest, and sexy as hell."

"And what if you do jump into bed with him?"

"I guess I'm afraid that I'll hate myself the next morning."

"You're right, that is a risk. So the question becomes, Is the risk worth the reward?"

"I never thought of it that way."

"Well, let's think of it that way now. If you do get involved with Jay, what's the reward?"

Barbara grinned. "He's a very sexy man and, to be perfectly honest, he turns me on. My insides get all squishy, my knees get weak, and well, I think it would be great."

"Okay, what's the reward if you tell him no."

Barbara considered for a few minutes. "I won't have any regrets the next morning."

"You won't?"

Barbara sipped at her cold coffee. "I will have regrets. I will regret all the things I didn't do."

"I think my job is to make you see all sides of this problem. You know what side I'm on. I think good sex is the best thing going. You're a big girl, and perfectly able to understand what you're getting yourself into, and you're no virgin. You understand, as I'm sure Jay does, about safe sex, condoms all that. You know how I feel, but it must be your decision."

Barbara pictured the scene, Jay stroking her hand at dinner, kissing her fingers. She'd read enough novels to know that once the hormones kicked in, resistance was futile. Then it wouldn't be her responsibility. "He'll convince me. I know he will and I'll do it."

But Jay didn't pressure her. Villa Josephina turned out to be a small Italian restaurant in Tuckahoe, with a round hostess who obviously knew Jay from frequent visits. They were seated at a table off to one side. Barbara took one look at the extensive menu and, her mouth dry and her appetite gone, she let Jay order for both of them. At first, Barbara was quite nervous and unable to do justice to a wonderful shrimp appetizer, but as the meal progressed she relaxed. Through the courses they talked. About everything but sex. Barbara began to feel like she was having dinner with an old friend, not a would-be lover. And, although he was a sensual man, he wasn't turning her on. As a matter of fact, she thought he was making an effort not to even indirectly refer to anything sexual. He had even dressed in a dark green flannel sport shirt and shaker sweater, muting any sensuality.

"I would offer you a brandy," Jay said to Barbara as the waiter brought small cups of strong espresso, "but I don't want alcohol to cloud your mind. Or mine, for that matter."

"Is that why you didn't order any wine?"

"I know what's going through your head. I know that this is a difficult decision for you, and I want you to be clear-headed." It was his first reference to the topic that had been so much on Barbara's mind. He took her hand across the soft blue tablecloth. "Whatever you decide is fine with me, but it must be your decision."

Barbara lowered her gaze.

"Okay," Jay said. "I understand."

He hadn't convinced her, pressured her or made her decision any easier. And without a push, she didn't think she could go through with it. She sipped her coffee. "Thanks. I think I'd like you to take me home," Barbara said.

Quickly Jay paid the check and drove Barbara back to her house in Fleetwood. He walked her to her door and said, "Do you think we might just have dinner together once in a while? I haven't enjoyed an evening this much in a long time." A boyish grin lit his face. "And maybe you'll change your mind."

"Kiss me," Barbara said, uncertain as to where the words had come from.

Jay looked startled, then put his hands on her shoulders. Drawing her close, he brushed his mouth across hers. He touched the tip of his tongue to the joining of her lips, then cupped her face with his hands.

Barbara placed her palms against Jay's chest and relaxed into the kiss. He was an expert, softly taking her mouth and possessing it. He explored and tasted until she parted her lips and allowed his tongue free access. Slowly she slid her hands up his chest to the back of his neck, holding him close. His fingers slowly slid up the sides of her neck and tunneled through her thick hair, caressing her scalp.

Finally he leaned back, his eyes caressing her face. "You kiss like an expert," he said. "I thought of you as being so innocent."

"I don't know where that came from. It must be that you do that to me," Barbara admitted.

Jay ran his fingers through her hair. "You know this silver stripe is incredibly sexy. Are you a witch?"

"No, of course not."

"What would you do if you were? Right now."

"That's an interesting question," Barbara said, smiling ruefully. "I think I'd make it tomorrow morning."

Jay cocked his head to one side. "Why?"

"Because tonight is causing me so much confusion. By tomorrow morning decisions would have been made."

"Do you want me to make the decision for you?"

"Yes." She paused. "No."

"What do you want?"

She looked into Jay's eyes and a slow smile spread across her face. "I want you to come inside with me."

Barbara watched Jay's eyes light up. "Are you sure?"

Barbara let go of Jay long enough to find her keys and unlock the front door. "Yes, I'm sure."

They walked into the house and Barbara put their coats in the living room. Then she slid back into Jay's arms and raised her face to his. He accepted the invitation readily. He brushed soft kisses on her eyes, her cheeks, her mouth, all the time keeping his hands on her back.

Barbara realized what she wanted. Her body was alive, impatient, unsatisfied. She ran her hands over the back of Jay's deep green sweater, then slid under it to touch his soft flannel shirt and the hard flesh beneath. She wanted, needed, him to make the next move. Push me, she cried. Seduce me. "Please."

"Oh, how I want you," he moaned, kissing her deeply again. When he pulled away, he looked around. "You know, living rooms are nice, but how about a nice horizontal surface? I want to make long, slow love to you, not paw and pet like teenagers."

Barbara motioned toward the stairs and together they walked up.

A small light was burning in the corner of the cozy room. Her bed was covered with a patchwork comforter, one pattern of which matched the curtains. Another of the patchwork fabrics covered the armchair on one side of the room, and the polished wood floor was covered with a multicolored braided rug.

This room is cleaner than it has been in weeks, Barbara realized as they entered. Maggie must have tidied up after I left for dinner. She glanced at the bed. Maggie had even changed the sheets. She had planned for this. She had known or hoped that Barbara would be here, like this, with Jay. Thanks, Barbara almost said aloud. She smiled silently as she watched Jay pull off his sweater. "Can I take that?" For want of something to do, she folded it and put it on a chair.

Jay came up behind her and slid his hands around her waist. "I know this is awkward for you," he said, his lips against the tender skin beneath her ear. "Let me lead. I promise you will like where we go together." He held her back against his hard chest and Barbara could feel the heat of his body against hers. He nuzzled her neck, planting small soft kisses on the skin he could reach. Then he turned her in his arms and again pressed his mouth against hers. She smelled his after-shave, spicy and mixed with the natural male smell of him.

Slowly the heat began to build. He kissed her over and over until all she was aware of was his mouth. She felt him press his lower body against hers so she could get used to his arousal. When he pressed, she found herself pressing back.

Jay stepped back and untied her scarf, then slowly unbuttoned her soft pink blouse. He pulled the blouse's tails from her burgundy skirt and slid the garment off her shoulders.

Barbara stood in a haze, wondering how Jay would see her, glad she had allowed Maggie to talk her into wearing her new, more daring, white lace underwear. She started to raise her arms to cover herself, but she heard Jay's voice. "Oh, my," Jay said, his eyes roaming over her body. "I expected you to have a nice figure, but you're really beautiful."

Barbara knew she weighed more than she should, but the look in Jay's eyes said he thought she was desirable. Her arms fell limply to her sides. Jay placed his hands on her ribs, then slowly slid them upward toward her breasts. "Your skin is so soft, like warm satin." His fingers reached Barbara's full breasts, still encased in the silk-and-lace bra. She felt him stroke her flesh softly, the touch muffled through the fabric. Go faster, she screamed in her mind. Push me onto the bed and fuck me. Get this waiting over with.

"No rushing," Jay purred as if reading her mind. "It's

hard for me to wait, but this first time for us this night will live in my mind for a long time. I want it to be perfect. I want you to want me, not to get it over with but because your body feels empty, hollow, needy."

"But . . ."

He covered her protest with his lips, his thumbs now stroking her nipples through the cloth. Barbara knew how tight her nubs had become, and she felt the wet swelling between her legs. Jay kissed and rubbed, then held her tight while he found and opened the clasp of her bra. He let the garment drop to the floor and admired Barbara's firm breasts. He bent, touching the tip of his tongue to each crest in turn, until Barbara's knees threatened to buckle. She heard a low moan and realized that it came from her.

Jay knelt in front of her, unfastened her skirt and pulled it down. "Oh, honey," he said, seeing the matching panties and garter belt Maggie had insisted upon. "This is so sexy. I want to go slowly but you are making it very difficult." She wore the panties over the garters, so Jay lowered the tiny wisp of fabric until she could step out of it. Then he guided her to the bed with the stockings and garter belt still in place. "I think making love to a woman with stockings on like this is one of the sexiest things," he purred.

She stretched out on the bed, rubbing the sole of her nylon-covered foot over the quilt. She watched as Jay removed his shirt, then she looked at the body now revealed. He was tanned, but looked like he hadn't worked out in years. No perfect athletic body. Just a man's chest covered with tightly curled hair. Not intimidating, she thought. She saw that Jay had already removed his shoes and socks and was unzipping his pants. I wish I were brave enough, Barbara thought with the part of her brain still capable of thought. I would sit up and help him pull off his shorts. Maybe, she thought. Maybe.

Jay, now naked, stretched out beside Barbara on the wide double bed. He kissed her again, then bent down and licked a swollen nipple. "Oh, yes," Barbara purred. "Yes." Hesitantly she cupped the back of his head and held him as he suckled. Shivers echoed through her body, centering now deep in her belly. She felt herself getting wetter and wanted him to touch her. Soon, she thought. Soon I'll be brave, able to touch what I want. Able to ask, show, guide.

Jay placed the palm of his hand on her belly and, over the lace of the garter belt, lowered it to the thatch of springy hair below. "So hot," he purred. "So hungry." His fingers probed, finding her hard clit, her swollen lips, her wet center. "I want you to come for me, baby. I want to watch you as you take your pleasure." He rubbed, using all his senses to discover exactly what she liked, what sent her higher. "Oh," he said, "you like to be touched right here."

"Oh, yes," she moaned, now incapable of any thought. "Yes."

"Open your eyes and look at me. I want to see your eyes when you come."

It was difficult, but Barbara opened her eyes and looked at Jay. His concentration was complete. He was stroking, rubbing, probing, all the while not taking his smoky eyes from hers. Barbara spread her legs still more, making it easier for him to reach all the places she had learned about in the past week. She couldn't speak, so she tried to tell him everything with her body and he learned quickly. Slowly he insinuated one finger into her wet channel. "That feels good, doesn't it?" he said as she gasped.

"Oh, yes," Barbara said, her eyes closing.

"No baby," he said. "Don't close your eyes. Look at me."

Barbara forced her eyes open. "It's hard," she said.

"I know, but it makes you think about something other than my hand. I want my face to fill over your mind while I fill your body." Slowly a second finger joined the first, then his thumb began flicking over her clit. "Yes, I can watch your eyes glaze with the pleasure I'm giving you. You're so hot, so hungry. I like it that I can do that to you. I can fill you, stroke you." He leaned over and licked her nipple. "Even bite you." He lightly closed his teeth on her tender flesh, causing small shards of pain to knife through her breast. "But the slight pain is exciting, isn't it?"

It was, she realized. The combination of sensations was electric. "Yes. It's good."

"I knew it would be."

He dipped his head and, as his fingers drove in and out of her pussy, he spread her legs wide and flicked his tongue over her clit. "Oh, God," she cried, her voice hoarse, all but unable to drag air into her lungs. She came as only her own fingers had been able to make her come before. He kept pulling her along, bringing waves of pleasure to her entire body. As she continued to spasm, she felt his hand withdraw. With his mouth sucking at her clit, she felt him awkwardly move around the bed, then heard the tear of paper. Briefly he sat up and, as Barbara's body throbbed with continued pleasure, unrolled a condom over his erection. He crouched over her for just a moment, then drove his hard cock deep into her. "Honey," he cried as she twisted her stocking-covered legs around his waist. "Honey, now! Yes!"

His back arched and he groaned as he pistoned into Barbara's wet body. Harder and harder he pumped until, with a roar, he came deep inside her. Her legs held him tightly against her as the waves of orgasm claimed them both.

It took several minutes for their bodies to calm and for their breathing to slow. "Oh, honey," Jay said. "That was sensational. I didn't expect you to be so responsive. You are a very sexy lady."

Barbara preened. She was feeling like a sexy lady, and she wanted to be a sexy lady. She wanted to be able to do to a man what Jay had just done to her. She had never even considered anything like that before. Conservative, mousy Barbara. Not anymore.

Chapter 6

"It was like a revelation. I understood things. I want to be a sexually free woman. Not necessarily like you, Maggie," Barbara said the next morning as she devoured a piece of toast, "but I want to feel free to do anything sexually I want."

"That's quite a change from the frightened and uncertain woman who left here last evening."

Barbara's eyes sparkled, her skin glowed. "I know, and I have no idea where it came from. But as Jay and I were making love, I just knew. I want to learn. I want to experiment. I want to do things that I never even knew existed." She giggled. "I don't even know that those things are, I just know there's more to sex than I've ever imagined."

"What about Jay? Won't he teach you?"

"Of course and I want to learn with him, but now I want to know everything, taste everything. Taste everyone." She looked down, then laughed. "You know what I mean. I guess the genie's out of the bottle and I don't want her to go back inside."

Maggie's grin spread from ear to ear. "I'm so happy for you, Barbara. I just knew that once you discovered good sex, you'd be unstoppable." She'd known no such thing, but what the hell. She was winning and, although Angela wanted marriage and a home for Barbara, it was, after all, Barbara's decision. And it seemed she had made it. "So you and Jay had it good last evening."

"Oh Lord, it was cosmic. We made love, then talked for a while, then made love again." She smiled, remembering the second time.

"God Barbara it's such a turn-on to watch someone like you open up."

It was about midnight and they lay side by side on Barbara's bed, the quilt thrown over them. It had only been an hour since her last orgasm, and already she was excited again. "I don't know how to express all the things I'm feeling."

"I can imagine," Jay said, his hand holding hers. "Your excitement is contagious. I'm not usually so quick to recover, but feel." He placed her hand on his again-erect cock. "Feel what you do to me."

"I like that. But I'm not responsible for your excitement."

"And who else is in this bed with me." He reached over and inserted one finger between her legs. She was wet. "And you are as excited as I am."

"It's just that we made love only an hour ago."

"And . . . ?"

"I should be lying here in some kind of afterglow, not lusting like an animal."

"I guess we're both animals then. And what are you lusting for?"

Barbara giggled. "I guess I have to admit that I want you again."

"I'm glad you do. What would you like?"

"You know."

"You want me to make love to you again." Jay raised himself up on one elbow and looked down at Barbara. She nodded almost imperceptibly. "Tell me," Jay urged. "Say yes."

"Yes."

"What would you like me to do? What gave you pleasure?"

Barbara pictured Jay's hands on her breast. And his mouth. That was what she wanted. But she couldn't say the words. "Everything you did gave me pleasure."

"Cop-out. Not an answer. What did you like best? When I nibbled your ear? When I stroked your tits? When I rubbed your cunt?"

Barbara's face went red. "Everything. Just love me."

"Maybe you need a lesson in words. Saying the words is very erotic. It's difficult and embarrassing, but it's also very exciting. Dirty words. Words your mother told you never to say. Words like 'fuck' and 'pussy' and 'dick.' Maybe you need a lesson on how to say those dirty words and ask for what you want." He placed his free hand flat on her belly and leaned his mouth against her ear. "What would you like this hand to do?"

Barbara was silent.

"Do you want it on your tits?"

She nodded slightly.

"Say it. Say, 'I want your hand on my tits.' "

"I can't say that," Barbara said, trying to contain the nervous giggle that threatened to erupt.

"Yes, you can and you will." He moved his hand upward until his fingers surrounded her breast. He moved his fingertips slightly, rubbing her ribs, nowhere near where she wanted his hands. "Say, 'Touch my tits.' "

"Touch me."

Jay shook his head. "Not good enough. Say 'tits.' Say it or I won't touch you."

His fingers were making her crazy. Her nipples were hard little buds aching for his hands and his mouth. She knew how good it had been just an hour before and she wanted it again. But could she say those words? She formed the word "tit" in her mind, then almost strangled on it. She couldn't get it out.

Jay's tongue was in her ear, licking and probing. Then he whispered, "Touch my tits. That's all you have to say."

His mouth was driving her wild. "Touch my . . . tits." There, she had said it.

"Such a good girl," Jay purred, his fingers squeezing her breasts and playing with her nipples. He pinched hard enough to make her gasp, but there was a stab of pleasure, too. "Now you probably want me to suck them, too. Tell me."

"Yes, please," she moaned.

"Say, 'Suck my tits.' "

"Suck my . . . tits." It was easier this time. "Please. I need your mouth."

"Oh, honey," Jay said, his mouth descending. He licked and sucked, and bit her. It was all ecstasy. For several minutes Jay played with her breasts, stroking, kneading, suckling. "God, you taste good," he purred. "But now it's time for more. You're hungry for me. You want my hands in your pussy. Say 'pussy.' "

Hearing the word made her back arch, the need almost overwhelming. "Jay, please touch me. I want you so much."

"I know you do. I know you want me enough to say the words. 'Touch my pussy.' "

"Touch my pussy. Jay, please."

"Oh, yes," Jay said, his fingers now busy driving her higher and higher. "Now I want something from you," Jay said. "Open your eyes." She did and saw his hand around his cock. "I want you to suck me the way I did it to you."

"I don't know how," Barbara said, suddenly cold and frightened. She had heard of women who"gave good head." There must be a knack to it. She couldn't, didn't know how.

"That's all right, I'll teach you." His hands still in her crotch, Jay turned, then knelt on the bed, his cock now only inches from her mouth. "Open your mouth. Just let me rub my cock over your lips so you get the feel of it." He stroked her lips with the velvety tip of his hard erection. "I'll teach you the best way. Do you want me to lick your pussy?"

"Yes."

He lay beside her, his head near her cunt, his cock only an inch from her mouth. His fingers continued to work their erotic magic. "Say 'pussy.' I know that as much as you deny it, saying those words makes you hot. Say it."

"Pussy," Barbara whispered.

"Such a good girl. Now I'm going to lick you. Try to duplicate what you feel with your tongue and my cock. If I lick slowly . . ." He gently licked the length of her slit. ". . . I want you to lick me slowly. Do it for me."

She used her fingertips to guide his cock close to her mouth. "Like this?" she whispered. She started about halfway down his shaft and licked to the tip as if her were a lollypop.

"Oh, God," he groaned. "Oh, honey."

Barbara was amazed at her ability to give him pleasure. She licked again and felt his sharp intake of breath.

Jay licked Barbara's clit lightly and she licked the tip of his cock the same way. Jay breathed hot air on Barbara's pussy and she breathed hot air onto his wet flesh. When Jay sucked her clit into his mouth, she was almost unable to think clearly enough to suck his cock, but when she did, she was rewarded with his moan. "Lady, you're a quick study."

Barbara could feel the vibrations of his voice against her hot flesh. "I hope so," she purred, hoping he could feel the same thing.

"You are a witch," he said, getting to his knees. He turned, put on a condom, crouched over her and plunged into her body. When his cock was deeply embedded in her cunt, he lifted and turned them both until she was straddling him. He held her hips and alternately lifted her and plunged her down onto his shaft. Harder and harder he drove into her, drove her onto him. "Say 'Fuck me good,' " he cried.

"Oh, Jay, fuck me good," she cried as she climaxed.

"Yessss," he hissed as he, too, came.

* * *

Barbara had been spending most of her weekends with Jay for more than a month before she saw Maggie again. One evening at the beginning of May, while Barbara was pouring herself a beer to go with the just-delivered pizza, Maggie walked into the kitchen.

"How have you been?" Maggie asked, dropping into a chair.

"Great. I've missed you." Barbara crossed to Maggie's chair and gave her a great bear hug.

"I haven't missed you, because, for me, I just saw you yesterday. How long has it been, and how is Jay?"

"It's the eighth of May and my dates have been great. We fuck like bunnies."

"Fuck. Such language." She tsk-tsked. "The Barbara I knew would never have used a word like that."

"I know, and I do keep it to a minimum except with you and Jay. But that's what it is, really. Wild, animal fornication, and it feels wonderful."

"That's terrific," Maggie said, taking a slice of pizza. She had discovered that she could eat what she wanted and food tasted great, although she had no concept of what happened after she swallowed. "I'm happy for you. Are you and Jay permanent? You know, forever?"

"Oh, Maggie," Barbara said, sitting across from her friend and taking a few large swallows of her beer. "I don't understand all this."

Maggie chewed, then said, "What's to understand? You said you guys were great together."

"I know, but it's not enough, somehow. I don't know. I've probably made love more in the past few weeks than I did in the previous thirty-one years. And I like Jay." As Maggie raised an eyebrow, Barbara continued. "I do. Really. It's just . . . Oh, forget it. I can't explain it."

"You know, I have no idea who decides when I appear, but whoever it is and however it's done, it seems you need someone to talk to right now. Try to explain."

Barbara took another long swallow of her beer and considered her words while Maggie devoured a slice of pizza. "Okay, let me put it this way. Jay's a real nice guy, but he's, how can I put this, predictable. We go to one of three restaurants for dinner. When I suggest somewhere else, he's willing but not anxious, so I don't pursue it. After dinner we go back to his place. We both love old movies, so we watch one of the tapes he has, usually an old John Wayne flick. We share some wine, get hot and make love. All fine, but . . ."

"Dull?"

Barbara sighed. "Yeah. Dull. After that first explosive night, when we made love twice, it's once, we doze, then he takes me home. That once is fantastic, don't get me wrong. But I thought that great sex like that first night was the answer to some question I didn't know I had."

"Great sex is just that, great, but it's also not life."

"I don't understand," Barbara said, startled. "Didn't you say that marriage was too predictable? That variation and hot sex was the answer for you?"

"I did, and I believe that. But from what you've told me, your sex life has become predictable. Dull."

"Yes, but . . ."

"There's lots of good stuff out there. Maybe it's time for you to spread your newly acquired wings and look around. See what's out there. There are lots of fish in the sea, my love."

"You mean men."

"I do. Look around. I'll bet there are guys who you see every day, and who you don't give a second look to who would be fun to fool around with."

"Fool around with?"

"Yeah. Get some experience. Steak is nice, but pizza is good sometimes, too." She lifted her slice in a mock salute. "You didn't cook tonight, I see."

Barbara laughed. "I've been spending more time thinking about life and less time cooking. There is more to life than gourmet meals that I prepare myself, for myself." She picked up a slice of pizza and took a large bite. Then she got up, crossed to her spice rack and returned with a jar of crushed red pepper. "Just a little spice to give my slice some pep."

"That's what your life needs, too," Maggie said. "There are as many pleasures as there are creative couples in the world."

"You're right. I want to experiment. I want to do everything."

"And what about Jay. Does he think you're exclusive?"

"Not at all. He's seeing at least one other woman. You know, when he told me, I thought I'd be jealous, but I'm not. We're having fun and he's having fun with Joyce. I keep waiting for misery, possessiveness, but I just don't feel that. I'm happy he's happy."

"Sounds healthy to me," Maggie said. "And what about Steve. Has he asked you out yet? Have you asked him?"

"He hasn't asked me and I haven't asked him."

"Why not? You want to be with him, don't you?"

"Yes. But I want to play for the moment and I don't want to complicate things with what might turn into something permanent." She sprinkled red pepper on another slice of pizza. "And anyway, he's still seeing that knockout. That Lisa person."

"Do I hear jealousy?"

"Maybe a little. It's not like Jay. Jay's a game. I want Steve to be serious. But not just yet. I have things to do and learn first, so we can be great together."

"I really do understand." Maggie remembered her first experiences after she and Chuck split. She had discovered that she loved sex. Good, rolling-in-the-hay, giggling, having-fun sex. "Remember the tape I gave you, the one that started all this?"

"Mmmm," she purred, "how could I forget?"

"Well, there are more in the series."

Barbara sat up, here eyes round. "There are?"

Maggie reached into her pocket and withdrew an audiotape. "This is another tape by the man who made that first one. These are erotic stories, published in an unusual way, using his bedroom voice. He's got a store in the city and sells them there and through the mail. Maybe you'll meet him sometime. He's a wild guy with a fantastic imagination." She placed the tape on the table between them. "That first one is unusual. Each of the remaining tapes is a story of people making love in new and exciting ways. Some you'll find exciting, some not. But the tapes will allow you to vicariously experience many of the things that couples do together. You can play them and see what turns you on, then go out and try to experience it."

Barbara took the tape.

"I'll be going, and you can play the tape at your leisure." Maggie stood up and walked toward the door. "How are they going to keep them down on the farm . . ." she said as she left through the kitchen door.

"How indeed," Angela said to Lucy as they flipped off the computer screen. "What did you get us into?"

"Be real, Angela," Lucy said. "You knew this might happen, and I'm glad it did. All that stuff about marriage. It's not right for Barbara, at least not yet. She's got some wild oats to sow."

"And this sudden need for her to get into kinky sex." Angela fixed Lucy with an icy stare. "Do you mean to tell me you had nothing to do with that?"

"It didn't take much." She grinned. "I guess the devil made me do it."

"Listen, I thought we had a deal here. There's a lot riding on how Barbara's life goes from here. We agreed that there would be no meddling."

Lucy looked only a bit chagrined. "I know. I couldn't help it. I just goosed her a little. I want to see her fly. I want to see her learn about good, hot sex. A good roll in the sheets beats anything going, including marriage and fidelity."

"What you want isn't the issue here. It's what she wants. Free will is everything. If humans lose that, decisions like Barbara's become meaningless."

Lucy sighed. "I know. I'm sorry. I just couldn't help myself."

Angela patted her friend's hand. "Okay. I guess I understand. It's hard to have any resistance to temptation where you come from. But promise me. No more."

"Okay. No more."

Barbara turned on the tap to run a tub full of hot water, sprinkled a handful of bath salts beneath the water stream, then undressed. All the while her gaze kept returning to the cassette player which already contained the tape Maggie had given her. When the tub was full, she turned off the water and stepped in. Before settling into the water, she pushed the play button. The familiar sensual wail of the saxophone filled the room. She rested her head against the rim of the large tub and closed her eyes.

As they walked, Jason and Carolyn felt the cool water wash over their burning feet. The sand was white and had soaked in the sun all day. Now, as the golden disk set, the sand radiated heat into the soles of their feet, up their legs and into their bodies. Gulls wheeled and dove into the surf hunting for their evening meal and crying their brief song over and over.

The narrator's voice was sensual, soft, warm, like listening to warm heavy cream, Barbara thought as she listened. She let the voice and the story wash over her, as though she were there, seeing it, feeling it. It played like a movie in her head.

As they walked slowly along, Jason draped his arm over Carolyn's shoulder and slid his fingers down the edges of the top of her brief bikini. He allowed his fingertips to brush the swell of her lush breasts.

Carolyn loved the look and feel of Jason's lean body. As she looked over at him, it seemed that the pink and orange light of the setting sun made Jason's skin glow as though lit from within. She wrapped her arm around his waist and felt his muscles move beneath his warm flesh as they walked along the deserted beach.

"How did we get so lucky?" Jason said.

"Fifteen raffle tickets and someone's lucky fingers," Carolyn answered.

Surreptitiously Jason slid his fingers under one of the two tiny pieces of green fabric that made up the top of his wife's bikini and touched Carolyn's nipple. "Someone's fingers are still lucky."

Playfully Carolyn batted Jason's fingers away. "Stop that, silly."

"Why? This entire stretch of beach is deserted. All ours. 'Each cottage has its own deserted beach for lovers to share,' the brochure said."

"I know, but it feels so public."

Jason grinned. "I know. That's what's so erotic. Even though I know there's no one who can watch, it's like we're in public." With a gleam in his eye, Jason quickly untied the two knots that held Carolyn's top on and threw the fabric onto the sand. "Your breasts are so beautiful in the light of the setting sun."

Carolyn was surprised at how sensuous and exciting it felt to be half naked with the evening breeze making her nipples tighten. With a brazenness she hadn't felt before, she turned to Jason and swayed from one foot to the other, rubbing her erect breasts against his chest.

Jason pulled the rubber band from the single braid that held Carolyn's long red hair and buried his hands in the luxuriant silken strands. He cradled her head, bent down and pressed his lips against hers, filling her mouth with his tongue. Her tongue joined his and they touched and explored.

"Ummm," he purred, "you taste salty. Are you salty all over?" He leaned down and licked the valley between her breasts.

"Oh, Jason, you get me so excited. But it's so exposed here."

"That makes me hotter." He licked first one breast, then the other. "You skin is so warm." He bent and filled his palm with the water that lapped around their feet. Slowly he trickled the cool liquid over Carolyn's

chest, and before she could react to the cold, he licked the salty drops from her nipples.

Carolyn was getting very hungry and, somehow, the idea of making love in the open added to the appeal. What the heck, she thought. It's a deserted beach. "Two can play at that," she said, filling one hand with water and dribbling it over Jason's hot shoulders. She touched her tongue to a rivulet and followed the water's path through the downy hair on his chest and down his flat stomach. The water trickled to his navel, just above his tight elastic bathing suit and she dipped her tongue into the indentation.

Jason's head fell back as Carolyn swirled her tongue just above his throbbing erection. He reached down and pulled off the bottom of her bikini and his trunks. "I want to love you right here, with the calling of the gulls and the foaming water and the setting sun shining on your body."

Jason laid Carolyn on the sand and stretched out beside her, the waves lapping to their knees. He tangled his fingers in her pubic hair, feeling a wetness that had nothing to do with the ocean. "You're as anxious for me as I am for you," he murmured in her ear. "Open for me and let me love you." He felt her legs part.

Carolyn couldn't have kept her legs together had she wanted to, and she didn't want to. She needed Jason inside her so she pulled at his shoulder until he covered her body with his.

He filled her and let her slippery body engulf him. He moved in and out, feeling both her body and the play of the waves against his legs. He wanted her to climax, needed it so he could come as well. He slid his fingers between their bodies and found her swollen clit. "Yes," she purred, "rub it. Touch me while you're inside me." His sentences were punctuated with sharp intakes of breath. "Baby, yes." She reached between them and placed her fingers over his, guiding them to the places she needed to feel him. "Right there."

It took only a few strokes more until he felt the clenching of her body around him and he could let his orgasm happen. And as it did, he held his hips perfectly still letting the semen spurt from his body into hers, experiencing her spasms of pleasure on his cock.

"Oh, darling," he whispered, feeling the water swirl around them. "That was unbelievable."

"Ummm, it was," Carolyn said. "And we still have three days here. Let's go inside and take a shower together. I understand that water can be very invigorating."

Barbara was breathless, her fingers relaxing after a frantic orgasm. As the music swelled, she thought about what she had heard. The woman asked for what she wanted. And it seemed natural and right for her. And it's right for me as well, Barbara realized.

The following Saturday, she and Jay had dinner at Villa Josephina and, at Barbara's suggestion, had an after-dinner drink at a small club around the corner. They danced on the tiny dance floor and, loose and ready for something new, Barbara thought about the evening to come. Yes, she thought, it was her turn to lead. "How about a bubble bath later?" she murmured into Jay's ear as they danced.

"That's an interesting idea," Jay said. "But my tub isn't really big enough for that."

"Mine is," Barbara said.

"You want to go to your house after?"

"That's what I had in mind."

"Ummm. I guess you've got a few ideas of your own. Sounds sensational."

Back at her house a while later, Barbara tuned her radio to an all-light music station and, while Jay opened a bottle of champagne, she filled the tub with hot water and placed several candles around the bathroom. As she lit a match, she thought about all the wonderful things she had learned in that tub. Tonight? More new experiences, this time with Jay.

"May I come in?" Jay said, standing in the bedroom doorway.

Quickly Barbara lit the candles and turned off the water. "Sure. I'm in here."

Jay walked into the bathroom with two flutes of champagne. "I love the atmosphere," he said, handing Barbara one of the glasses. He touched the rim of his glass to hers. "Here's to new adventures."

"New adventures," Barbara said. They undressed slowly, watching in the candlelight as each part of the other's body was exposed but not touching each other. "You're gorgeous," she said as she looked at Jay's naked body. She remembered the evening when, at the instructions of the man on the tape, she had discovered her own body in that tub. She wanted to get to know Jay's body as well. "I would like to touch you," Barbara said.

Jay stretched his arms out at shoulder level. "I would like that," he purred.

Barbara used her fingertips to touch places on Jay's body she had never explored before. She discovered that he was ticklish beneath his arms and down his sides. She found the almost downy texture of his chest hair a contrast to the wiry hair in his groin. She flicked his male nipples with a fingernail and watched them tighten. She turned him around and stroked his back with her palms, then scratched a thin line down his spine to a small patch of hair in the small of his back.

She had never taken the time to know his skin and what lay beneath, from his forehead to the soles of his feet. "You are a wonder," Jay said. "You make me feel sexy, yet soft and dreamy all at once. Strong and masculine, yet weak and almost submissive."

"I like that," Barbara said. "I like making you feel all different kinds of things." She took his hand and guided him to the tub. Together, holding hands, they stepped into the still-steamy water.

The tub was large enough that they could sink beneath the surface until only the tops of their shoulders and their heads were not submerged. "How do you feel under that water, I wonder?" she said, rubbing soap on her hands. Then she rubbed his chest, arms, and legs, again wondering at all the different textures. When she was content that she had touched all of Jay's body, she handed him the soap. "Touch me now," she said.

Smiling, Jay took the soap and used lathered hands to caress all of Barbara's skin, from her underarms to the back of her knees. He washed her fingers, sucking each into his mouth, then lathering and rinsing each. Then he did the same with her toes.

She giggled when he rubbed the sole of her foot and found that, rather than spoiling the mood, Jay shared the laughter. Then the laughter turned into a splashing contest and finally, when the bathroom was soaked, they got out of the tub and bundled each other in big fluffy towels.

"This wasn't what I expected," Barbara said as she rubbed her hair dry.

"What did you expect?"

"In the movies, the people always get very passionate in the tub. This was just sensual and fun."

"Hot water makes me less than passionate," Jay said. "I get the ideas in my mind, but my cock refuses to cooperate." He took the towel from Barbara and rubbed her hair. "Have you got a hairbrush?"

In the bedroom, Jay sat Barbara on the chair at her vanity then, from behind her, began to slowly brush her hair. Barbara closed her eyes and allowed the sensuous moment to engulf her. The mesmerizing strokes of the brush lulled her almost to sleep. "Open your eyes, sleepyhead," Jay said. "No nodding off here."

"Ummm. But it feels so good." She opened her eyes and looked in the vanity mirror. Jay stood behind her, his skin still glowing from the warm water, a towel fastened around his loins. Slowly she watched Jay remove the towel from around her shoulders. Then he took the brush and scratched the bristles along her collarbone.

"Hey," she said. "That hurts."

"No, it doesn't," Jay said. "It feels like it should hurt, but it doesn't. Watch what I'm going to do." He scraped the bristles across the flesh of her breast, then scratched the tip of one nipple. He repeated the action on her other breast, then down the center of her belly.

It didn't hurt. Quite the contrary. She felt her clit swell and her lips part and moisten. Two could play at that game, she thought. She took the brush from Jay's hand, then turned and rubbed the bristles through Jay's chest hair and down past his waist. She considered, then did it. She scratched Jay's semi-erect cock with the sharp spikes. Rather than being a turn-off, as she had feared, his cock jumped, getting harder while she watched.

She turned the brush in her hand so she could brush it up the inside of one of Jay's thighs, then scratch it over his testicles. Groaning, Jay grabbed her wrist and pulled her to a standing position. He took the brush, threw it into the corner, then dragged her to the bed.

"Not so fast," she said, laughing.

"Yes, so fast." He pushed her down on her back and, with one quick motion, unrolled a condom over his cock. Then he grabbed his erection in one hand. "You did this, now let me put it where it belongs." He crouched over her and with one thrust buried himself deep in her pussy.

Barbara wanted to feel him from a different angle, so she pushed at him until he was on his knees, her pussy still impaled on his cock. He supported her buttocks in his hands as she twined her legs around his waist. "Now, baby," she said. "Fuck me."

Her request was more than granted as he withdrew, then plunged in full length. She wanted, needed, stimulation for her breasts, but, rather than wait for Jay to touch them, she cupped her flesh and pinched her nipples. Because of their unusual position, Barbara's clit was completely exposed. She wanted Jay to touch it. "Rub my clit," she said, and Jay's fingers found her immediately. He rubbed and, as she pinched her hard nipples and Jay's long strokes filled her cunt, she came, hard, with a long, loud moan.

"Oh, Barbara," Jay said. "So good. So good." And with a scream, he came, too.

They lay silently side by side while their breathing returned to normal. "I can't believe how far you've come from that timid woman I first made love with," Jay said.

"I can't believe it either," Barbara said, pulling the quilt over them. "Thank you."

"Don't thank me," Jay said. "You are a wonderful partner. We fit so well together, in all ways."

Barbara giggled. "I love the way we fit together."

An hour later, as Barbara listened to Jay's car pull out of the driveway, she thought about what Jay had said. She was a different person and she liked the person she had become.

The following evening, Barbara was back in her tub with another of CJ's wonderful tapes. She settled back in the water, now confident that the tape was going to bring her at least one orgasm. The voice filled her head.

It was warmer than usual that evening in the health club so Jack removed his T-shirt and continued to lift. Twice twenty reps with a thirty-pound weight in each hand ought to finish it off. He glanced at the clock. Almost nine-thirty, he saw. He had had a business meeting so he had begun his workout later than usual. "I thought the club closed at nine," he muttered.

Jack was well built with a smooth, muscular chest, well-developed arms and legs and an angular face. His short sandy beard covered a hard, granitelike chin. Long hair, slightly darker than his beard, was caught in a rubber band at the nape of his neck. His eyes were deep blue and a sheen of sweat covered his body as he lay on his back on the bench, lifting the barbell rhythmically. "Fifteen . . . sixteen," he counted.

"It's way past closing time," a woman's voice said.

"Seventeen, eighteen. Can I just finish?" he asked.

"Sure," the voice said, and as he continued to lift, he

thought little more about it. When he finished the first thirty, he rested for a few moments, then began on the second series. "You're taking advantage of my good nature," the voice said.

"I didn't realize you were still there," Jack said, almost dropping the weights. "I'm sorry if I'm inconveniencing you."

"You're the last one here," the voice said. "I'm waiting to close up."

As Jack started to sit up to return the weights to the rack, he looked behind him. She sat on another weight bench, wearing bicycle pants, a sports bra and a tight tee top with the name of the club across the front. He had never seen her here before. "I'm really sorry."

"How sorry?"

"I beg your pardon?"

The woman stared at Jack, her eyes never leaving his. "How sorry are you? I think you should make it up to me."

Was that an invitation? Jack thought. Is this beautifully built woman making a pass at me? He was certainly willing. "What did you have in mind?" he asked, looking over the woman's body. She was small, with tight breasts, slender, well-muscled thighs, and good definition in her upper arms. Her hair was cut very short, with tight red curls, and her eyes were green. She wore no makeup on her ivory skin and freckles dusted the bridge of her nose.

The woman stood up and walked over to the bench. She pushed her hand against Jack's chest until he was pressed back down onto his back. She put the weight Jack had been using on the floor beside his right hand. "Hold that and don't let go," she said. Jack wrapped his hand around the cold bar while the woman took the second hand weight and placed his left hand on it. "Don't let go or everything's over," she said.

Jack lay on his back on the narrow bench, his hands stretched toward the floor, his hard cock pressing up-

ward against his shorts. God, he thought, is this really happening?

"My name's Nan," the woman said, "and I've been watching you. I think you'll be easy."

"Easy?"

"I think you will do anything I say, when I say it, and nothing more. I think you will do it all willingly because I'm going to do things to you and with you that we will both like. A lot. And you want me to do that, don't you?"

Jack could hardly catch his breath. "Yes," he whispered.

"Good. Here are the rules. You will keep your eyes on me at all times. Look nowhere else unless I tell you to. And keep those weights in your hands. If you let go, I will stop and leave at once. Do you understand the rules?"

Jack swallowed hard. "Yes," he whispered.

"Good. Let's see how hard you are already." She reached down and grabbed Jack's hard cock through the silky fabric of his workout shorts. "I knew you'd be easy. So hard." She grasped his cock and squeezed, moving her hand slightly up and down. "Too hard, I'm afraid. I don't know whether you will have enough self-control for me. Do you have self-control?"

"Yes," Jack said, barely able to breathe.

"We'll see. You are not to come. Period. If you do before I tell you to, I will leave. Immediately. Your cock is mine to control. Do you understand that?"

"Yes," Jack whispered, staring into the woman's deep green eyes. "Yes."

"All right. Let's test that control you say you have." Nan pulled off her tee top and bra and cupped her small tight tit with her hand. "I'm going to put my nipple into your mouth. You're not to suck, lick, or anything. Just keep your mouth open."

Jack opened his mouth and felt her large nipple between his lips. He wanted to suck, to caress the warm flesh with his tongue, but he thought of her warning and her challenge to his ability to master his desires. More intense than the urge to suck was his need for the woman not to leave. He kept his lips parted, her engorged nipple brushing his tongue. She moved, rubbing the nub against his lips, his cheeks, his chin. "Stick your tongue out, but don't move it."

He stuck his tongue out and she rubbed her nipple over the rough surface. He wanted to suckle, but he used all his concentration to keep his mouth still.

"Such a good boy," Nan said, and she straightened. "You might have more promise than I expected." She stepped out of her shorts, leaving herself dressed in only her sneakers and white socks. She straddled the bench with her back to him, and lowered her wet pussy to Jack's mouth. "The rules haven't changed. Do nothing." She wiggled her hips, and the aroma of her hot cunt filled Jack's nostrils. He licked his lips, but valiantly kept his tongue from caressing the swollen flesh so close.

She lay down along his body, her cunt still less than an inch from his mouth, her mouth close to his cock. Quickly she shifted one leg of his shorts and pulled his cock free. It stood straight up from his groin. "You can't see me too well from there," she said. "Look in the mirror."

Jack had forgotten that one wall of the free-weight area was mirrored. He turned slightly to his right so he could just see around Nan's thigh. The sight was incredible. A naked woman was lying along his body, her breasts caressing his belly, her mouth just above his straining cock, her warm breath making him quiver. Her smell filled him. Her weight pressed him down. His hands gripped the weights until his knuckles went white, his muscles strained to push his cock into this woman's waiting mouth.

"You'll wait until I'm ready," she said. "Make me ready. Lick me."

He did gladly, sliding his tongue over the length of

her sopping slit. He tried every trick he knew to give her pleasure, sucking her clit into his mouth, flicking the tip his tongue across her then slowly laving the entire area. He pointed and stiffened his tongue until his mouth ached, then stabbed it as far into her pussy as it would go.

"My, my," Nan said, her breathing rapid, "you do good work. I think you deserve a reward."

Jack felt her hot mouth draw his aching cock deep inside. It would only take a moment of that level of intense pleasure for him to come. "You'll make me come," he groaned.

"You better not come," Nan said. "You've got a job to do. If you make me come first, then, and only then, will you be allowed to climax. Do you understand that?"

Jack moaned and clenched his muscles tightly. "Yes," he whispered, trying to concentrate on cold showers and snow-covered mountains. He licked and sucked, his mind divided between giving pleasure and trying to control his need to climax. Slowly he felt Nan's thigh muscles tighten. He tried to concentrate on which of the things his tongue was doing would make her come. When he rubbed his lips over her clit, she quivered. When he blew a stream of cold air over her swollen lips, her thighs clenched around his head. Yes, he told himself, I can do it for her. As he felt the ripples through her belly and the spasms of her vaginal muscles, he knew he could hold back no longer. He filled her mouth with his semen, coming for what seemed to him like hours.

It was several minutes before either of them moved. As Nan stood up, she said, "Damn, you're good. That was wonderful." She moved behind him.

Jack took a deep breath and let go of the weights. He flexed his aching fingers and picked up a small towel that lay on the floor. "Terrific." He sat up slowly, wiped his face, drying the sweat and enjoying the lingering smell of Nan's juices. "How about going back to my place? We can pick up a pizza and continue this when we recover." He took the towel away from his face and looked around in amazement. The gym was empty. Although he looked throughout the large facility, Nan seemed to have vanished.

Jack worked out late every night for several weeks, but eventually he had to admit that he would never see her again. But he had the memory of that one incredible night, a night he would never forget.

As the story ended, the room filled with the mellow tones of the saxophone, Barbara lay in the tub and rubbed her fingers furiously between her legs. When she came it was swirls of all colors, bright and silent.

As she relaxed, she lay in the cooling water thinking about the story she had just heard. There was so much out there, so much sexual fun for people to share. Next weekend she was seeing Jay again. Could she wait? She wanted to experience everything now. Right now.

Chapter 7

The following morning, Barbara showed up at work dressed in a soft rose knit suit. Although the line of the suit itself was quite conservative, the way it clung to her body as she moved was enough to ignite fantasies in a few of her office mates. And, for the first time, as she looked at the men she passed in elevators and hallways, she noticed the appreciative glances she received. Branch out, she thought. Date. Make love because it's fun and easy.

Midmorning she went to the ladies' room and looked at herself carefully in the full-length mirror. Not a raving beauty, not even conventionally pretty, she realized shaking her head, but there was a spark there now. She smoothed her skirt over her hips and adjusted the jacket's neckline slightly to reveal just a bit of cleavage. Not bad, she told herself. Not bad at all.

"Hi," a voice said as she walked back to her desk. "I don't think we've met. I'm Alex Fernandez. I'm from Gordon-Watson's West Coast affiliate."

"Nice to meet you," Barbara said, watching the man's eyes coolly appraise her. "I'm Barbara Enright."

"Well, Barbara Enright, I'm only here till tomorrow afternoon. I know I should take my time, but when I see something as delectable as you, I can't see beating around the bush. How about a drink after work?"

"You don't waste any time," Barbara said, grinning at the man's audacity. But he was gorgeous, medium height, with deep brown eyes and brown curly hair that looked like combing it was useless. He was wearing the office costume, dark suit and white shirt, but his tie was a wild print of orange and purple. Feeling bold, she reached over and touched his tie, pressing just hard enough so she knew he felt the slight pressure of her fingers. "Nice tie."

"Thanks. So how about that drink?"

She thought about it for only a moment. "I'd like that. Tonight?"

"If you're free," Alex said, his eyes holding hers. "Since I'm going back tomorrow, we don't have too much time. Listen, I have lots of work to do, but I can probably be out of here by seven."

"Let's see how the time works out as the day progresses," Barbara said.

About four-thirty Barbara found Alex in the law library. He had his head buried in a three-inch-thick tome and several others littered the table around him. "I have a few things to do. Why don't I stop back here around seven and we can see about that drink?"

Alex looked up and smiled slightly. "That'll be great," he said, looking at his watch. "Better make it about seven-thirty."

When Barbara got home, Maggie was waiting for her. As Barbara made coffee, she told Maggie about Alex. "I'm tingling all over," she said finally. "And I initiated it."

"Don't get carried away," Maggie said, then giggled. "Hey, listen to me. Which side of this am I on?"

"Oh, Maggie, I won't get carried away. It's just that this

is so much fun. Flirting. Picturing every man I see without clothes. Wondering how he would be in bed."

Maggie patted the back of Barbara's hand. "I know, and I'm with you. Just be careful. Condoms and like that. And never do something that you don't want to do just because someone else wants you to."

Maggie looked at Barbara's watch. She had stopped wearing one because it never told the right time anyway. Whenever she went through the revolving room in the computer building, time got all shifted around. "It's getting late and you need to shower and make yourself gorgeous. Why don't you go meet Alex and let things flow from there." Maggie made a few suggestions about how to make the evening progress the way Barbara wanted it to, and Barbara listened carefully. Then she stood up. "I think I will do just what you suggested," she said. "And let the devil take the hindmost."

In the computer room, Lucy raised her arms in the air. "Yes," she hissed. "Right on, Barbara."

"Shut up," Angela growled.

It was almost eight when Barbara locked the office's heavy outer door behind her and dropped the keys back into her purse. She put her coat on her desk, then picked up the shopping bag she had brought with her and walked toward the library. About halfway down the hall she stopped. Could she do this? It had sounded like a fantastic idea when she and Maggie had talked about it, but now, in reality, she felt like she was about to make a fool out of herself. Alex probably wanted to talk to her about office politics or something.

Suddenly the door to the library opened. "Barbara," Alex said, seeing her standing in the hall. "I was beginning to think you'd stood me up." A grin lit his face.

"I'm sorry I'm late. I got held up." No, she wouldn't do it. She couldn't.

Alex walked toward her, then glanced down at the shopping bag. He peeked in the top, looked at her and smiled.

"Champagne," he said, a slight catch in his voice. "Do some shopping on the way here? Is that a gift for someone?"

Now or never. "Actually, I thought you might be getting thirsty. All those books and all."

"What a great idea," Alex said, his eyes widening. "I was just going to get a soda, but this will go down much more easily. Got glasses?"

"I certainly do," Barbara said. As she slowly followed Alex back into the law library, she wondered whether he might have misunderstood. But what was there to misunderstand? An empty office. Champagne.

As Barbara closed the door behind her, Alex pulled the champagne bottle and two flutes from the bag. "What's this?" he asked, pulling out the tape player Maggie had placed there. She had included a tape Maggie had given her that contained just the erotic background music from the tapes Barbara had become so intrigued with. He put the tape in the player and pushed the play button. As he opened the bottle, the soft-summer-night wail of a saxophone filled the room.

"Great music," Alex said as he filled the two glasses. He handed one to Barbara and, with the music filling their ears, they clinked glasses. "Wonderful," he whispered, swallowing some of the bubbly liquid.

Nervously Barbara emptied the glass and Alex quickly refilled it. She sipped a bit more and looked at him standing in front of her. From the look in his eyes it was obvious that he wanted what Barbara wanted. But how to begin? As the hesitation lengthened, she decided she could make the first move. She could. Then she squared her shoulders, took a deep breath and said, "Dance with me?"

"Ummm, yeah," Alex said, putting his glass on the large oak table. "Good idea."

Barbara held on to her glass like some kind of security blanket as Alex took her in his arms. Their feet barely moved and his body pressed against hers. "I love slow dancing," she whispered into Alex's ear, alternately confident and terrified. "It's like making love standing up."

"I do too," Alex said, shaking his head. "But I don't believe this is happening. Things like this only happen in movies. And never to guys like me."

"Do you want it to happen?" Barbara asked.

"Oh, yes."

Barbara leaned back and gazed into Alex's eyes. "So?"

After a moment's hesitation, Alex's face softened and his mouth pressed against hers. The kiss was at first tentative, then deeper until Barbara felt her entire body fuse with his. When he took her in his arms, she could feel the drumming of his heart, and hers. She placed her mouth beside his ear and hummed a bit of familiar music.

Hungrily Alex placed a line of kisses from Barbara's ear, along her jawline, to her mouth. As his mouth covered hers, he took her glass and put it on the table. Then he laced his fingers with hers and held her hands against her thighs. They stood, their feet moving slightly to the deep rhythm of the music, their mouths fused, her nostrils filled with the smell of his aftershave.

Barbara was soaring. The music, which she had come to associate with erotic experiences, filled her soul, Alex's mouth teased, his tongue probing and filling, his hands holding hers immobile.

Alex slid their joined hands to the small of Barbara's back and pressed so her belly and mound were pressed intimately against his obviously hard cock. Barbara moved her hips slightly and heard Alex groan. She changed the position of the kiss slightly and tangled her tongue with his. He shuddered.

They danced until the backs of Barbara's thighs touched the edge of the large conference table. She boosted herself slightly until she slid onto the table, knees spread. Now she understood why Maggie had insisted that she change into a short denim skirt that zipped up the front. She wore a light green scoop-necked T-shirt and a denim vest that barely closed.

As Alex stepped between her knees, Barbara wrapped her legs around Alex's thighs and linked the high heels of her leather boots behind him. Between the effect of the music, the champagne, and the intensely hot look in Alex's eyes, she felt bold and daring. Her legs still around Alex's, she pushed books and papers aside until she could lie back on the cool wood.

With a groan, Alex pulled her shirt up so he could cover her lace-covered breasts with his hands. "Oh, sweet," he said, his voice hoarse. He found the clasp at the center front of her bra and deftly opened it.

"I knew you'd be gorgeous, but I had no idea . . ." he said as her breasts spilled out and filled his hands. He bent over and kissed her chest and ribs, finally covering her aching nipples with his wet mouth.

As he pulled and nipped, shafts of pure pleasure stabbed through her body. Unable to wait much longer, he grabbed the bottom of the skirt zipper and pulled it upward until the skirt was only held around her waist by a single button. "Oh, shit," he groaned when he discovered she wore lace garters to hold up her stockings but no panties. "Oh, shit." His eyes glazed as he stared at her naked pussy. "Oh, shit."

Quickly he pulled down his slacks and underwear. "Protection," Barbara said.

Alex pulled a condom from his wallet and opened the package. "Let me do that," Barbara said, standing up. She pushed Alex into a chair and unrolled the latex over the hard cock that stood straight up in his lap. When he started to rise, she said, "Let me do that, too." She straddled his thighs and slowly impaled herself on his erection.

"Oh, shit," Alex said again. "Yes, yes, yes."

When the length of him was inside her, she planted her feet firmly on the floor and levered herself up, almost off his cock, then allowed her body to drop again. Up and down, in and out, she established a carnal rhythm.

She allowed her head to fall back and surrendered herself to the music, the champagne, the heat of her desire. She reached between their bodies and rubbed her clit and the base of his cock. It took only another minute until Alex climaxed, and soon after Barbara reached her peak as well.

Panting, Barbara collapsed against Alex's chest, still covered with his white shirt and tie. "Making love half dressed is very erotic," he said. "I still have my shirt on and you're still almost wearing most of your clothes."

"God," Barbara said. "That was great." She rose and Alex quickly removed the condom with a wad of tissues. When he went to toss it into the wastebasket, she added, "Drop it into the bag. Why let anyone suspect what we've been doing?"

Alex tossed the tissues into the shopping bag as Barbara rose. She collected the champagne bottle and put it, the glasses, and the tape player into the bag.

"Leaving so soon?" Alex asked, picking up a few books and papers that had landed on the floor. "I'm running late, but we could have dinner in about half an hour."

As Alex pulled on his clothes, Barbara rezipped and tidied herself up. "I find that I'm not too hungry anymore," she said with a suggestive wink. "You satisfied my hungers just fine."

"Ummm," Alex purred, holding her and nibbling on her ear. "You aren't bad yourself."

"I'm going to catch a cab home and collapse from the pleasure of what we just did."

"I hope I'll see you before I leave."

"You might. And when you do, think about how good this was. And maybe next time you're on this coast we can do it again." Barbara picked up the shopping bag and looked around the library. "This room will never feel quite the same again," she said.

"I'll bet not," Alex said. "Sleep tight." He kissed her hard.

"Ummm," Barbara said. "Don't work too hard." As she opened the door, she looked back and marveled at the expression of pure satisfaction on Alex's face. She had put that there. Life was wonderful.

"Maggie, it was a trip," Barbara said the following morning as she poured coffee for herself and her friend. "It was sport fucking, it was no-strings lusting, it was more fun than I've had in years. And it was meaningless." Unable to sit still, Barbara paced the length of the kitchen, her cup in her hand.

"I know just how it makes you feel. Desirable, attractive, sexy."

"Yeah. All of that. No one has ever made me feel that way before. No, that's not really true. Alex didn't make me feel that way, *I* did. It's all inside me. Somehow I think it's always been there, that spark, that glow. It took you to make me see it." She walked up to Maggie, pulled her to her feet and gave her a giant bear hug. "I'm a sexy woman."

"That you are, yet you're also the same person you were three months ago, before we met."

"I feel like going to bars and picking up guys just to prove that I can do it. Then fucking their brains out, and mine, too, of course, just for fun."

"That's what sex is for. Fun. Sex with Chuck was never fun. It was okay, just not fun with a capital F. I never had fun like that until after my divorce."

Barbara sat down at the table and thought a moment. "Do you really mean that your marriage to Chuck was all bad?"

"Not bad, just boring."

"There wasn't anything good about it?"

"Marriage is for fools who are willing to settle for monotony and security."

"My parents had a good marriage, I think, until my father died. I think they were truly happy. I can remember that they used to disappear into the bedroom to 'go over finances.' They would close the door and giggle. Giggle. My mom and dad. They were truly happy."

"Maybe they were the one in a thousand," Maggie said.

"What about Bob? Wasn't that good?"

"Funny, it was the exact opposite of my marriage to Chuck. Hot sex but nothing else. It's impossible to have both hot sex and a good friendship in the same relationship."

"I hope you're wrong . . . Anyway, back to last night. Did I tell you about the tape? It was wonderful, so dreamy and erotic."

"Did you do some slow dancing? I always like to start an evening with a little concentrated body rubbing."

"Yeah, we did. And you're right about that. It is a great way to start things."

"But Alex is history?"

"He'll be in the office this morning, but I have several errands to run for Steve so I'll probably get to the office after he leaves to go back to the Coast. Anyway, seeing him the morning after would probably be a letdown." She took a swallow of her coffee.

"And Jay?" Maggie asked.

"Oh, no, he's still very much around. He's a nice man and I enjoy sex with him, even if it is a bit predictable."

"Why don't you initiate something new? Something that turns you on more than what you're doing."

Barbara looked surprised. "You know, old habits die hard. I guess I thought I could do new things with others, but I never thought of taking the initiative with Jay. Maybe I could. But I'm still such a dunce when it comes to creative stuff. I wouldn't know what to try." She raised her eyebrow a bit.

"Are you manipulating me?" When Barbara smiled, Maggie continued. "You want another of my tapes, don't you? You know you could buy some books of good erotica. They will be full of new ideas."

"I know, but those tapes turn me on. And I love both the music and the voice of the sexy man who reads the stories."

"That's my friend, the one who gave me the tapes in the first place. I think I told you that he runs an erotic boutique in the city. You should go there and meet him sometime."

"I think he'd intimidate me. He's sort of a professional at sex, and I'm such an amateur."

"He's a wonderful, creative lover with a marvelously devious mind. You shouldn't be afraid of him. You and he would make beautiful music together. I'll see whether I can get the two of you together. In the meantime . . ." Maggie reached into her pocket and pulled out another audiotape. "I want you to save this one for twenty-four hours. Put it on your dresser so you'll see it tonight when you get home from work. Think about it, but don't play it until tomorrow."

"Why?"

"It's a bit heavier than the ones you've listened to before and I want you to be really excited. So no touching, no sneaking, just let the excitement build till tomorrow. Okay?"

"If you want, Maggie. You haven't steered me wrong up to now."

Maggie looked at Barbara's watch. "Aren't you getting late for work?"

Barbara looked down. "Oh, damn," she said. "It's almost eight. I'm going to be late for the first time in years."

Since Maggie had given her the tape, Barbara had been intrigued. A bit heavier, she had said. The next night Barbara put the tape in the player and pushed play. There was music and that wonderful voice. She became wet just hearing it. I'm getting like Pavlov's dogs, Barbara thought. That man doesn't have to say anything dirty. He could read the telephone directory and I'd probably come. She stretched out on the bed, closed her eyes and listened.

His name was William Singleton and he had been working on the plan for months. First, he combed the city for just the right women, prostitutes to be sure, but women of beauty and refinement. Women who entertained men and didn't just fuck them. He paid them well and, telling them exactly what he intended, he invited the three he selected to his home.

Over the following weeks, using exotic drugs and hypnosis, he trained the girls for many hours each day. Now he could show off his creations to his friends at a small exotic party he was throwing that evening.

He checked the living room and the dining room. "Yes," he muttered as he rearranged a flower here and a napkin there, "everything's ready."

He walked down the hall and opened the door to each

of three special bedrooms. In each room, a girl lay sleeping, resting for the evening ahead. Reclosing the three doors, William went downstairs to await his guests. It would be a long evening.

At eight o'clock, the doorbell rang for the first time, and by eight-fifteen there were four men in formal dress, including William, seated in the living room. Each held a drink in his hand; each talked nervously, anticipating the evening to come. Sir William Singletree was known for his erotic and highly unusual parties and his three best friends were anticipating a creative evening.

At eight-thirty, the doorbell rang again. The butler, dressed in tailcoat and patent-leather shoes opened the door. The woman who swirled through the opening was beautiful. She shrugged out of her floor-length royal-blue velvet coat and left it with the butler. She was dressed in an ice-blue satin evening dress which was draped dramatically over her left shoulder. Her right arm and shoulder were bare, which showed off the wide diamond cuff bracelet that was her only piece of jewelry. Her meticulously arranged chestnut-brown hair swept up from her long, graceful neck.

She crossed the living room and offered a perfectly manicured hand to each of the gentlemen, greeting William last.

"My dear," he said as he took Sylvia's hand and kissed her cheek, "I think everything is ready for dinner now."

Without another word, she gracefully crossed the room and disappeared down the long hallway.

"Sylvia is looking magnificent as usual," Marshall said. He was in his midthirties and the star of a successful TV series. Tall, with dark and brooding good looks, his life was a continual battle to keep women from throwing themselves at him. But willing women bored him.

"Absolutely gorgeous," Samuel agreed. At almost fifty, he was the oldest man in the group. Gray hair and

matching steel-gray eyes made him look the epitome of a business tycoon, which was exactly what he was.

"Yes," William said, taking obvious pride in the looks that his dinner companion got. "Sylvia is a beautiful and surprisingly resourceful woman."

Resourceful was a strange word to use for a woman, Paul, the third invited guest, thought. But leave it to William to use words in their most unusual connotations. Paul was about the same age and height as his friend Marshall but that was where the resemblance ended. Paul was a blue-eyed blond with hair slightly longer than was fashionable. A successful writer with three best sellers to his credit, he usually managed to look just a bit individual, and his sexual tastes were unusual as well.

William looked around at his three friends. Three totally different types, each with exotic sexual appetites like his own, but each with entirely different tastes. It would be interesting to watch how each one reacted to the evening's "entertainment."

Small talk continued to fill the living room until, about five minutes later, Sylvia returned, followed by three spectacularly beautiful women. Each was about twenty-five, one a blonde, one a brunette, and one a redhead. The women were dressed in identical evening dresses, strapless and unadorned, sweeping to the floor in a waterfall of silk. The only difference was that the blonde's dress was gold, the brunette's black, and the redhead's silver. Each was perfectly made up with an elaborate hairstyle that piled obviously long hair high on each woman's head.

The three guests stared. The women were all of medium height and well proportioned. "Good evening," they said, almost in unison.

"These are your dinner companions," William said. "Sylvia, introduce our guests."

Sylvia took the hand of the blonde in the golden dress and walked her over to where Marshall was standing.

"Marshall, darling," she said, "I'd like you to meet Kitt. I think you and she will get along wonderfully."

Marshall took Kitt's hand as she murmured, "It's so good to meet you."

Sylvia then walked the brunette toward Samuel. "Samuel, you and Ginny have a lot in common, as I'm sure you'll find out."

"I've heard a lot about you," Ginny said, "and I've been looking forward to meeting you."

Paul walked over to the girl with the incredibly red hair. "I've always loved redheads," he said to the girl. "My name is Paul."

"This is Cynthia," Sylvia said. "She's to be your companion for the evening."

Almost immediately, William said, "Dinner is ready. Shall we eat?"

As dinner proceeded uneventfully, perfectly prepared dishes arrived one after another, accompanied by perfectly selected wines. The eight diners discussed politics, books, sports, any subject that anyone was interested in. Each man marveled at how perfectly the woman he was with fit his tastes, both in looks and in interests.

When coffee and brandy arrived at the table, William stood. Raising his brandy snifter, he said, "A toast to a splendid evening to come."

They all raised their glasses, then drank.

"Shall we go downstairs?" William asked.

They crossed the living room and walked down the great curved staircase to the large well-carpeted area below. The three male guests had been in William's house many times before. His parties were legendary, and the best entertainment always took place downstairs.

The three couples settled themselves on large overstuffed sofas to wait for whatever entertainment William and Sylvia had planned.

The host and hostess crossed the room and, while Sylvia gracefully took her seat, William stood beside a table on which a line of glass bells of different sizes was ar-

ranged. With great ceremony, he took a small glass rod and tapped the bell at the near end of the row. A single clear note filled the room.

William looked at each of the three women. As he gazed, each man turned and looked at his companion. Each of the three identically dressed women stared into space, seemingly out of contact with the others in the room.

"Gentlemen," William said. "The ladies are unable to hear or see what's going on right now. They have been conditioned to the sound of these bells. When I ring this one, they all respond by going into a trance. When I tap the one on the other end," he tapped the bell, "they all return to us."

He looked at the three women. "Don't you, ladies?"

The women smiled and looked a bit confused, so Sylvia said, "You're feeling fine, aren't you, ladies?"

"Certainly, Sylvia," Kitt said. "We all feel wonderful."

William tapped the first bell and the three women again stared into space, their eyes distant and clouded over.

"Each one of these women has volunteered for a most amusing training program. Sylvia and I have spent weeks perfecting their behavior. We have done it as a present to each of you to thank you for your years of friendship and loyalty."

"You know you don't have to thank us," Samuel said. "We've always been there for each other."

"Well, I wanted to do this," William said, "so let's get on with it. Marshall, you get to go first."

Marshall looked a bit puzzled. "First for what?" he asked.

"I'll show you." William tapped a bell in the center of the row and said, "Kitt, take off your dress and show Marshall what is his for the evening."

Slowly Kitt rose. She looked into Marshall's eyes as she reached behind her and slowly unzipped her dress and gradually allowed it to inch down her body. Proudly she displayed a sensational body, covered with a golden corselet that cinched in her waist and cupped her breasts but left the nipples bare. Gold-colored garters held up matching stockings. Her shoes were also golden with high spike heels. She wore no panties and Marshall could see her blond hair between the garters.

"What do you think, Marshall?" Sylvia asked.

"She's magnificent, Sylvia." He sounded hesitant.

"Say what you wish," Sylvia said. "She won't remember anything we don't want her to."

"Well, you all know I don't like willing women. I like my women to fight me."

Sylvia chuckled. "We know that, dear. We know all your tastes. In our conversations with Kitt, we discovered that she has a matching fantasy, one that she's been reluctant to discuss with anyone. But we've used that desire to train her to fulfill your fantasy, while fulfilling hers at the same time." She looked around the room, catching Samuel's eyes, then Paul's. "The same is true of your dinner companions, gentlemen. Your tastes match perfectly. Now, I hope you two don't mind waiting? We'd like to play, one couple at a time."

The two others shook their heads. If William and Sylvia did know all their tastes, it was going to be an evening worth waiting for.

"Now, Kitt," William said, "listen to me. Marshall wants to fuck you. Do you want him to?"

Kitt smiled and allowed her gaze to roam over Marshall's body. "Yes. He's very sexy and I'm very hungry."

Sylvia said, softly, "The girls are all very hungry. Their bodies have been conditioned to become physically aroused at the sound of the bells." She looked at William, then at the three men. "We have found that sexual excitement, like anything else, can be conditioned. We have trained these girls to react in specific ways to different sounds." She looked at Kitt, standing proudly and displaying her shapely body. "How much do you want him? Tell him."

A slow, erotic smile spread over her face. "I want you to make love to me. I want you to fuck me now. Please fuck me."

Marshall looked disappointed. It was too easy.

"Don't worry," William said, "we understand." William tapped Kitt's bell twice. Instantly, Kitt grabbed her dress and held it in front of her as she backed away from Marshall. "I know who you are and what you want. You want to rape me." She licked her lips. "I've seen you looking at me all evening and I'm not going to give in. Don't you come near me," she snarled.

William looked at the smile that spread over Marshall's face. "Is this more to your liking?"

"Most certainly," Marshall said. "I've always had rape fantasies, but I would never actually commit rape, hurt anyone, you know. Are you sure that she really wants this?"

"You'll have to trust me. Each of these women has been selected for her sexual tastes and appetites. Don't worry. All of you," he looked around the room, "will get tremendous pleasure from what happens."

"If you're sure."

"I am. Now, she's all yours," William said.

Marshall stood and carefully removed his jacket and loosened his tie. He dropped the jacket on the sofa next to him but kept the tie in his hand. As he walked toward Kitt, he glanced around the room. Yes, he thought, there was everything he might need. He slowly stalked Kitt as she backed away from him. "Come here, Kitt, I won't hurt you."

"Stay away," she said.

"It will be easier for you if you hold still. I don't want to hurt you."

"I know exactly what you want, Marshall, and you won't get it from me without a fight." She continued to *back away from him staying just out of arm's reach.*

With sudden speed, Marshall took three steps, reached out and snatched the dress from Kitt's hands. Then, as she tried to scamper away, he snagged her wrist and pulled her to him. He twisted her arm behind her and tangled the fingers of his free hand in her hair.

Hairpins flew everywhere as long strands pulled free. Soon, still holding her squirming body, he wrapped a hank of long flaxen hair around his hand. He gently pulled her head back and pressed his lips against hers. She tried to twist away from his kiss, but his hand in her hair prevented her head from moving.

As he felt her press her lips together to keep his tongue out of her mouth, he said, "You aren't strong enough to resist me, you know."

Silently she glared at him, her lips sealed.

"Let me find out just how reluctant you really are," he said. He picked her up and dropped her on the nearest sofa. As she tried to twist away, he stretched his body on top of hers and reached his hand between her legs. He touched her pubic hair and slid a finger through her folds. He smiled. "You're soaking wet. You really do want me."

"Keep your hands off me!" she shouted.

Marshall hesitated.

"Marshall," William said, "just in case you need reassurance . . ." He tapped Kitt's bell. Instantly she was quiet. Looking puzzled about how she ended up on the sofa with her date's body stretched over hers, she gazed into Marshall's eyes and said, "Mmmm. You feel good against me. Are you going to make love to me?"

"Yes, darling, I am." Marshall nodded to William who tapped Kitt's bell twice. At the sound, she was a tiger again, squirming to get free of his hold. "God, I like it like this," Marshall said. He looked at Samuel and Paul. "Gentlemen, I could use a little help at this moment."

The two men got up and each held one of Kitt's arms.

Marshall held both her legs and together they carried her over to a low table. Samuel and Paul each pulled off his tie. They stretched Kitt across the table, face up, her head hanging off the end. Using their ties and a soft rope that William provided, they tied her arms and legs to the table legs. Then they stood up and surveyed the scene. Kitt was still dressed in the corselet and stockings, but her cunt and nipples were exposed, offered to the men for their use.

"Yes," Marshall said, "that's very good." He paused, looking at her squirming body. "William," he said, "you said that she'd be enjoying this. I want you to release her so we can both enjoy."

William tapped her bell again. "Kitt," he said, "listen to me." Kitt's body went limp. "Marshall wants you to relax and be yourself. Do you understand?"

"Yes," Kitt said, testing her bonds, "I understand. But I can't move."

"No, you can't. Does that upset you?" When she hesitated, he asked again, his voice soft, "Does it?"

Kitt looked at Marshall. "No. I find it very exciting, being tied up like this. But it's hard for me to admit it."

"I understand. Do whatever you like. If you say stop, you can be sure that I will."

Kitt smiled and again pulled against the ties that held her. "I really am at your mercy. What are you going to do?"

"Pleasure us both, I hope," Marshall said. Then he walked around the table stroking and scratching Kitt's belly, thighs, nipples. "You're so beautiful."

Quickly he undressed and knelt at the head of the table so his hard, erect cock was level with her mouth. "I want you to suck it," he said.

Kitt opened her mouth, then paused. With a gleam in her eyes, she turned her head away, her lips firmly pressed together. "Oh, yes, baby, get into the game. Fight me."

Marshall twisted his hand in her hair and pulled her

face around. "Open your mouth, bitch, and suck my cock!"

As she did as he said, he pressed his penis into her mouth. Suddenly Marshall knew she was enjoying what she was doing. He felt her lips tighten on his cock and her tongue slide over his skin. As he pulled back, he felt her create a vacuum in her mouth as she sucked. Still holding her head, he fucked her mouth until he came. Spurts of semen filled her throat and she swallowed, licking him clean.

As Marshall settled back on his haunches, he said, "What about her? She's so hot."

"What's your pleasure, gentlemen?" William asked.

"I'd like to watch one of the other girls get her off," Samuel said.

"Is that all right with you, Kitt?" Marshall asked.

"Would you like to watch?" she asked him.

"Oh, yes," he admitted.

Kitt smiled and nodded.

"That's a splendid idea," Sylvia said. "We haven't trained anyone specifically for that, so it will interesting to see how it works."

As William reached for another bell, Sylvia said, "Let me tell her. I think I'd enjoy doing that."

"Certainly," William said, tapping a different bell. A clear note, higher than any they had heard previously, sounded through the room. Ginny raised her dark-brown eyes and looked at William. "Ginny, you will listen to Sylvia like a good girl. You will hear only her voice and do whatever she says," William said.

Ginny turned toward Sylvia who said, "Dear, Kitt is so excited and she needs to come. I want you to pleasure her with your mouth."

William explained to the three men. "Ginny is our most adventurous woman. You must understand that I never ask any woman to do anything that is outside her nature."

During William's explanation, Ginny had sat quietly, not yet obeying Sylvia's instructions.

"Has she ever had any lesbian experiences?" Samuel asked.

"Several, according to her, and she enjoys it tremendously," Sylvia said, turning to the girl. "Ginny, I told you to do something."

"Tell me exactly what you want me to do," Ginny whispered. "I want to hear the words."

"All right, my dear. I want you to do whatever I tell you." Sylvia smiled. "Now, get up and go over to the table."

Marshall was holding Kitt's head in his hands, stroking her face. "We'll both enjoy what's going to happen," he whispered to her.

Ginny approached and, at Sylvia's instruction, knelt beside Kitt. "Now suck her nipples," Sylvia said. "Take one into your mouth and suck it, hard. Tug at it with your teeth."

Ginny bent over Kitt's body and began to suck her breasts, exposed above the corselet.

"Use your hands. Pull her tits out and caress them with your hands."

Marshall could hear slurping sounds as Ginny sucked.

"Now the other one," Sylvia said. Obediently Ginny switched to the other breast.

Kitt's hips thrust upward, reaching for something, a cock, a tongue. "She needs you, Ginny. She needs your mouth on her pussy to make her come. Lick and suck her pussy, Ginny, like a good girl."

Ginny moved around the table and tentatively touched the tip of her tongue to Kitt's cunt lips. "Lick the whole length of her slit," Sylvia said, "then flick your tongue over her clit. Good. Now stick your tongue inside and pull it out. Lick. Nibble at her clit."

Sylvia walked over and placed her hand on Kitt's belly, just above her pubic hair. "I can feel her hips moving," she said. "Lick faster. Flick your tongue over her clit, then pull it into your mouth. Yes. Make her come. I can feel it coming. Don't stop." There was a moment's pause, then Sylvia yelled, "Now! Suck hard now."

Marshall reached down and felt the tiny, compulsive movements of Kitt's hips. As she came, he pressed his mouth against hers and probed with his tongue. He thrust his tongue in and out of her mouth in the rhythm he could feel with his hand. Her climax seemed to go on for hours. When she calmed, Marshall untied her and cradled her in his lap.

As Ginny finished licking Kitt's body, Samuel stood up, unzipped his pants and pulled out his erect cock. He had to have her now. On a side table there was a jar of lubricant and he spread a handful on his cock. "Tell her to let me fuck her my way."

"She already knows," Sylvia said, "and she loves it that way. Offer Samuel what he wants, Ginny."

Ginny flipped her dress up over her back, raised her ass in the air and, still licking Kitt's pussy, parted her ass cheeks with her hands. All anyone could see were the same garters and stockings that Kitt was wearing, except Ginny's were black to match her dress.

Samuel found his cock getting even harder at her eagerness to give and take pleasure. God, he wanted her tight ass. He rubbed his lubricated fingers over her entire rear, then pressed the tip of one finger against her hole.

"Oh, yes, darling," Ginny said, holding very still. Samuel's finger pressed and released. Slowly, the pushing became a bit harder and the tip of his finger penetrated. Deeper and deeper his thrusting finger went, rhythmically forcing itself into her.

As the finger continued its assault, her hips began to thrust backward. "That feels good, doesn't it, Ginny. It's tight, but it makes your pussy hot." He reached around and fingered her sopping cunt with his other hand. "So wet. You're so wet."

Samuel stroked her pussy with one hand and fucked

her ass with the other. When he felt she was ready and he could wait no longer, he lubricated his hard cock and pressed the tip against her puckered hole, then thrust deep into her.

"It feels so good, darling. Do it harder," she screamed.

Samuel kept massaging her cunt and soon felt her rear muscles relax and her hips begin to buck. "Yes," he said, establishing his own rhythm, "move your hips while I fuck your ass and finger your cunt. Move with me."

"Oh, God," she screamed, "I'm going to come."

"We're both going to come, Ginny."

He fucked her ass and rubbed her pussy until they both came and collapsed on the floor.

Barbara stopped the tape and, panting from her orgasm, she went into the bathroom and got a glass of water. That I could get so hot from just a story . . . she thought. No wonder people buy dirty books and magazines. Then she stopped herself. Not dirty. Erotic. Delicious. She made a mental note to find a bookstore or newsstand and do a little shopping. When she was calmer, she lay back on the bed and pressed play again and the story resumed. She was instantly back in the basement with William and Sylvia.

William crossed to the bar and poured Sylvia and the three men a drink. They untied Kitt and put robes on the two spent girls. Then they sat them on the sofa and put them back into their trance.

William looked at Paul. "Yours is yet to come. I just want everyone a bit rested to watch the show."

Paul smiled and rearranged his clothing over his hard cock. After what he had already witnessed, whatever William and Sylvia had in store for him would be worth any amount of inconvenience.

After they had rested for a short while, William said, "Your treat is a bit different, Paul. Cynthia has been trained for a new experience. When she hears her bell she will listen only to my voice and she will feel exactly what I tell her to feel." William tapped a bell with a lower, more mellow tone. Cynthia sat up.

"Cynthia," William said, "it's very warm in here, isn't it?"

"Yes," she said. "Very warm."

"So warm that you think you'll never be able to get cool."

Cynthia started fanning herself with her hand. Her face began to flush and she blew a stream of cool air on her chest.

"That air you're blowing is hot and it's making you hotter. Even though this room is full of important people and you will be very embarrassed to do so, you have to pull the top of your dress down to get cool."

Cynthia looked around at the "important people" and looked very uncomfortable. "I'm so hot," she murmured, "I have to get cool." She pulled the top of her dress down and, like the other girls, she was wearing a corselet that bared her nipples, hers in silver.

"You're still so hot," William continued. "That's not helping. Your nipples are the center of the heat. They're so hot they're on fire. You have to cool them off. Your whole tit is so hot." Cynthia pulled her breasts out of the corselet, looked frantically around the room and spotted the ice in Paul's drink. She grabbed the glass, pulled out an ice cube and rubbed it over her breasts. "Yes, that feels better, doesn't it?"

"Yes." The word came out like a hiss. "Better."

"The ice is getting hotter from the heat of your breast. It's not cooling anymore. You need something else."

"What?" she asked, dropping the ice cube.

"Paul's mouth. That's the only cool thing in the room. But he might not want to suck your tits and cool them. You have to ask nicely."

"Please cool my tits," she said, offering her breasts to him. "Please."

Paul blew a stream of air across her nipples. "Yes," she purred, "that's cool. But I need your mouth."

Paul smiled and said, "You'll have to force them into my mouth." This was his oldest fantasy coming true.

She climbed into his lap and forced her swollen buds into his mouth. She pulled at his hair and his ears as she tried to force her whole breast into his mouth at once. He sucked and was in heaven.

"Now the other one, Cynthia. Let Paul's mouth cool it."

Paul alternated between Cynthia's pillow-soft, white breasts, filling his mouth and his hands with her flesh.

"Your tits are getting cool now," William said, "but the heat is traveling to your mouth. It's your mouth that is hot now."

Cynthia opened her mouth and panted, trying to draw in cool air. Then she picked up Paul's drink and took an ice cube into her mouth.

"That ice is still hot, Cynthia," William said. "There's only one thing here that's cool." She looked at him, puzzled. "Paul's cock. It's the only cool thing in the room."

Frantically Cynthia pulled at Paul's zipper until she could pull his pants aside and take out his cock. It was huge. Paul loved to have it sucked, but it was too big for most women.

"It's a huge ice cube, Cynthia," William said. "If you take it into your mouth it will cool you, but only where it touches. The rest of your mouth will still be hot."

Cynthia wrapped her hand around Paul's erection and opened her mouth as wide as she could. She took Paul's entire cock into her mouth, her tongue and hands moving ceaselessly. She bobbed her head, moving the "cold" cock around to cool each part of her hot flesh.

For five minutes, everyone watched as Cynthia sucked Paul's erection until it was hard for him not to come. "Make her stop," he cried. "I want to come in her pussy."

"The heat in your mouth is subsiding now, Cynthia." Cynthia's body slowly relaxed and she sat up. "Your body is warm again all over. You'd better take off your dress."

Cynthia pulled off the dress that had been bunched around her waist.

"That's better," William said. "Now the heat is flowing back, this time in your pussy. It's like hot honey running down inside your belly and flowing out of your cunt, making it warmer and warmer."

Cynthia spread her legs as she "felt" the honey flow. "Spread your legs as the honey streams down your thighs. You need something cool. The honey is making you hot. Paul's cock is still the only cool thing in the room. Sit on it. Take it inside you."

Cynthia climbed onto Paul's lap and impaled herself on his cock. "Move it around to cool your entire cunt," William said. "Up and down so it cools the sides of your passage. There's cool juice inside that prick. Tighten your muscles to squeeze out the cool juice. Squeeze and relax, squeeze and relax. That's the best way."

Paul could take no more. With a scream he came deep inside her. "Yes, you did well," William said. "Cold juice is spurting into your pussy and putting out the fire. But you must hold Paul's cock inside you or you'll get hot again."

Paul looked at William, exhausted. He had no idea what William had in mind, but he was spent.

"Have you ever felt a woman come?" Sylvia asked Paul. "Really felt it? Well, we've always thought that we could make one come just from the sound of William's voice. The only way we'd be sure is if she came while your cock was still inside and you could feel her climax. Are you game?"

Paul looked at Cynthia still sitting in his lap. He knew she couldn't hear him or Sylvia. "Yeah, sure. I'm game. But I don't think you can do it. Orgasm isn't trainable."

"We think it is. Let's put it to the test. I'll let the other women listen, too. You can all enjoy your date's excitement."

He tapped another bell. All the women looked at William. "Now, ladies, don't move any part of your body, just listen to my voice. You will feel exactly what I tell you to feel. Do you understand?"

Cynthia and the other women nodded. "I understand."

"You feel hands on your breasts. One hand on each breast is kneading your flesh. It feels so good. Lean forward just a bit so your breasts will press into the caressing hands." Paul felt her strain forward. "That's good. The fingers are twisting your nipples now. It's painful, but it is also exciting. The pinches have taken on a rhythm, first one side then the other. They are pulling at your nipples, milking your breasts. Those hands are making you so excited."

Paul could feel Cynthia's body swaying with the sound of William's voice. The voice was so exciting that each of the other two men were playing with the breasts of the women now sitting on their laps.

"The fingers are creating tiny electrical charges that are sparking through your tits. Hot electrical sparks that excite you and make your pussy wetter. You can feel the sparks through your ribs and your belly. Tiny pinpoints of pain and pleasure are traveling over your skin, lower and lower through your belly and now over the insides of your thighs.

"The sparks are tiny caresses now, flicking soft touches up the insides of your thighs. Now those flickers are on your pussy, pulsing over your clit."

Almost simultaneously the other two men entered their women and began pumping in sync with William's voice.

"Your clit is pulsing with the sensation. You can feel the tightness grow in your belly as your climax approaches. That tightness is traveling to your pussy."

Paul could feel his cock swell as he tried to remain still. He could feel Cynthia's juices soaking his thighs.

"Feel those pulses all over your body, in your breasts, in your mouth, in your ass. Those pulses are your orgasm approaching. You want to resist but you can't. The pull of the pulses is too strong. The pulses are pulling your orgasm from you.

"Tell me, are you going to come?"

"Yes," each woman screamed. "I can feel it . . . right now."

"Then come now. Let the orgasm come. Let the pulses flow through your cunt."

Paul screamed as he felt Cynthia's climax suck at his cock. He couldn't keep his own orgasm back and he climaxed again.

No one was sure how much later, William tapped the bell that released the women from their trances. He and Sylvia tossed blankets over the exhausted couples and turned down the light.

"Good night, everyone," William said. "Sylvia and I are going upstairs."

Chapter 8

It was several weeks before Barbara saw Maggie again. She had dated Jay frequently and had had dates, and been to bed, with three other men—one from her office, one a neighbor, and one a man she had met at the supermarket. She had also played the tapes frequently and found that, thanks to the attitudes of the people in the stories, she had become accepting of sex in all forms, and was able to suggest games and activities that proved both stimulating and rewarding.

In mid-June, Barbara arrived home from work one evening to find Maggie in her kitchen, cooking. After long, almost tearful hugs, Barbara stepped back, looked at her friend and said, "It's been such a long time and I've missed you. God, things smell good in here."

"I've missed you, too," Maggie said. "And I'm making corned beef and cabbage. I couldn't resist."

"You must have shopped. How did you do that? Could people see you?"

Maggie looked shocked. "They must have been able to, but I have no clue how. I never even thought about it. I just went to the supermarket and picked up a few things." She shook her head. "People must have seen me. The woman checked me out without a blink. And I had money in my wallet."

"But in the mall, no one could see you but me."

"Things in this plane of existence work strangely to say the least. When is this?"

"It's June."

"It looked springy," Maggie said. "But I cooked this anyway. It was in my mind when I arrived at the A&P."

Barbara lifted a piece of cabbage from the pot and tasted. "Wonderful. I'm glad you did. And I'm incredibly glad to see you."

Maggie hugged Barbara again. "Me too, although I just left you a few moments before I showed up at the supermarket."

Barbara opened the refrigerator door and spied a six-pack of Sam Adams. She looked toward Maggie questioningly. "My favorite. One for you?" At Maggie's nod, she pulled out two bottles.

"Sure." She pushed a long fork into the slab of meat in the pot. "Let's give this about fifteen more minutes."

The two women sat at the kitchen table and each poured a beer. "How have you been, Barbara?" Maggie asked.

"I've been great," Barbara said. "Lots of dates, lots of good healthy sex."

"Steve?"

"No. Not him. Despite all the great clothes and keeping myself looking good, he pays almost no attention to me, except as a very useful piece of furniture."

"Have you asked him out?"

"No. We did have dinner one evening, but it was with a client and his wife. I guess Lisa, Ms. Knockout, isn't the kind you take to dinner with a guy with oodles of old money. You should have seen his wife. Her jewelry was older than I was."

"And nothing remotely date-like from Steve?"

"Not a whisper. He didn't even take me home, just put me into a hired car and told the driver to take me wherever I wanted to go."

"We really have to do something about that, don't we?"

"Yes, we do. But I have another request first. Those tapes?"

"I gave you all I had," Maggie said.

"You told me that the man who made them has a store in the city. I think, well . . ."

"Yes? Out with it."

"Well, I'd like to meet him."

"His voice really gets to you, doesn't it?"

"His voice fills my erotic dreams, which, of course, I'd never admit to having except to you. What's he like?"

"He owns an erotic toy, book, and what-have-you store in the Village. He's a free spirit with a great understanding of the secret desires everyone has. And he exploits that knowledge in his stories and the items he sells in the shop. He's wonderfully creative in everything he does. And I do mean everything."

"You've been to bed with him?"

"Beds, boats, tables, CJ makes love wherever the fancy strikes him. But yes, I've been with him many times."

"Was he a customer?"

"He doesn't ever have to pay for it. He has whatever he wants, whenever he wants it. And frequently he wanted me. And I wanted him. So we did. I met him when I first went into his shop to buy a few things."

"I don't want to make love with him, I just want to see the man who goes with that incredible voice."

"The shop is called A Private Place." Maggie wrote down the address on a piece of paper. "Take one of the tapes as sort of an introduction. And keep an open mind and be ready for anything, that is, if you're so inclined."

"Oh, Maggie," Barbara said. "That's not why I want to meet him."

"Whatever you say." She took a long drink of her beer and the conversation shifted.

The storefront was unremarkable, a large window with a display of erotic books, but nothing overt enough to offend any passers-by. The words *A Private Place* were lettered on the window in ornate gold script, and there was a small sign in the corner of the window that proclaimed *C. J. Winterman, Prop.* CJ. Yes, that voice. Hours 11:00 to 5:00 Tues., Thurs., and Sat. He certainly works only when it suits him, Barbara thought.

That Saturday afternoon, as she stood looking in the window, Barbara rubbed her sweating palms together. She was nervous as a teenager, yet she dearly wanted to meet the man who had been part of her fantasies since Maggie gave her the first tape. She took a deep breath, inhaling late spring air, then glanced at her watch. Almost five o'clock. Only a few minutes until closing, but the sign read Open. She pushed open the door and heard a small bell jingle.

The store was well lit, with racks and shelves filled with sex toys, erotic games, books, greeting cards, everything the creative lover might want. She slowly toured the shop, pausing to giggle at several get well and birthday cards, then trembled a bit in front of a display of bondage equipment. As she crossed the front sales area, she overheard a young couple discussing which vibrator they should purchase.

"Do you think that's powerful enough?" she said.

"I don't want the kind that plugs in," he responded. "You're limited by the length of the cord."

"I like this one. It has a clit tickler," she said.

"If you like it, then we'll get it." The man handed a woman behind the counter a credit card as Barbara looked over a display of whips and leather harnesses.

"These are cleverly arranged so that you can strap on a dildo leaving your hands free for other pleasures," a voice behind her said.

It was his voice, the voice from the tapes. It hummed through her, making her knees weak and her pussy wet. She swallowed and turned slowly. He was about her age, average height with very curly brown hair and a sweet, almost cherubic face. His smile was open and warm. No wonder people buy stuff here, Barbara thought. He seems so innocent, as though everything in here must be ordinary. "You must be CJ," she said.

"Is that a guess from the sign in the window, or have you been here before?"

That voice. That incredible voice.

"Actually neither. I know your voice from some tapes I've been listening to." She withdrew a tape from her pocketbook and showed it to him.

"Oh." His face lit up as he grinned. "Yes. But these are part of the special edition, ones I made up for my friends." He pointed to the gold rim around the label. "See. This is how you tell. Where did you get this one?"

"That's a bit of a long story. Let's just say I got a few of them from a wonderful woman named Maggie."

"I haven't seen Maggie in a long time. I miss her. How is she?"

How to handle this one? Barbara wondered. "Actually, Maggie passed away last summer."

"I am so sorry. She was an amazing woman. Were you good friends?"

"Oh, yes, very good friends. But that was long ago."

"And were you and she kindred spirits?"

Barbara knew exactly what he was asking. Was she a hooker? "We weren't in the same line of work," she answered. "But we shared a lot of the same feelings." Was that an invitation? She hoped so. Much as she had denied it to Maggie, she had to admit that she wanted this man as she had never wanted anything.

"And what can I do to help you?" CJ asked.

"CJ," a voice called, postponing her answer. "It's after five and my husband's waiting outside. Unless you need me, I'm leaving."

"Have a nice evening, Alice," CJ called. "And turn the sign as you leave."

"I guess you're closing now," Barbara said, unable now to ask for what she wanted. The moment was gone. "I'll be leaving, too."

"Since you're a friend of Maggie's, you're welcome to wander as long as you like. Were you looking for anything special?" He placed his hands on her shoulders and turned her toward the display of leather-and-metal harnesses. "These are usually bought by dominants, for training sessions with their subs. Do they interest you? " He spoke with his mouth close to her ear, his breath warm, his hands on her shoulders.

"Yes," she whispered.

"You're trembling. Tell me what has you so excited. The idea of wearing one of those and doing deliciously evil things to someone?" When she remained silent, he continued. "Or maybe having someone wear a harness like that and overpower you."

Barbara couldn't move, couldn't speak. She was unable to control any parts of her body. All her thoughts were concentrated on his hands, his mouth, and her aching pussy.

"Did you want to buy one for your lover? Male or female?"

"Not for a lover," she croaked.

"For yourself?"

"For you." The words slipped out, but she was glad she had said them.

"Ah." His breath was warm against her ear. "You have a fantasy about me. Maybe in the fantasy I am wearing something made from heavy leather straps with metal rings and buckles, holding you down while I violate your body." Barbara couldn't answer. "You are helpless, unable to prevent me from doing whatever I want to you. Is that what you want?" Silence. His mouth remained against her ear, his tongue licking the edge. His arm slipped across her upper chest and pressed her back tightly against his chest. "Is it?"

"Yes," she whispered.

"Good girl," he purred. "Don't move." He nipped at her ear with his teeth, then left her. She heard him pull down the shades and put the chain on the door. He returned to stand behind her. "Now no one can come in and disturb us. Come with me."

Barbara moved like an automaton, following his slender frame through a curtain and into the back of the shop. They passed through a storage area and into another room. CJ closed the door and slid a bolt home. "Now we are truly alone. You are here of your own free will, are you not?"

"Yes," she whispered.

"Do you understand about safe words?"

Barbara remembered that Maggie had explained that if anyone used the pre-agreed safe word during any bondage session, everything stopped. She nodded.

"I use a slightly different system." He placed a Ping-Pong ball in Barbara's hand. "If you drop this, I will stop anything and everything, no questions asked. Do you understand?"

Barbara looked down at the small white ball in her hand. "Yes," she said, unable to say anything more even if she wanted to. The inside of her mouth felt like cotton, her knees were jelly, and her insides were trembling so hard it was difficult to concentrate on anything else. But she was so turned on, she felt as if she could come on command.

"And do you promise me you will drop that if anything, and I do mean anything, bothers you? It's most important that I have your word on that."

"You have my word," she said.

"Good." CJ flipped a switch and the room filled with the music that formed the background on the tapes. Then he opened a small closet in the corner of the room, grabbed some clothes and stepped behind a shoulder-height screen. "Get undressed," he said, his head above the top of the screen. "I want you completely naked." When she hesitated, he snapped, "Now!"

Barbara put the ball down, quickly removed her clothes, put them on a chair and picked up the ball again.

"Let me see you," CJ said, still behind the screen. "Stand up straight, stretch your arms up over your head and spread your legs."

Barbara separated her feet slightly and raised her arms.

"Wider," he snapped.

Barbara spread her feet wider and stared at CJ's face, the only part of him she could see.

"Nice," he said, obviously fumbling with clothes behind the screen. "Good legs, nice hips. Show me your tits."

"What?" Barbara said.

"Put the ball down and hold those tits for me so I can see how full they are." When her hands remained in the air, he said, "Do it now or leave."

Barbara put the ball on the small chair at her side, then cupped her breasts. The room was warm but she was shivering, from need, from lust, and from a sliver of fear. What had she gotten herself into?

"Pinch the nipples and make them hard. Show them to me."

Embarrassed but so aroused, she pinched her nipples until they swelled.

"Nice titties," CJ said. "Big and soft. You'll do nicely." When she went to put her feet together, he said, "Not in my presence. Your feet will always be apart, your body ready for me. Do you understand? Get the ball, then come here."

He stepped from behind the screen, now dressed in a deep brown harness. Wide straps of what appeared to be hard, unyielding leather crossed his bare chest and a leather pouch cupped his penis and testicles. He wore leather sandals that laced up his slender, yet muscular legs. He wore wide silver cuffs around his biceps and a leather collar around his neck. Whatever led me to see him as an angel? Barbara wondered. In this outfit, he was all power and control.

Holding the Ping-Pong ball, Barbara crossed the room and stood before CJ. He stared at her legs and glared. She looked down, then separated her feet.

"Stand with your chest against the wall."

She moved so she stood facing a bare wall, then felt his hand on her back, pressing her tightly against the cold surface. He raised her arms above her head, spread about as far apart as her feet. "How much of this do you want?" he asked. "I can make you cry or beg, I can hurt you or just control you. What do you want? This is the last decision you will make."

Barbara thought. She wanted to try everything. She didn't know whether pain would be a turn-on, but she had the ball in her hand and she trusted CJ completely. "Everything," she whispered. "I want to try it all."

"Good girl," he said. Then she felt the snap as cold metal cuffs were locked onto her wrists and ankles, then CJ attached the cuffs to the wall. She couldn't move. Then CJ placed cotton balls against her eyes, and covered them with a blindfold. She could see nothing.

"Now," he said, "we begin." He inserted his finger in her slit. "Such a hot slut," he said. "So wet. Let's cool you down a little."

Barbara heard noises, then jumped as something very cold pressed against her heated lips. The frozen object was inserted into her channel. "Some ice should cool you off a bit. You're much too excited." He rubbed another ice cube over her slit, numbing her flesh, yet heating her belly.

"God, that's too cold," she said.

"You will say nothing, or I'll gag you, too." When she shuddered, she felt a wad of cloth stuffed into her mouth, then another cloth stretched between her teeth and tied behind her head. Then he rubbed her clit and laughed. "You want this. Your body tells me everything."

She did want it. She wanted to give everything over to this man with the magic voice. He could do everything to her, all the things she had only dreamed about. Cold water trickled down her inner thigh but she couldn't move to wipe it off. Her mind traveled to the ball in her hand. She wouldn't drop it. Not yet. Maybe not at all.

"Now, let's see how you like this part." Suddenly she felt a hard slap on her right buttock. Then one on her left.

She groaned, making strange strangled sounds around the gag in her mouth. Again and again, his hand landed on her heated flesh. She burned. She throbbed, yet she was also incredibly turned on. The music filled her mind and the pleasure/pain filled her body. She could control her body no longer and she climaxed. Without anyone touching her pussy, without being filled with anything but an ice cube.

"No self-control," he said, laughing again. "I like that, but you're much too easy. Maybe now that you've come once, you'll be more of a challenge." Barbara felt CJ rub some lotion on her hot buttocks, kneading and caressing her skin from the small of her back to her cheeks. Some of the liquid trickled into her slit, oozing over her asshole and joining with the water still running from her icy cunt.

When her flaming ass was a bit cooler, CJ unclipped her cuffs from the wall and led her across the room. He placed her hands on a table of some kind, then pushed her so she was bent over the soft leather cover, her feet on the floor, her upper body cradled in the soft fabric, her arms hanging down. Still holding the Ping-Pong ball, her hands were cuffed to the front legs of the table and her ankles to the rear two. There were openings in the table so her breasts hung freely.

She felt fingers pulling on her nipples, then lightweight clips attached to the hard, erect flesh. "Just so you won't forget your tits," the wonderful voice said. Then he continued. "I know you can't talk, but shake your head. Have you ever been taken in the ass?"

Barbara shook her head.

"Oh, a virgin. That's wonderful."

He left her lying across the table, unable to move, her blindfold and gag in place, tits hanging, with the clips attached. Although it was difficult, Barbara used the moment to catch her breath and come down from the earth-moving climax that had ripped through her while he was spanking her. But although she had come once, hard, she knew she was close to coming again.

Then she felt his mouth beside her ear. "I have a dildo in my hand. It's quite slender, but wide enough to fill your ass. Remember the ball in your hand. I will know if it falls."

Barbara felt him stroke her back, then press his hand against her waist. "I'm going to rub some lubricant on now." The sound of his voice, telling her what he was going to do was unbelievably erotic. "Your ass will feel so filled, so fucked. It will feel strange, but wonderful." He rubbed cold, slippery gel over her ass, sliding his finger in just a tiny amount. Then he slowly inserted a slender plastic rod into her previously unviolated rear.

"No," she tried to say around the gag. "Don't." But she didn't drop the ball from her hand. "No."

"Oh, yes," he purred, slowly driving the rod deeper into her body. When it was lodged inside her, he stopped and left it there.

"Oh, God," she mumbled. Then his finger was rubbing her clit and she came again. She couldn't help it. The orgasm ripped through her, making her entire body pulse.

"Such a good slut, but again too easy. But it's my turn now." A moment later, he said, "I just want to assure you that I'm using a condom, so you don't have to worry." His cock rubbed against her cunt, moving the dildo that still filled her ass. His hips and groin pressed against her burning ass, forcing the dildo still deeper into her ass. He plunged his cock into her pussy and she came yet again, her spasms clutching at him. It took only a few thrusts for him to bellow his release.

A while later, CJ released Barbara's wrists and ankles, then removed the blindfold and gag. "You're so receptive. It makes me crazy when you come like that."

"So good for me, too," Barbara said, her breathing still ragged. "It's never been any better."

The silence broken only by the music, they dressed. There was no talk of dinner. She realized they had never even kissed. "Please come to my store again," CJ said as he opened the outer door. "There are several more things I can show you and some I'm sure you could show me."

"Maybe," she said, not being coy, just unsure whether she would repeat the experience. "I don't really know."

"That's fine," he said. Then he placed two tapes in her hand. "For another time," he said. "I just made these recently and they both focus on performing for an audience. If you're ever interested in living out this type of fantasy, let me know." With the tapes she saw that he had handed her his business card. "CJ Winterman A Private Place Unusual Items and Entertainments of All Sorts." It contained the store's address and a phone number. "The number rings here in the store and in my apartment upstairs."

Barbara put the tapes and the card in her pocket. "Thank you," she said, walking toward the door. "For everything."

That night Barbara lay in bed and put the tape into the player. The expected music filled the room and CJ's voice, a voice she could now put a face and a body to, began to spin his latest tale. She let herself drift into the story.

The club was warm and the lights low as the music began for the last show of the evening. Marianne stood at the side of the small stage, ready for her first effort at entertaining the patrons at the Exotica Club, a totally nude review club a few miles from her home. She had practiced her act and thought she could give them a good show. After all, she had watched the performing often enough.

It had all begun a year earlier when the club first opened. Her husband Matt had frequented a similar club in the city before their marriage and had often told her about the wild dancing at the storefront club he had gone to. When the Exotica Club opened, she and Matt had been among its first patrons. A bit raw at first, the club's entertainment had improved. The comedians had become increasingly talented, the singers more professional, and the dancers more skillful in their movements. Now, a year later, shows were sold out weeks in advance and lines formed early in the evening to get the few tables or spots at the bar that might become available.

Thursday night had evolved into Talent Night, when anyone could sign up for a spot on the program and, after much urging from Matt, Marianne had finally listed herself among the performers. As she stood in the wings watching the first woman take her turn, she looked into the audience. Matt sat at a table right in front and Marianne watched him gazing at the slender, small-bosomed woman who strutted around the stage to "The Stripper." She removed her clothing slowly but a bit awkwardly, Marianne thought. The next act was a new, young comedian whose routine was filled with expletives and was quite funny. He was followed by a male dancer and a woman in a slinky dress who sang several erotic songs.

Finally, as a couple performed a tango, almost copulating right on the stage, Marianne realized that she was next, and last, on the program. The couple's performance was followed by cheers from the audience. As she looked past the lights, she could see several couples engaged in sexual play, hands in crotches rubbing, caressing. She took a deep breath and squared her shoulders. You ain't seen nothin' yet, she thought.

The lights dimmed and a stagehand pushed a large washtub onto the center of the stage and set a short stool beside it. Marianne picked up a basket of old clothes and, as the lights brightened and some soft music began, she walked slowly to the center of the stage. She was wearing a small pinafore that barely concealed her breasts and covered the front of a short skirt that came only to midthigh. She was barefoot, her long blond hair was braided, and she wore almost no make up.

As background music played, she put her basket down, sat on the stool, her knees widely spread so the audience could see the crotch of her white panties, and took a pair of men's brief's from the basket. She glanced at Matt and saw him grinning from ear to ear. She knew how much he loved watching her and, although there were probably almost a hundred people watching, Marianne performed for him alone.

She took an old-fashioned wash board and started to scrub the pants, sloshing water everywhere, including all over herself. After a moment, she stood up and tried to sluice the water from the top of her pinafore. All she succeeded in doing was wetting the entire front so her breasts were easily visible. "Oh, my," she said, looking innocently into the audience. "Oh, my." She covered her breasts and giggled, then looked into the laundry basket. She found a white T-shirt she had put there because not only was it too tight but it had been washed so many times it was almost transparent.

She turned her back to the audience, took off the pinafore and put the T-shirt on. "Better?" she asked softly as she turned back to the gathering. Her breasts were clearly visible and her dark nipples were pressing against the front.

"Yeah," some yelled.

"Take it all off," yelled others.

"I couldn't do that," she said sweetly, batting her eyelashes. "I'm not that kind of girl."

There were whistles and groans, cheers and calls of, "Yeah, right."

"I have to get back to work," she said and sat back on the stool, giving the audience another clear view of her crotch. Again she washed an item and again sloshed water everywhere. By now, whatever had been partially hidden by the T-shirt was fully revealed and her skirt was soaked as well. "Oh, my," she said again, holding her skirtfront and squeezing water from the fabric. "Oh, my."

The watchers silenced, waiting for her to remove more clothing. She turned her back to the audience and unbuttoned her skirt, letting it fall around her feet. All the while, soft music played in the background. Finally she turned back to the sea of eyes watching her, now wearing only the soaked T-shirt and a pair of tiny white panties.

"Oh, yeah, lady. Right on."

Again she sat and washed another garment, now soaking herself. "Oh, my," she said as she stood up and watched water run from her body. "Oh, my." She slowly ran her hands over her skin, ostensibly scraping the water from her legs and belly. Then she wrung out the front of her T-shirt, smiled sweetly to the audience and shrugged. With agonizing deliberation, she pulled the soaked shirt off, eventually revealing her white skin, her breasts, and dark, dusky nipples. She appeared to try to cover herself, then shrugged and apparently gave up. Then she slowly she removed the ribbons that held her hair and fluffed it free. It fell almost to the small of her back and she slowly ran her fingers through it, arranging it so it flowed down her chest, and almost, but not quite, covered her breasts.

Now, as she sat on the stool, she was only clad in her panties and her hair. She picked up another piece of wash and sloshed it around in the tub. Now her panties were almost transparent, allowing the audience only a partially screened view of her blond bush. "Oh, my," she said, standing again and looking at her panties. The audience roared and screamed, then silenced as she looked at them. They could see that this was more than just a strip show. She was letting them peek at an embarrassed girl, making them delighted voyeurs.

She slowly slid the panties down her legs, bending so those in the audience couldn't see her crotch. She remained crouched and looked at the faces of the crowd. Then she looked at Matt, who was quite obviously rubbing the bulge in the front of his trousers. She could feel an answering tingle in her pussy. "Oh, my," she said again, then stood up, allowing the people to see her nude body. "Oh, my," she said again as she looked around. The audience was strangely silent, as if not wanting to disturb the sweet young girl and her laundry. Although several couples were making love and one woman knelt with her partner's cock in her mouth, all eyes on the show. Wow, Marianne thought. This is great. I can turn people on. I love this and it makes me so hot.

Giving the audience a good view of her bush, she once

more sat down and dropped the another piece of laundry into the water. Water flew everywhere until she was dripping. She stood up and rubbed her body to remove the water. Then she rubbed her crotch as if to remove the last of the water. "Oh, my," she said, rubbing her flesh. "Oh, my."

As she had planned, water had splashed on several people in the front of the audience, including her husband. As faces peered up at her, she walked to the edge of the stage, then slowly made her way down to the level of the tables, a small towel from the laundry basket dangling from one hand.

Several large men stood around the periphery of the room watching to see that everyone followed the club's rules. A performer could do anything to anyone in the audience. Those watching could do nothing to or with a performer without being invited.

She and Matt had discussed things that might happen and they had agreed that Marianne could do anything the mood compelled her to. Matt would enjoy watching her antics. He knew that she loved to play and that she would end the evening with him. He also knew that she loved him totally. That was enough reassurance for him. She could play to her heart's content.

She made her way to Matt and sat on his lap. "Oh, my," she said, wiping water from the front of his shirt. Then she wiped the front of his slacks, pressing all the places she knew would delight him. Under her breath, she asked, "Still all right with this?"

"Oh, yes, baby. Have fun."

Marianne stood up and moved to another man, who stared at her in rapt attention. "Oh, my," she repeated, wiping the man's face and shirt. As she rubbed his pants, she felt his hard cock. Slowly she crouched between his spread knees and unzipped his fly. With little urging, his cock sprung forth. "Oh, my," she said, clear appreciation in her voice. She curled her fingers around his large erection and rubbed, watching small drops of fluid ooze from the tip. "Mmmm," she purred, and she continued to caress his staff.

"You don't know what you're doing to me," he groaned.

"I certainly do," she said as semen erupted into her hand. "Oh, my." Minutes later, she wiped her hand and moved away. Two women were stretched out on a double lounge chair at one side of the room. As Marianne watched, they rubbed breast to breast, their hands working in each other's pussy. She walked over and tweaked two nipples, then inserted fingers of both hands into two wet pussies.

For several more minutes she wandered around the room, touching, rubbing, caressing, then she walked back up on the stage. She splashed water onto her face and allowed some to dribble onto her breasts. Her right hand rubbed her clit while her left palm slid over her nipples. She sat on the stool, her legs spread, her head back, so everyone could watch her stroke herself. And she did, she watched Matt out of the corner of her eye. He was really excited, she realized, and so was she. It had stopped being just a show. If she rubbed in just the right place . . . She stroked and caressed and then inserted two fingers into her pussy. Men and women were watching while sucking and fucking each other and Matt had his naked cock in his hand. All eyes were on her.

She moaned. "Oh, God," she yelled. "Oh, now."

As she came, a small part of her still watched Matt and the others, all approaching or just past orgasm. "Yes," she groaned as she climaxed, her juice running down her fingers. She sat for long moments as the audience remained almost completely silent. Then it erupted in applause and calls of "Way to go, baby" and "Lemme have some." Several husky men surrounded the stage to prevent anyone from getting too close.

Slowly the lights dimmed and Marianne left the stage, her breath slowly returning to normal, her knees still weak. Matt found her in the dressing room, tossed her onto the floor and drove his cock into her, unable to stop until he erupted inside her slippery pussy.

"Oh, my, baby," he said later, as he lay beside her. "Oh, my."

Barbara lay on her bed as the music filled the room. She had just climaxed for the third time during the story, glad she had learned to masturbate for lengthy pleasure and multiple orgasms, not just to scratch her itch. She thought back on what had excited her the most about the story. Performing? Giving a stranger a hand job? No. What had driven her quickly over the edge was the picture that formed in her mind of the two women.

The following evening, Maggie and Barbara sat in the living room sipping wine. "I know I sound like a commercial, but I have to say it. You've come a long way," Maggie said.

"Yes, I'm a very different person that I was when we first met."

"Are you happy?" Maggie asked. "Or at least happier?"

"I'm having so much fun, but I don't know whether it's a life."

"I don't quite understand."

"Neither do I right now, but I do know that this is an interlude, a time of change. I'm not the person I was, but this isn't the person I will be eventually either." When Maggie looked at her questioningly, Barbara continued. "Sport fucking is wonderful for right now. I'm learning about sexuality and sensuality, but not really about relationships. I don't love any of these men I'm with. I lust for them and it's exciting to be together, but none of them are people with whom I could spend a life. There's not a lot outside of the bedroom."

"I had love. It isn't much either," Maggie said, a bit of bitterness in her voice.

"What did you have exactly? With your husband, I mean. Weren't there any good times? What did you two have in common?"

"Sure there were good times. We played golf together, and tennis. We liked pizza and Kentucky Fried. We were both rather nonpolitical, but once a guy ran for the state assembly we really believed in. We campaigned, went door to door." Maggie gazed into space. "Yeah, there were good times."

"The sex was always bad?"

"It was nothing."

"Even at first? You told me yourself that first times are the best. Wasn't that true with your husband? Do you remember the first time you and he ever made love?"

Maggie smiled. "Yeah, I do. It was in my living room. I still lived at home and my parents were out. Chuck and I sat on the sofa supposedly watching TV. He touched me and kissed me until we were both crazy."

"Were you a virgin?"

"I was, believe it or not. I was almost eighteen and still untouched."

"And Chuck?"

"Oh, he had been with a few girls. But he didn't know very much."

"So it was lousy?"

Maggie considered Barbara's question for a long time. "No, actually it was cosmic. It's been so long that I guess I had forgotten. If I must be honest, it was pretty good for the first few years. Then along came," she deepened her voice like a radio announcer, "*the other woman*. I was really angry."

"And why not? He didn't tell you anything about it."

"Actually, he did. He felt so guilty that he confessed all. They had been friends for several months at work, then he got snowed in at the office. She lived nearby and offered to let him stay on her sofa. One thing led to another and that was that for my marriage."

"Did he want to leave you or did you throw him out?"

"A bit of both. We were both bored and, if I have to be brutally honest, we were both ready to move on."

"So it wasn't as one-sided as you led me to believe."

"Maybe not. I'm not ready to admit all that just yet."

* * *

In the computer room, Lucy snapped off the computer screen. "You goosed her, didn't you. You helped her to remember how it really was in her marriage. That's cheating."

"It is not," Angela snapped. "I just prodded some actual memories. I didn't create anything that wasn't already there. I wouldn't cheat. After all, look at who I represent."

"You cheated."

"And you didn't, goosing Barbara into believing free sex is fun just for itself."

"Well, it is."

"That's neither here nor there. We still have a bet, and Maggie's future will depend on the next few weeks."

A lanky, angular man walked into the computer room. "Hey. What is this place?" he asked.

"Well that's a change from 'Where am I?' " Lucy said, returning to her seat and changing the focus of her computer to the life of the newcomer. "And this place is a little hard to explain."

Chapter 9

It was several days before Barbara had the time and sexual energy to play the second of the two tapes CJ had given her. The story was, if anything, more erotic for her than any of the ones she had heard so far.

It was to be an initiation of sorts, several men to be accepted as full members of the exclusive Hathaway Group, a collection of wealthy men in their twenties and thirties who spent one evening a month at a retreat, devoting themselves to pleasures of the flesh. The annual initiation ceremony was eagerly anticipated by both the initiates and the existing members of the Group. Although several of the women at the meeting were hired, many were volunteers who had enjoyed the hedonistic activities of the Group at previous gatherings. In all, there were almost thirty men and more than a dozen women.

Although all the women would have their share of

sexual fun, Scott Hathaway, the leader of the group, had selected one to take the central part in the initiation ritual. The Carnal Sacrifice she was called. As all the men stood around the raised platform, Scott extended his hand and led the honored woman to the stage.

Alyssa walked forward and took Scott's hand, her diaphanous white gown flowing around her long, shapely legs. Her breasts, barely covered by the sheer fabric, were high and full and her almost white hair flowed down her back like a pale curtain. Her face was carefully made up and she had applied perfume to all the erogenous zones of her body. She climbed the two steps to the platform and turned to face the audience. Men dressed in flowing black robes with crimson cowls stood with arms draped over the shoulders of bare-breasted women. Four men were bareheaded, and would receive their ceremonial cowls when they had completed the ritual. Everyone stared at the dais with lust-clouded eyes.

On the stage was a velvet bench, specially designed for the men's pleasure. And, after bowing to the crowd, Alyssa allowed Scott to remove her gown, leaving her gloriously naked. She stretched out on the bench on her back, her arms at her sides, her legs spread. Scott slowly rotated the table so the audience could see every aspect of the woman spread invitingly before them. Mirrors reflected from above and around the dais, and several video cameras projected images on large screens around the room. The room lights dimmed and spotlights brightened to illuminate the body on the stage. Alyssa was surprised at the heat that raced through her as one spotlight was adjusted to shine directly on her open pussy lips.

As the group watched, Scott tied Alyssa's wrists and ankles to rings in the bench with soft velvet strips. Then he released a section of the table so her head fell back, and adjusted the bottom of the bench so her legs were still more widely spread.

"Let the initiates come forward," Scott said, and the

four would-be group members climbed the two steps. "Disrobe," Scott said and the men removed their robes. They were nude beneath and all had hard erections. "Take your places."

Each man moved to a different spot, one to her head, one to each side, and one between her thighs. Each man unrolled a condom over his cock. "Each of you will have the advantage of the condom, which mutes the sensation. The one who comes first will have to spend another year as an initiate, as Barry has had to do this year." He patted the shoulder of the man who stood at the woman's head. "Actually, Barry, I don't think you minded at all, going through all the training for a second time. As a matter of fact, I think you might have lost on purpose." Everyone, including Barry, laughed.

"Now, you all know the rules. First you will rub oil into Alyssa's skin, all over her body. Then each of you will slowly take Alyssa, one in her mouth, one in each hand, and one in her pussy. Then you will remain unmoving while Alyssa does whatever she can to make you climax." He looked down at the men and women in the crowd below. "Those of you who want to copulate while you watch what is happening may certainly do so. 'Whatever gives pleasure' is our motto. And, gentlemen," he said, speaking to the four initiates, "if you can make our Carnal Sacrifice come, without coming yourself, then you all pass the initiation test automatically. But once you are inside her, you cannot touch her."

Alyssa lay on the bench, listening to the leader give his speech. Last year she had watched from the audience. The man she had been with had pointed out each man and how he was pleasing the woman on the stage and how he was being pleased as well. As they watched, she had become hungrier and hungrier until she begged the man to take her right there on the floor. Now she was on the stage ready for the ultimate pleasure.

"Gentlemen," Scott said, giving each man a bottle of oil, "you may begin."

Alyssa closed her eyes as eight hands rubbed warm oil on her belly, her breasts, her thighs. Hands kneaded, stroked, fondled, and pinched. Several fingers invaded her pussy, opening her, readying her for what was to come.

"Enough," Scott said. "Enter her."

And she was filled. One cock slowly thrust into her mouth, the latex not diminishing her pleasure. One cock was pressed into each waiting hand and she closed her fist around each. And finally one slowly filled her pussy. Then each man stood completely still and Scott said, "The job of the Carnal Sacrifice is to make them come."

Alyssa smiled inwardly and licked the cock in her mouth. Since she couldn't move her hands because of the bonds, she squeezed her fingers, one after another, to pump those two cocks, and she clamped her vaginal muscles to squeeze the cock so deep in her pussy. She was so excited it was hard to concentrate on making the men come, without coming herself. She wanted to lie there and revel in the sensation of being so full. So many men were part of her at one time.

She opened her eyes and saw that Scott was moving around the table with a video camera in his hand, taking close-up shots of the cocks. She discovered that she could see the TV screen on which the images were projected in the mirror on the ceiling above her.

It was so erotic, the vision of her body invaded by so many men. She watched the men in the mirror, their eyes closed, concentrating on not allowing their body the freedom to come. As she sucked, she heard the man whose cock had penetrated her mouth hiss. Yes, she realized, he was close. But so was she. Although the excitement was almost unbearable, she couldn't come yet, not until one of the men came first.

She increased the movements of her hands, her mouth, her pussy muscles. She hummed softly so the buzzing was echoed in the cock in her mouth. Then the man between her legs blew on her clit. That was enough. Her back arched and she came. Almost simultaneously, both the cock in her mouth and the one in her right hand erupted as well. Only moments later, while the spasms still filled her belly, the other two men came, their groans and howls filling the room.

Now that the contest was over, the cock in her cunt pumped hard, hips slamming into her groin. The men at her sides bent over and each took a nipple in his mouth. The man at her head cupped her head in his hands, holding her still and pumped into her throat. Several people in the audience moaned as they came as well. The room smelled of sex and sweat and animal lust.

Alyssa came and came and came, unwilling to allow the pulses that throbbed through her body to end. Over and over cocks invaded her, men moving around the table taking additional pleasure from her mouth, her hands, and her cunt. It was an orgy of sensation she prayed would never end.

When the men were spent, they withdrew and Scott said, "Since it was impossible to tell who came first, I will declare all the men members of the Group. And I will take my turn with our carnal sacrifice." He pulled off his robe and, unrolling a condom over his large cock, he moved between Alyssa's legs. She watched as he adjusted the leg sections of the table until her legs were in the air, her bottom exposed.

"You know what happens now."

"Yes, my lord," she said, her body throbbing with both echos of her climax and her need for more.

"Only one part of you remained uninvaded. That part is mine. Do you agree?"

"Yes, my lord."

He covered his cock with lubricant and touched his finger tip to her anus. "Are you a virgin there?" he asked, rubbing lubricant on her hole.

"Yes, my lord."

"Yet you are willing?"

"Oh, yes, my lord."

Someone else held the camera so Alyssa could see the tip of Scott's finger slowly enter her tight hole. The feeling of fullness was both unpleasant and wildly erotic. Part of her wanted to expel the invading finger, part wanted to drive it deeper. Slowly, as she watched the monitor in the mirror, the finger went deeper and deeper, stretching and oiling her for the eventual penetration. Scott withdrew the finger, then used his thick thumb to open her still further.

She had been anxious to try this type of sexual fun, yet had been a bit unsure as well. She was no longer doubtful. It was magnificent. "My lord, I am ready for you," she cried.

As he held the tip of his cock against her puckered opening, he rubbed her clit with his other hand. Then in a single, slow stroke, he filled her. She came with the first stroke, screaming her pleasure for all to hear. Scott pulled back, then thrust into her again. Over and over he filled and emptied her ass until he, too, succumbed to the pleasure of the fucking.

As he left her body, someone announced that anyone who wanted any part of the carnal sacrifice's body could take it. Many did, in her mouth, in her hands, her pussy, her ass. She lost track of the number of times she came or the number of men she pleasured.

Later, she was released from the bench and given a cooling drink. Then two women lovingly massaged her body to relax and refresh her. Finally, when she was ready, she rose and walked through the room to the applause and cheers of all assembled. She had given and taken the ultimate pleasure, and that, of course, was what the group was all about. "Alyssa," Scott said as he handed her a glass of champagne, "you were wonderful. I don't know when we've had a better initiation ritual."

"Thank you," Alyssa said.

"Would you consider being the Carnal Sacrifice again next year?"

Alyssa smiled. "It would be my ultimate pleasure."

Barbara thought about the most recent tapes for the next few days, imagining herself on stage like Marianne, performing for a bunch of strangers. Could she do that? It was an intriguing possibility. And, of course, she did want to see CJ again. And this was, after all, no-holds-barred sex. A week after she left the store, she called CJ.

"Well, hello, hot woman," CJ said. "I have been hoping all week that I'd hear from you."

"I just thought I'd call and thank you for the tape. I really liked that club scene."

"Do you think you could dance like that?"

"I don't know. It's an intriguing thought, but I think I'd chicken out at the last minute."

"You're an honest woman, Babs."

Barbara reacted automatically to hearing the name that Walt and Carl had called her all those years ago. The humiliation of the situation, the flash of Walt's camera. She could almost smell Carl's All Spice aftershave. But this was CJ's voice, a voice that had come to mean hot, erotic sex, and the sound of it made her wet. Should that experience have felt all that terrible or was it just that she didn't have a life then? She didn't have any idea what good sex was all about. But then neither did Carl or Walt. All these thoughts flashed through her mind in an instant. "I like to think so," she said into the phone.

"I have a group of friends who get together once a month, sort of like the Hathaway Group in the story. Women are invited to participate in the various activities. There's a party next weekend and I wondered whether you'd like to come."

Barbara hesitated. What CJ was describing sounded like an orgy. Was this what her sexuality was leading her to? Was this the culmination of her months of learning about herself? Voices filled her head. Do it, it will be fun. It's a sin. Enjoy. You'll be punished.

"If I can chicken out at any time, I think I'd like to."

"I promise you that any time you say so, I will take you home. Instantly. No questions asked, no recriminations."

"It sounds very interesting."

As arranged, Barbara arrived at CJ's shop at five the following Saturday afternoon, prepared for anything. CJ had promised her that nothing would happen without her permission, but, if she were willing, all kinds of new experiences awaited her. As she walked into A Private Place, his assistant was just leaving and CJ was finishing with his last customer. She stood, gazing at the bondage equipment while the customer debated whether to buy a green or a red dildo.

"Barbara, come over here and help us," CJ said loudly. When she approached the counter, he asked, "Which do you like better?"

Barbara looked at the two dildos on the counter, then at the display beneath the glass. "Actually, just to confuse you, I like that black one. It looks dangerous and erotic, and makes me think of black lace underwear and high heels."

The man who stood beside her looked at her, then said, "I'll take the one the lady likes. If my girlfriend glows like this lovely woman does at the thought of that black dildo, I'll be a lucky man."

Barbara grinned as CJ wrapped the dildo in red lace gift paper. With a thank-you, the man put the package into his pocket and left. As the customer closed the shop door behind him, CJ locked it. He walked to Barbara, placed his hand on the back of her neck and kissed her softly. "Welcome. This is going to be one wonderful night." He placed her hand against the crotch of his black jeans, cupping his hard cock. "I'm looking forward to it."

His voice turned her on like few things in the world. Without hesitation, Barbara placed CJ's hand against the crotch of her jeans. "Feel the heat? I'm looking forward to tonight, too."

CJ laughed. "You're quite a brazen bitch," he said. "Come into the back." He led her into a room she hadn't been in the last time, invited her to sit down and poured her a glass of white wine. Then he deftly opened a dozen oysters for each of them, and served them with lemon and a cocktail sauce spiced with lots of horseradish. "They say wonderful things about oysters, but I don't believe that nonsense. I just like them. We'll be eating quite a bit later, but I thought this would hold us for now."

Barbara picked up a shell and, with loud slurping noises, slid an oyster into her mouth. "I love them, too," Barbara said. She licked her lips with exaggerated movements of her slender tongue.

"The way you eat those makes me want to fuck you right here, right now. But there's a long evening ahead of us and anticipation makes it that much better."

They chatted amiably, ate and drank and, by the time they had finished, Barbara was no longer turned on. She merely felt warm and comfortable.

"As I told you, I would like to dress you up for the evening," CJ said finally. "But first, I have a question for you. Have you ever thought about shaving your pussy?"

Barbara thought for a moment. "I haven't, but I wouldn't mind, if you'd like me to."

"I'd like to shave you myself. It's very sexy for a man to look at a shaved pussy. It's so brazen somehow, so inviting and obvious. It would be perfect for this evening. If you don't ever want to do it again, you can let it grow. I will warn you, it might be a bit itchy as it grows out."

"I'll risk it. It sounds kinky."

CJ beamed. "Great. Take your jeans and panties off and sit here," he said, indicating a leather director's chair.

Slightly embarrassed at casually undressing before a man that, despite their previous activities, she hardly knew, Barbara removed her jeans, panties, shoes, and socks. She sat in the chair and CJ draped her legs over the arms so her pussy was exposed and vulnerable. Then CJ brought a pair of scissors, pan of warm water, soap, a razor, and a handful of towels.

While Barbara watched, he cut her pubic hair very short,

then rubbed the short stubble and 'accidentally' brushed her now-exposed clit. From not turned-on to ravenous in only a moment, she thought. Barbara swallowed hard but tried to look as casual as CJ. Then he made lots of soapy lather and rubbed it over her pubis. Slowly and with infinite care, he shaved off all the hair, his probing fingers and the gentle rub of the razor making Barbara tremble with need.

He washed the area with a soft cloth, then smoothed on some antiseptic lotion. Then he rose and returned with a large mirror that stood on a wooden stand. "Look at your wonderful pussy," he said, adjusting the mirror so Barbara could see her hairless mound. CJ was right. It was obvious and erotic, like an opening begging to be filled. CJ stroked one finger along her naked slit. "It makes you hot looking at yourself, doesn't it?"

"Yes," she breathed, her voice barely audible.

"Then you need to be filled." CJ disappeared, then returned with a dildo like the one she had recommended to the customer. "Remember how Alyssa could watch the men as they fucked her? Now, watch in the mirror while I fuck you with this." He held the dildo against her opening, then slowly, while Barbara watched, fascinated, slid it into her body.

Barbara was shaking from the intensity of the twin sensations, watching herself being fucked with the dildo and the feel of the large member penetrating her. "May this be the first of many tonight," CJ said, kneeling between her legs and tonguing her clit until she came, her juices trickling over her now-exposed skin. "You are the most responsive woman," CJ said, rubbing her clit and thrusting the dildo in and out as tremors shook her. "And you are so beautiful when you come."

Unable to speak, Barbara just moaned.

A while later, CJ stood up and said, "If you're calmer now, we can get you dressed for the party." He looked at his watch. "It starts in an hour."

Barbara took a deep breath and took her legs from the

arms of the chair. Smiling, she said, "What would you like me to wear?"

CJ reached for a box on a table and handed it to her. "The idea of presenting you to my friends wearing this makes me hot, but it will only work if it turns you on as well." Barbara opened the box. Inside was a black latex body suit with long legs, long sleeves, and openings where her breasts and pussy would be. "Picture yourself in that," CJ purred. "You would look amazing. Are you game?"

Barbara gazed at the garment. Her large breasts and now-hairless crotch would be exposed, but the rest of her body would be tightly encased in the stretchy fabric. It sounded delicious. She nodded and CJ smiled. "You delight me," he crooned, handing her the suit. "I need to change, too."

While CJ was in another room changing for the party, Barbara slowly wiggled the tight suit on over her skin. Zippers tightened the sleeves and legs until, when it was in place, it fit like her skin, with only her breasts and pussy exposed. She looked at herself in the mirror and was amazed at the wanton woman who looked back at her. "Oh, Lord," she said to her reflection. "Barbara, what have you done to yourself?"

"Made yourself into the most desirable woman I've ever seen," CJ said from behind her. She turned and saw that he was dressed in a similar black latex outfit, only his had short sleeves, thigh-length pants, and a full crotch. His swollen shaft beneath was hard to miss. "The feel of the latex hugging my cock keeps me erect all night." When he placed her hand between his legs, she felt something around the base of his cock. To her puzzled expression, he said, "I wear a cock ring to keep me from coming before I'm ready."

"Oh," Barbara said.

"Now, sit back here," CJ said, motioning her to the leather chair. "I want to do your finger-and toenails."

With great care, CJ polished her now-long fingernails and her toenails with polish that was almost black. Then he asked her to close her eyes while he applied additional makeup and arranged her hair over her shoulders. She could feel him stroke the silver streak.

When he was done, he angled the mirror so she could look at herself. She opened her eyes and stared. He had used deep green shadow, heavy mascara, and deep, almost-black lipstick. She looked like an animal on the prowl. Where's the woman who Maggie met that first night? she wondered. Gone for now, she answered herself.

"Do you approve?"

"Very much," she said.

He handed her a pair of calf-high, black patent-leather boots, with spike heels. "I think these should be about your size," he said, and she slipped them on and stood up.

"Oh, yes," he said, slowly lowering himself until he was crouched at her feet. "Mistress."

Mistress. He was inviting her into his fantasy, she realized. He wanted her to control him. Did she know how? Her confusion must have shown on her face. "You'll learn how, if you're willing," he said. "There will be many there willing and able to teach you. And I will serve you." He got a cloak from the closet and draped it around Barbara's shoulders, carefully arranging her hair over the collar. "If you will allow me to lead," he said.

"Yes," Barbara said, standing up straight, now taller than he was in her high heels. "Do that."

In silence, they took a taxi across town to an old loft building in Soho. Although the taxi driver gave them a few odd looks, the trip was uneventful. CJ paid the driver and opened the door for her. They entered an old elevator and ascended two floors. When the doors opened, Barbara looked around, her eyes widening.

The room took up more than half of the loft and was furnished with tables and chairs, single and double lounges, and soft sofas. There were benches with straps and rings attached, stocks, and items that Barbara could only imagine uses for.

There were about two dozen couples, a few dancing, several sitting around tables, others in various stages of copulation. Music played in the background, similar to the music on CJ's tapes, with deep, pulsing rhythms that echoed in Barbara's soul.

As CJ removed Barbara's cloak, two men got up and walked over to them. "Who is this goddess?" one asked.

"My mistress," CJ said.

"And she allows you to speak on your own?"

"Occasionally," CJ said. "When I have pleased her sufficiently. Her name is Barbara."

"Good evening," she said, slowly getting acclimated to her surroundings and trying to figure out exactly how to behave.

"Good evening, Mistress Barbara," the two men said.

"CJ. It's good to see you," a woman called, motioning them over. The men led CJ and Barbara to a small table. "My name's Pam," the woman said as Barbara sat down. "And this is Tisha," she said, indicating the other woman at the table. "You're new to our little group."

"Yes, I am," Barbara said.

"My mistress is new to everything about this," CJ said. "But she wants to learn."

"Wonderful," Tisha said. A tiny blonde, she wore a genuine-looking policeman's uniform, with a pair of handcuffs dangling from a clip on her wide leather belt. "Let me show you what wonderful things my pet can do." She snapped her fingers and spread her legs. Barbara saw then that, like her outfit, the crotch of Pam's navy-blue pants was missing. "I like my men to be able to service me whenever I like." One of the men who had greeted her now knelt between Tisha's legs and began to lick her pussy. Tisha picked up her glass and sipped, trying unsuccessfully to look unaffected. "He's gotten too good at this," she said, panting. "Shit," she yelled, and Barbara watched as waves of orgasm overtook her.

Pam laughed. "He seems to be able to bring her off with almost no effort. I don't know whether she's that hot all the time, or he's that good." It was all Barbara could do not to stare at the woman speaking. She wore a kelly-green lace teddy that barely covered any of her athletic, ebony body, with thigh-high, green lace stockings and green satin heels.

She also wore dark-green, elbow-length fingerless gloves. Even sitting down, Barbara could tell that she had to be over six feet tall. And gorgeous.

"She certainly seems to enjoy it," Barbara said.

"And why not," Pam said. "It's the best. I understand you're new to this type of fun and games."

"Yes," Barbara said, not sure what she was supposed to do.

"Watch what goes on around you and do what you think will give you and CJ pleasure."

"God, that was good," Tisha said, rejoining the conversation. "Get me something to eat," she said to the man who was now sitting on the floor at her feet.

"Yes, Mistress," he said, rising and moving to the buffet table. Pam looked at the man beside her and he quickly got up and followed.

Barbara looked at CJ. "I'm hungry, too," she said in what she hoped was a sufficiently authoritative tone. "Get me something."

CJ tried not to smile. "Oh, yes, Mistress," he said, and left the table.

"CJ's never brought a mistress here before," Pam said. "Usually he's the dominant one."

"How can someone be dominant one time and like that another?" Barbara asked.

"Many people enjoy both sides of dominant/submissive behavior. Others only enjoy being in charge, or surrendering." She smiled, encouraging Barbara to trust her. "What do you usually enjoy?"

"I don't really know. I've been tied up and I loved that. I've also listened to a lot of CJ's tapes and all the stories really turn me on. But I've never actually been in anything like this before, on either side."

"How wonderful to explore," Pam said. "To try it all out for the first time. I envy you. First times are so hot."

"I like to run the show," Tisha said. "I can't get into letting someone else tell me what to do."

"And I love it when someone tells me what to do," Pam

said. "It's so liberating. I don't have to think about anything. Just do as I'm told."

Tisha gazed at Pam, her eyes wandering over the other woman's lush body. "Maybe I'll take you up on that offer before the evening is done," she said. She looked at Barbara, and the heat in her gaze made Barbara look down. "You, too, love."

The three men returned with plates of food and, as Barbara watched, Tisha held out a bit of meat and the man at her feet ate it from her hand. "Oh, this is Pet. That's what I call him since that's what he is."

"Hello," Barbara said.

Pet inclined his head, but said nothing.

"And this is Mack," Pam said, patting the man at her side on the head. "He's such a good boy."

"Thank you, ma'am," the man whispered, obviously pleased at the compliment.

Barbara took a shrimp and offered it to CJ. He stared at her, the heat in his gaze almost stinging her naked nipples. Then he took the shrimp from her fingers with his teeth.

Together, the three couples ate and talked. Actually, the women talked, the men remained silent, eating only when a morsel of food was handed to them.

Despite the thoroughly bizarre situation, Barbara was surprised at how much she liked the two women. They were honest, sexually open, and easy to talk and listen to.

When they finished, a man in a tuxedo walked to the center of the dance floor and announced the entertainment for the evening. Several men danced Chippendale-style, and a woman did amazing things with two thick candles. There was a Don't Come contest during which three men were teased until finally one erupted onto the floor. After he cleaned up the mess, he was escorted into another room by his mistress for what Barbara was told would be suitable punishment for his lack of self-control.

Then a naked man was led to the stage and his arms and neck were locked in a set of wooden stocks. Women from the audience used hands, paddles, and a hairbrush to spank his ass until it was bright red.

When the lights rose again, several couples moved toward a door at the far end of the room. "They are going to have ceremonial whippings and other heavy pain games. Some people like that sort of thing, but since many do not, whippings and things like that are held at in another, soundproof room. Not my thing," Pam said.

Barbara didn't think she would enjoy watching or participating in pain for pleasure games. "Me neither," she said, glad she wouldn't lose her new-found companions.

"Barbara," Tisha said, "I can see that CJ is enjoying being the bottom, the submissive, but you don't seem comfortable with the role of top."

Barbara sighed. "I guess I'm not. I'm just not used to giving orders." She turned to CJ. "I'm really sorry. I know that having me control you would turn you on, but, well . . ."

"Don't apologize," CJ said. "Something that doesn't turn you on, no matter how much the thought of it might excite me, won't make me happy."

"Would you like to be the one controlled?" Tisha asked.

Barbara felt heat rise and thought she might actually be blushing. "I don't know."

"Yes, you do," Tisha said. Then she quickly changed the subject. While they sipped club sodas, the women made small talk. Barbara felt the heat of Tisha's stare frequently over the next half hour. At one point Tisha spent several minutes staring at her nipples. Barbara felt her nipples tighten and her pussy get wet from the heat of Tisha's gaze. "Excuse me," she said, disappearing to the ladies' room.

When she returned, she saw CJ whispering in Tisha's ear. "Barbara, CJ tells me that he would love to watch you make love to Pam. Under my orders, of course. I think you want that." Tisha stared at Barbara. "Sit down!" she snapped. Barbara sank into a chair.

"Spread your legs!" Seemingly without any control from her brain, her knees parted. "Wider." She spread her knees farther.

"Good," Tisha said, smiling. "And, if I'm so inclined, I might even let the men join you later. If they are very good, that is."

Oh God, what had she gotten herself into? Barbara wondered. But she flashed back to the scene in on of CJ's tapes. The dancer who had been able to make two women so hot that they made love in public. She shivered.

Tisha leaned toward Barbara. "The safe word is Cease. Do you understand?"

Barbara remembered the ball she had held when she and CJ had played the last time. She nodded.

Tisha took a police whistle from around her neck and blew into it. "I think we need an audience." Several other couples brought chairs and surrounded the table. "Now, Pam, kiss her."

Obediently Pam turned and cupped Barbara's face in her hands. Softly she brushed her lips across Barbara's, her tongue teasing and probing. Barbara sighed, closed her eyes and relaxed. This was very strange, but arousing. She allowed herself to be pulled into the situation. She touched Pam's cheeks with her fingertips, just brushing the soft skin. She moved her mouth and pressed it more firmly against the other woman's. The smell of Pam's musky perfume filled her nostrils.

Pam leaned forward and rubbed her lace-covered breasts against Barbara's naked nipples. Tit against tit, the two women slowly stood up, their bodies intertwined.

"Massage each other's tits," Tisha said. "Tweak those titties."

As Barbara's hands rose to touch Pam's breasts, she felt Pam's large hands on her bare flesh. "Barbara, pull out Pam's tits." Barbara pulled the cups of Pam's teddy aside and filled her hands with warm flesh. She had never felt anything like this before. Soft hands on soft breasts. Hers. Pam's. White fingers on black skin. Black fingers on white skin. Her knees almost buckled from the heat of it all.

She heard movement around her and opened her eyes to find a lounge chair now beside her. "Barbara, sit there,"

Tisha said, and Barbara gladly collapsed into the chair.

With a few snaps of her fingers, Tisha moved Pet to one side of Barbara and Mack to the other. "Suck," she said, and suddenly two mouths suckled at Barbara's breasts.

"Do her, Pam," Tisha said, and Pam laid, her chest on the bottom of the lounge chair, her mouth on Barbara's clit. "Look, Barbara. See what's happening." When Barbara's eyes remained closed, Tisha said, "I said, open your eyes!"

Barbara opened her eyes.

"That's better. But don't come," Tisha said. "Don't you dare!"

Barbara looked down. She was still tightly encased in the latex suit, the black rubber shining under the lights. Sweat pooled beneath her arms and on her belly, but the feeling was sensual, not uncomfortable. Two men suckled at her breasts, their fingers kneading her flesh. She could see Pam's face, turned up to her, her tongue dancing over Barbara's naked pussy.

Tisha didn't want her to come. But how could she keep the orgasm from building in her belly? She gritted her teeth and tried to fight the myriad of sensations trying to control her body.

"Stop!" Tisha's order could not be disobeyed.

Barbara took a deep breath as the mouths left her. Tisha looked at her. "Get up." When she did, Tisha ordered, "Pam, you sit there." Once Pam was stretched out in the lounge chair, her thighs spread wide, one leg on either side of the chair, Tisha leaned over and removed the crotch of Pam's teddy. "So wet," she said, then snapped her fingers, and the men resumed their places, now sucking Pam's nipples.

"Now, Barbara, lick her the way she licked you. Do it while we all watch."

Could she lick a woman's pussy? Ordinarily, Barbara thought in a small, conscious place in her mind, no. But she was so hot that anything was possible. She knelt at the foot of the lounge chair, lay on the bottom section and pressed her aching breasts against the rough fabric. She rubbed like a cat, trying the relieve the itching hunger in her swollen nipples. As her face neared Pam's steamy pussy, the odor of the woman's excitement surrounded her. She looked at Pam's shaved mound and saw the swollen outer lips, parted to reveal the hard clit between. She pointed her tongue and licked, marveling at the shudder that ran through Pam's body. She tasted Pam's juices. So this is what I taste like, she thought, filling her mouth with the salty tang.

Feeling increasingly brave, she explored every fold, each hollow. Using the things she understood about her own body, she quested the spots that would give Pam the most pleasure. "Finger-fuck her, Barbara. Make her come." She inserted one finger into Pam's sopping pussy, smiling at the moans and animal cries that Pam couldn't control. A second finger joined the first and, knowing what she herself enjoyed, Barbara spread the two fingers, stretching Pam's channel.

Suddenly something was behind her and there was a hand in the small of her back pressing her against the chair. She felt something slippery being spread on her ass and cunt.

"Is she hot?" Tisha asked.

Someone at her back rubbed her opening. "Soaked. Hot enough to fire."

"Do it."

As Barbara fingered Pam's pussy, she felt something rammed into her ass. A dildo? A cock? She couldn't tell. Then there was a mouth on her cunt. Whose mouth, whose cock? She had no idea. Nor did she care.

"Don't you dare come until Pam does." Tisha said, swatting her ass hard, once. "And Pam, don't you come until Barbara does."

Barbara needed to come. She was trying to concentrate on making Pam climax and not on her own needs screaming inside her. Not yet, she told herself as her mouth worked on Pam's clit and her fingers fucked her cunt. Just a little more. She used the index finger of her other hand to rim Pam's asshole. As she slowly circled, she could feel the tiny spasms that heralded the woman's climax. But she felt her own orgasm building as well.

"Ah!" Pam screamed as she came, and Barbara's orgasm erupted seconds later. Wave upon wave of electric pleasure washed over her. She put her head on Pam's belly and allowed her fingers to softly caress Pam's calming body. Now her cunt and ass were empty, but she felt someone press against her from behind.

She turned and watched CJ rub his latex-covered cock between her spread ass cheeks, his head thrown back, his hips bucking. Tisha reached down the front of his tight bicycle pants and quickly removed the cock ring CJ had put on earlier. It took only a moment until, rubbing against Barbara's ass, he screamed loudly and he came, his cock still inside the latex shorts.

Barbara rested, then, through a haze, she felt herself guided to her feet and her cloak replaced around her shoulders. She vaguely realized that she was being told how much everyone enjoyed her presence and she numbly said good night to the people she had met.

CJ directed the taxi to her car, and then, while Barbara dozed, he drove her home to Bronxville, Tisha and Pet following in their car. He kissed her firmly at her door. "They are waiting for me. I'll call you."

"Mmmm," Barbara said, opening her door. "It was amazing. I've never experienced anything like this."

"I'm glad. It was great for me, too. I never know where these parties will lead, but it's always wonderful. Tonight was particularly terrific because I know how much you enjoyed it, too."

"You weren't disappointed because I couldn't . . . you know."

"Whatever you enjoy is great, and the things you find you don't, we won't do. It's really quite simple."

"Thank you," Barbara said, kissing him again.

"Good night." CJ climbed into the waiting car and Barbara closed the door behind her and went to bed.

Chapter 10

"I think I reached the ultimate of something last evening," Barbara said the following morning as she and Maggie sat over coffee. "It's the best time I've had in maybe forever, but after I got home I thought a lot about it, and about me."

"Thinking's always dangerous," Maggie said dryly, "but tell me about it."

"I think that I understand myself a lot better than I did a few months ago. Last evening was wonderful, but that was outside of the real world. It's not life."

"And what is life."

"For me, life is having mad, wild sex with one person, someone I know and like. Someone who pleases me inside and outside of the bedroom. CJ is a wonderfully creative lover, but that's all. He's sort of out of context." Barbara slumped. "This is really hard to explain."

"I think I understand."

"But your life with Chuck wasn't life either. What I need

is equal parts friend and lover. What's depressing me is that I'm not sure something like that really exists."

"I'm not sure either," Maggie said, lacing her fingers. "But all you can do is try."

"Which do you think comes first, the friendship or the sex?"

"I think for there to be really good sex, there has to be a level of trust and friendship, a desire to please the other person. It can develop over a period of months or just in a day. Take you and Jay. From what you told me, you started the relationship for sport fucking, but it was a lot more than that from the start."

Barbara looked puzzled. "But I wasn't in love with him nor he with me. And we weren't and aren't exclusive by any means."

"All that is true, but there was a lot of genuine caring and concern, each for the other. No one was taking anything at the expense of the other. Right?"

Barbara cocked her head to one side. "Right."

"That's not love, but it's the kind of caring necessary for really good sex."

"I never thought about it that way."

"Actually, neither did I until now," Maggie admitted. "But as I think back to my good and bad bed partners, it's true."

"I guess Jay and I did have a lot of mutual respect and caring. Just not enough to build a life on. So then, what is love?"

"You think I know? I haven't a clue. To be completely honest, I think I have been in love a few times. Not just in lust, but really in love. Caring about someone else's happiness more than my own. Maybe it was that way when Chuck and I were first married." Then she thought about Paul and their last phone conversation the night of her heart attack. "And there was a guy who wanted to run away with me. He was a banker type and twenty years my junior. It never would have worked, but I did love him, in my own way."

"I've never felt that, and I want it. I guess I'll just have to keep looking."

"What about Steve."

Barbara smiled. "Maybe it's time I found out what Steve is really like. I've been in love with him from a distance, whatever that means, for a long time. But, what I understand now is that from a distance is easy. It's the up-close-and-personal stuff that's hard."

"And it's more difficult with someone who you're going to see every day, whether it works out or not."

"I know. I keep wondering whether it's worth it. It doesn't seem so important or intense now."

"Do you want to find out?" Maggie asked.

"I think I do."

Later that morning, Maggie left the kitchen and, as she had dozens of times before, found herself in the revolving door. Instead of pushing to see when she would emerge, she stopped in the dark and said aloud, "Lucy, Angela, I think we need to talk."

"Push the door," a voice said and, when she did, she found herself in the computer room. "Yes?" Angela said.

"I was wondering what there is left for me to do. Barbara has discovered herself and I think she's a happier, more complete woman. She's going to ask Steve to dinner and maybe they will end up together, just like you wanted. So what more is there?"

Lucy looked at her. "Do you think Steve is right for her?"

"How should I know?" Maggie snapped. "I'm trying to do what you asked me to do when you gave me this assignment."

"I still think Steve is perfect for Barbara," Angela said.

"Not a chance," Lucy said. "And Maggie, there are still one or two things left that Barbara will need your help with."

"If you say so," Maggie said, turning toward the door. "I just want to do the best job I can, you know."

"Of course. Just a few last loose ends. We'll send for you when we know the outcome."

"Hers or mine?" Maggie said.

"Both," the two women said in unison.

Barbara arrived at Gordon-Watson at her usual time the following Monday morning. She had taken particular care with her wardrobe, selecting a sheer white blouse and short tan linen skirt. She topped the blouse with a brown linen vest so that the sheerness of the blouse and the lacy bra she wore beneath were only evident when she unbuttoned or removed the vest. She wore sheer stockings and brown suede pumps. She took care that her makeup was sexy yet understated, then applied a new, musky perfume behind her ears and in her cleavage.

She settled at her desk and by nine-thirty was deep into a will she was assembling from a set of stock paragraphs. "Good morning, Barbara," Steve said as he approached her desk.

She looked up and held his gaze just a bit longer than usual. "Good morning, Mr. Gordon."

"What's on my calendar for today?" he said, breezing past her desk.

Barbara picked up her laptop, then followed him into his office. She settled into a soft leather chair, crossed her legs and slipped one shoe off then lifted it with her toe. Then she clicked a few keys on her computer. "You've got the Harris deposition at ten-thirty, lunch with Jack Forrester at twelve-thirty, and, if the deposition doesn't go too late, you can go over Mr. Carruthers's will and the McManister closing documents for tomorrow. And, whenever you have time, I have a list of phone calls you need to make." As she looked up, she saw Steve gazing at her swinging foot. She smothered a smile as she shifted in her chair, moving so her skirt rode up to midthigh. "Do you have anything for me?" she asked with mock innocence. When he didn't answer immediately, his eyes following her foot and the dangling shoe, she said, "Mr. Gordon?"

"Yes?"

"Did you hear me?" Barbara asked.

Obviously snapping back to reality, Steve said, "Of course." He picked up a pencil from his desk and tapped it on the arm of his chair. "Barbara, I've been meaning to talk to you. You've seemed different recently."

"Different?" She slowly unbuttoned her vest and allowed the sides to part.

"More . . ." He looked her over from head to toe, his gaze lingering on her breasts. "More, I don't know. Just more."

She lowered her head so she looked up at him through her lashes. "I hope I can take that as a compliment."

"You can." He looked her over again. "Listen, maybe we can have dinner sometime."

"Are you asking me out on a date?"

Steve hesitated, then said, "I guess I am."

"Well, I'd love to have dinner with you, Mr. Gordon." Barbara giggled. "I guess I should call you Steve now."

"I guess you should." He stood up and walked around and positioned himself behind Barbara's chair. She could feel him touch her hair. "You know," he said, "you're quite something. I'm surprised at myself for not really noticing before now."

Delighted that they were finally going to get to spend some time together, Barbara said, "Shall we say Saturday?"

She could feel Steve playing with the silver streak in her hair. "Saturday sounds great. How about Indian?"

Afraid she would spoil the mood but unwilling to eat very hot food, Barbara said, "I'm not a big fan of curry. How about sushi?"

"Raw fish?" He made a face. "I know a great steak place."

Barbara grinned. "That sounds wonderful." She was glad they had found common ground.

"And Saturday I have tickets for the City Center Ballet. I was going to ask my mother to join me, but I'd much rather have you by my side."

Barbara remembered several trips to the ballet with her mother years before. She had found it stultifying. "The ballet might be nice, and if you already have the tickets . . ." She wondered whether the gorgeous Lisa enjoyed the ballet.

"I try to get there every week or so during the season, but I can tell from your voice it isn't your idea of an enjoyable evening. I'll just give the tickets to my mother and we can go wherever you like." He sat down on the chair beside her and placed a hand on her knee. "Where would you like to go?" He gazed deeply into her eyes. "I mean, if you could go anywhere."

Barbara thought. She had read the entertainment section of *The New York Times* just yesterday. "There's a Woody Allen film festival."

"Oh," Steve said, taking a deep breath. "That would be fine."

Barbara could tell he viewed Woody Allen the way she viewed the ballet. "Maybe just a small, intimate place where we could talk," she said quickly. "We could take some time and get to know each other. And maybe do some slow dancing."

Steve's face brightened. "That sounds wonderful. But I have to warn you, I don't dance."

Barbara stared at Steve. She had been in love with him for so long. But in love with what? He was handsome, well dressed, and very intelligent. But what did they really have in common? "What do you enjoy doing? Tennis? Golf?"

"Actually, I love swimming and I lift weights. And, of course, I really like sports. But you already know that."

She had gotten enough last-minute tickets for sporting events over the years for him that she should. But she had never made the connection. "That's right. Of course. You particularly like boxing."

"I love a good heavyweight match," Steve said, taking her hand. "I guess you probably don't like that sort of thing, but you could learn. It's an acquired taste, like anchovies."

"I hate anchovies, and I think the idea of watching two men beat each other's brains out for money is barbaric." She pulled her hand back.

"We don't have to like the same things, do we?" He

cupped her chin and pulled her face toward him. He kissed her softly on the lips. "I'm sure there are some things we will enjoy doing together very much."

She closed her eyes and leaned into the kiss. His lips were warm and moist and his tongue slipped between her teeth to caress her. Suddenly she felt his hand on her breast, squeezing and kneading her tender flesh like bread dough. His other hand began to unbutton her blouse. "No," she said, leaning back. "I don't think this will work."

"But, baby . . ." Steve said, reaching behind her neck to cradle her head. He kissed her harder, forcing her head back.

She placed her palms against his chest and pushed him back. "Steve, Mr. Gordon, I don't think this will work at all. I'm really sorry. It was a mistake." She stood up, put the laptop onto Steve's desk and rebuttoned both her blouse and vest. "This was really a big mistake."

"Oh, baby, don't say that. I'm sorry. This shouldn't have started in the office. Not here where there's no privacy. I understand. Let's talk about it Saturday."

"No, Mr. Gordon, let's not. Let's not see each other Saturday. This isn't going to work. I'm really sorry."

"But . . ."

"Look. We've worked well together for all these years. This is just going to spoil it. Let's just keep this as a business relationship. I like working here and I do the work well. Let's just leave it at that."

Steve stood up and heaved a deep sigh. "I think you're underestimating how good we could be."

She floundered for the right words to tell him to go away without losing her job. "Maybe I am, Mr. Gordon, but I'd rather keep a good relationship here in the office than spoil it with a extracurricular fling, no matter how good it might be." Or how awful.

"I'm disappointed."

"So am I, but I think it's for the best." She retrieved her laptop. "Did you have anything more for me or should I begin placing those phone calls? We can probably get a few things done before the deposition."

Steve looked Barbara over from head to toe. "Well, maybe you're right." Slowly Barbara left the office and walked toward her desk. Then she turned, looked at the sign beside the door. Steven Gordon. She shrugged, then grinned.

"Babs," a voice cried from the end of the soup-and-canned-vegetable aisle in the supermarket a few weeks later. Barbara had stopped in after work to pick up something for dinner. "Babs," the voice said again. "Imagine running into you here."

She looked around for the source of the slightly louder than necessary voice. Striding toward her was a person she hadn't been able to forget. "Hello, Walt," she said softly.

"Babs, you look terrific," Walt said, leaning forward and grasping Barbara by the shoulders. He looked her over from left and right, then from head to toe. "I haven't seen you in a long time. You've changed." He reached over and fingered the streak of white hair above her ear. "And this is very sexy."

Barbara gritted her teeth and tried not to glower at the man whose face she had last seen in the glare of a camera's flash bulb. I certainly have changed, she said, trying not to let all the humiliation rush back. "I haven't seen *you* in a long time."

"What have you been doing with yourself?" he asked, his smarmy smile trying to give the impression that they were old friends.

In as few words as possible, Barbara told him that she was still working at the same place and that her mother had died more than a year ago. "Nothing much else has changed." At least nothing she wanted to discuss with him.

He flashed his most charming smile. "Well, I think you look wonderful. Why don't we have dinner some evening and catch up on old times?"

"I'm really quite busy these days," Barbara said, her fingernails digging into her palms.

"If you're still at the same place, I must still have your

number. I'll give you a call. I'm sure we can work something out. I really want to see you."

I don't want to see you, she thought. "I don't think it will work out," she said, turning her back and pushing her shopping cart toward the front of the store.

"Good, I'll call you."

"You know, Maggie, almost every sentence began with 'I.' He's such a prick."

"I wouldn't insult wonderful erect pricks like that," Maggie said with a twinkle in her eyes.

Barbara burst out laughing. "Thanks for that," she said. When she could talk again, she said, "I needed you to put everything back into perspective. God, he's such a jerk."

"He certainly sounds like one. But he did notice how wonderful you look." She winked. "He's obviously a very perceptive guy."

Barbara giggled as she considered how far she'd come. "I don't think I look that different," she said, "but I feel so differently about myself."

"That's so much a part of how you look. Confidence, a positive image of yourself, and, don't overlook the sensuality that's so much a part of you now."

"I guess Walt saw that," Barbara said. "He looked me over like I was the blue plate special. It made me want to punch his lights out, then take a shower."

"But does it still hurt? Think before you answer."

Barbara considered, then said, "Yes, I guess it does. But I'm so different now. It shouldn't hurt anymore, but when I saw him in the market, my stomach clenched and it was as though that evening happened only a day ago."

"Maybe you need to exorcize the evil spirits."

"I'd love to. But how?" Barbara asked, flexing her fingers to try to work out the sudden stiffness.

"Revenge is good for the soul occasionally," Maggie said. "Women have weapons, you know."

"I couldn't," Barbara said, her brain suddenly scrambling,

searching, planning. Maggie raised an eyebrow and Barbara smiled. "Could I?"

"This has to be your decision," Maggie said.

Barbara knew that this was, indeed, her decision. Could she do it? Even the few moments she had spent with Walt had done a job on the self-confidence she had built up over the last months. She thought about the men she saw now on a regular basis, Jay, CJ, and the others. What did they see when they looked at her?

The two women were silent for a long time, then Barbara sighed and silently nodded. She was not the same person Carl and Walt had humiliated that night years ago. She was happy, and, although she had yet to find someone who gave her everything she wanted in life, she knew that finding him was possible. And in the meantime she was having fun.

She nodded more strongly, then grinned. "I want to smash the slimy son of a bitch into pulp," Barbara said. "Starting with his overactive cock." She was quiet again, then said, "And I think I have the germ of an idea. Will you help me?"

"Do you need to ask?" Maggie said, her grin widening. The two women talked for hours until they had every aspect covered. All that remained was for Barbara to pick up a few items on her next visit to CJ's store.

The following evening Walt called, as Barbara had known he would. "Babs, I have been thinking a lot about you since we ran into each other the other day."

"And I've been think about you too, Walt," Barbara said, her voice soft and mellow.

"I was wondering about dinner on Saturday. I happen to be free and I thought we could talk about old times."

Old times indeed. The bastard acted as though they had had a wonderful, but unfortunately interrupted, dating relationship. She was spending the evening with CJ on Friday, so Saturday would work fine. "That should be all right for me," she said.

Walt sounded a bit taken aback as he said, "Sure. Great. I wasn't sure you'd be available."

"Well, you're in luck, Walt. How about the Peachtree Lounge?" she said, selecting the most expensive restaurant she could think of. She could almost picture Walt considering whether she might be worth a hundred-and-fifty-dollar dinner.

"Uh . . . okay. That's sounds fine."

He was hooked. "Can you pick me up about seven?" Barbara suggested. "You remember where I live, I'm sure. And will you make the reservation?"

"Of course. The man should make the reservations anyway. And let's make it seven-thirty on Saturday. I'll be looking forward to it."

Barbara bit the inside of her mouth to keep from laughing. Seven-thirty. She suspected that Walt had to make a point of making the decisions. "That's fine. I'll see you then."

On Saturday afternoon, Barbara settled into the tub and pulled out one of her favorite tapes. She played it and masturbated to several satisfying orgasms. As she dried herself off, her sensual awareness was at its height. She selected a new, basic black dress with deceptively sexual lines and spread it out on the bed. Surprised that Maggie wasn't here to help her, she picked out a black satin-and-lace teddy, thigh-high black stockings, and high-heeled black shoes. Heavy silver earrings and several bangle bracelets completed her outfit. She brushed her hair, then arranged it so, although it was high on her head, it was held with only three combs that could easily be removed. She used a curling iron so that the silver streak curved against her jaw and caressed her neck as she moved.

As she looked at herself in the full-length mirror, she knew she had created exactly the image she wanted. And without any help from Maggie. "Nice work," she told herself.

Walt rang the bell right on time. She opened a second-floor front window and called down, "The door's open. Make yourself comfortable and pour a drink if you like. I'll be down in a few moments." Although she was completely ready, she sat in her bedroom for almost half an hour. As she finally walked downstairs, Walt was pacing the living room. As he turned and saw her, his expression turned from annoyance to appreciation. "My God," he whispered. "Babs, you look . . ."

"Thanks," she said as she handed Walt her light jacket so he could drape it around her shoulders. She leaned back into him just slightly so he could inhale the exotic scent she had carefully applied behind her ears.

"I never imagined you could look like that," Walt said. "It's amazing."

"I thought a lot about you after we met last week and I realized that you never got to know the real me." She walked out the front door and locked it behind her. Walt walked around and got into the driver's seat of his Ford while Barbara opened her door and got into the passenger seat. As she fastened her seat belt, she allowed her skirt to slide up her thigh. She patted Walt's leg. "I think we're going to have an interesting evening."

They drove the short distance to the restaurant in silence. At the entrance, a valet opened her door and assisted her out, with an appreciative look. They entered the large room with a soft blue, nineteenth-century southern decor and were seated side by side on a blue-and-white patterned banquette. As they settled, Barbara reached over and grasped Walt's thigh, just above his knee. "I'm glad this evening is finally here."

Walt blinked his eyes several times and leered at her as the waiter arrived to take drink orders. "We would like a bottle of wine," he said without consulting Barbara. "White."

"I'd like to see the wine list," Barbara said.

"Of course, madam," the waiter said. "I'll send the sommelier over."

"I didn't know you knew anything about wine," Walt said.

Barbara thought about the financial analyst who had

taught her to appreciate fine wine. And a few other things as well. "There's a lot about me you don't know," she purred, wondering whether Walt would be sickened by the incredibly predictable dialogue.

He leaned forward, hanging on her every word. Beneath the tablecloth, he reached over and placed his hand on her stockinged knee. Rubbing her index finger up and down his inner thigh, she glared at him until he removed his hand. It had become clear that she could do what she wanted, but he had to keep his hands to himself. Slowly, she allowed herself a slow smile. "Later."

When Walt placed both his hands on the table, Barbara saw they were shaking.

"The wine list," the sommelier said, handing her a leather-covered tome.

"Goodness, this is quite a list," she said. She leaned forward so Walt could get a good view of her cleavage. "Walt, are you having beef, fish, chicken, what?"

She could see his gaze reluctantly rise from the shadowed valley between her breasts. "I thought I'd have a steak," he stammered.

"Good." Still caressing his thigh with one hand and holding the wine list with the other, she discussed the wine selection with the sommelier for almost five minutes.

"You have wonderful taste, madam," the sommelier said as she finally selected a 1984 California Cabernet from an obscure vineyard. "I'll get that right away."

As he disappeared, Barbara returned her attention to Walt. She licked her lips and watched his eyes follow the path of her tongue. "I hope you don't mind, but I found a wonderful wine at a ridiculous price. I'm sure it was a mistake on the list. Only thirty-five dollars. It should have been at least fifty."

Walt was in a daze and seemed not to hear anything Barbara said. Barbara talked and Walt listened through the pouring of the wine. Since Walt seemed incapable of concentrating, Barbara ordered the meal: a creamy carrot soup, sirloin steaks medium-rare with baked potatoes and sour cream, broccoli, and green salads with the house vinaigrette dressing.

During the meal, Walt spoke very little, totally distracted by the frequent presence of Barbara's hand on his leg. Her hands, her looks, her very posture were designed to keep him off-balance. Sensual, inviting, yet taking charge at every opportunity, she was creating exactly the atmosphere she wanted.

As the plates were cleared and the last of the wine poured, Walt said, "How about we go back to my place after? We could continue this wonderful evening there. I even put clean sheets on the bed."

Barbara bit her lip to keep from laughing. He still thinks he's choreographing this evening. "I have a better idea," she said. "I have some wonderful things to play with at my house."

"Oh" was all Walt could say.

"But let's have coffee first." Barbara let the tension build for another half an hour before she signaled for the check. Moments later, Walt signed the credit card slip.

They waited only a moment outside the restaurant as the valet got Walt's car. As the valet started to hand Barbara into the passenger side, she walked around to the driver's seat. "I think I'll drive. Okay, Walt?"

"Sure," Walt said hesitantly.

Barbara got behind the wheel and saw that Walt hadn't fastened his seat belt. "Here, let me help you." She leaned across Walt's body and, as Walt gazed down the front of her dress, she grasped the seat belt and pulled it across his chest and snapped it into place. "There," she said, patting his chest.

"But I'm caught," he said, realizing that his arms were trapped.

"I know," Barbara said, and tapped him on the chest again, "and I like it that way." She pressed her lips against his, licking the surprised 'O' his lips formed. He stopped trying to free his arms from beneath the belt, the tent in his slacks growing each minute.

Again in silence, they drove to Barbara's house and she let them in the front door. She remembered the first evening she had had a man in her house, her first evening with Jay. So much had changed. "Come upstairs with me," she said, "and let's have some fun."

Eagerly Walt followed her up the stairs and into her room. "Now," Barbara said, "I really like to play. And I think you do, too."

"Oh, I do," Walt said, unbuckling his belt.

"Not so fast," Barbara said, slapping his hands hard. "In here we do things my way." She watched Walt consider the situation. Would he go along? To increase his incentive, she licked her lips slowly, then reached out and squeezed the hard ridge in his pants. "It will be wonderful. I promise."

Walt dropped his hands to his sides. "I'm sure it will."

She was in control. When she had first thought up this idea, she had wondered whether she could pull it off. She had been very reluctant to assume control at CJ's party, but now it seemed comfortable. Different situations, different views, I guess. "Good boy," she said. "Now that we understand each other, strip."

"What?"

"You heard me. Strip."

"But . . ." He stared at her, obviously unsure.

Barbara met his eyes and tapped her toe on the carpet until Walt's gaze dropped to her shoes.

Awkwardly, without a word, Walt quickly pulled off all his clothes until he stood in the middle of Barbara's bedroom naked. He's actually not badly built, she thought, but she also noticed that his erection had softened. She wanted to keep him continually hard so he would do anything she wanted. She pulled the combs from her hair and shook out the dark mass, allowing it to fall around her face. She separated out the silver strands with her fingers and twisted them around her pinky.

"Let me give you a taste of what's to come," she said then. Still fully clothed, she quickly knelt at his feet and sucked his semi-erect cock into her mouth. He was hard again instantly.

After only a moment, she stood again and lifted her skirt. She motioned him to his knees and pulled the crotch of her teddy to one side. "Now lick me."

Eagerly he licked at the hot, wet places between Barbara's legs. Although he seemed to pay no attention to what pleased her, he did lick many of the places she enjoyed. She'd get hers this evening, she vowed, in more ways than one. "Use your hands, too," she said and felt his fingers probe her pussy. As she wiggled, his fingers slipped toward her anus. "Umm," she said, "I like it back there, too."

As she took her pleasure, she looked down and saw that Walt had one fist around his erection. She leaned over and slapped first his hand, then his cock. "Mine," she snapped. "And don't forget again."

"But . . ."

"No buts. Your hands and your cock are mine. Unless you want to leave, of course."

Walt groaned "No," and his shoulders sagged. He was hers.

"Good. Get on all fours. I like the feel of my pussy on your back."

Reluctantly Walt knelt on his hands and knees and Barbara stepped over him and rubbed her wet pussy on his spine. "It's like horseback riding," she said as she settled her weight on his back. "It always gets me hot." She had never been on a horse in her life, but it sounded good. "Move underneath me," she said. He moved a bit and she purred, "Mmmm, that's good." Slowly he seemed to get into the game and began to arch his back and wiggle his hips so his spine rubbed against Barbara's wet lips.

"You are very good at this," she said. She dismounted, reached beneath him and squeezed his cock. "And you certainly seem to enjoy it." She left for a moment, and returned with a tube of lubricant. "I love hard cocks," she said, rubbing the cold gel all over his erection and balls. "You feel so hot, so hard. I've never known anyone so hard."

She watched him preen, the oily bastard. Still rubbing his cock with one hand, she slid one finger of the other to the sensitive area behind his balls and stroked. Gradually, her caresses worked her fingers closer to his anus. "So hot, baby," she purred as she rubbed his puckered hole. She had no idea whether he'd ever done anything like this before, but whether or not he was experienced, he seemed to be enjoying her ministrations. She lightened her touch on his cock so he wouldn't come just yet.

"A horse needs a tail," she said, "and I have just the thing." She quickly found an anal plug with a slender neck just below the flange and a dozen strands of leather attached to the base. She imagined that some used the dildo end as a handle for the whip, but she knew what she wanted to do with the device.

Still on all fours, Walt looked at the item in Barbara's hand. "You're not going to hurt me with that, are you?" he said.

"No, baby," she said, rubbing her slippery hand over the flesh-colored plastic handle. "I am going to fill you as you may never have been filled before."

"I don't know," he said.

Barbara looked at his cock, now harder than ever.

"Yes, you do. It's dirty and evil, but the idea of having something invade your ass excites you." She leaned beneath his groin and rubbed his swollen cock. "You can't fool me, so don't try. Just be quiet and let me do this."

Walt shuddered but remained silent. Gently Barbara massaged Walt's rear hole with the tip of the dildo, then pushed it inch-by-inch into his rear passage. When it was deep inside, held by his tight sphincter, the leather strips made it look as though her horse indeed had a tail.

Again Barbara straddled Walt's back, undulating so her pussy rubbed against his heated flesh. "Such a good mount," she said, gazing off into the corner. She reached into her crotch and fingered her clit. "Ummm," she purred loudly. "Good horsy. Buck for me, horsy."

Walt arched his back and, with only a few more strokes, Barbara came, her wetness soaking Walt's skin.

"When does it get to be my turn?" he moaned.

Barbara caught her breath, then stood up and crossed the room. She pressed a few buttons on a small remote control, then flipped on the TV. "We'll see what you want after you've watched this hot video." She pressed the remote's rewind button then pressed play.

After a moment of snow, the image of Walt on his knees before Barbara filled the screen. Staring at the sight of his head moving against her crotch and hearing the sounds of her purrs and his pleased grunts, Walt stood up and walked, naked, toward the TV. As Walt watched himself get down in his hands and knees, he growled, "You taped the entire thing?" He reached behind him and yanked the dildo from his ass, his face turning bright red.

"The entire thing," Barbara said. She pressed fast-forward, then slowed the picture again as a clear shot of Walt, with the tail hanging from his rear, filled the screen. The camera zoomed in on the dildo in Walt's ass.

"How did you get it to zoom like that? Shit. Someone must have been holding the camera."

Maggie had been controlling the camera at that moment, but Walt would never know or understand that. Barbara let the tape play for another few moments. Then she said, "Now, go home."

Walt's breathing was raspy and his entire body shook. His eyes wildly searched the room. "How? Why?"

Barbara slowly shook her head. "You poor, stupid bastard. You don't even remember the trick you and your friend Carl played on me several years ago. The car? The camera?" She watched as recognition slowly changed his expression. "Good. I see you remember now. That was me. And you humiliated me in ways you couldn't even imagine." She smiled ruefully. "And you didn't even remember it."

"Okay. I'm sorry," Walt said as he pulled on his pants. "Really. I am. Now give me that tape." He prowled the room looking for the camera.

"I'm sure you are sorry. Now. But sorry isn't enough. Be a good boy and get out of here."

"Not without that film"

"The film is only part of it. The friend who helped me with the camera also took lots of still pictures. Like the ones you took of me that night. Those photos of you and your lovely tail are long gone." There were no such pictures, but Walt would never know that.

Walt stopped searching the room and pulled on his shirt and jacket. "What are you going to do with them?"

"Actually, nothing." She retrieved the camera from its hiding place behind some ferns on her wardrobe and pulled out the cassette. "You didn't do anything with the photos you took that night, so here . . ." She handed the cassette to Walt. "I'll hold on to the stills. Just having them is a symbol of something for me."

"You won't show them around?" Walt said, stuffing the cassette into his jacket pocket.

"No. Unless you get out of line, that is. So run along. Go home." She thought about the condition of his deflated cock and what she hoped were very uncomfortable balls. "And jerk off."

Walt stared at her for a long moment, then shook his head. "Amazing," he said. "Just amazing." She left, and Barbara heard him pound down the stairs and slam the front door behind him.

"It's all gone," Barbara said to Maggie later that evening. "All that leftover anger and frustration are gone. I don't even hate the poor slob anymore."

"I'm glad. Did he believe you about the still pictures?"

"He did. Just like I expected him to. Thanks for aiming the camera for me. I didn't even mind it that you were watching."

"I only watched for a few minutes." She patted Barbara's hand. "You were great."

"It all felt good. And maybe Walt will think twice before he plays tricks on women again."

"I hope so. What's up for you now?"

"Just more of life, I guess," Barbara said, stretching out of the bed in her bathrobe. "I saw a T-shirt recently. It said, 'So many men and so little time.' "

Maggie laughed. "Well, babe, I've got to go."

"Okay. See you soon."

"Yeah," Maggie said, knowing it was a lie.

Maggie pushed through the revolving door and, as she thought she would, ended up in the computer room, wearing the soft white gown she had been wearing on her first visit. This was it, she knew. Up or down. And how had she done? She didn't really know.

"And we don't know either," Lucy said, as always reading her mind.

"Yes, we know you did your job," Angela said.

"And you did it well," Lucy chimed in.

"But the outcome is not quite what either of us anticipated," Angela added.

"Outcome?" Maggie said, making herself comfortable in a chair facing the women's desk.

"Oh, that's right," Angela said. "You left Barbara after her evening with Walt."

"That was seven months ago," Lucy said.

"Seven months? Oh," Maggie said. "It's funny. I miss her even though it seems only a moment ago."

"Well, once we knew you were gone permanently, we fixed it so she wouldn't miss you."

"Fixed it?"

"We erased you," Lucy said.

"You what!" Maggie yelled, jumping from her chair. "You erased me?"

Angela walked around the desk and patted Maggie's shoulder, pushing her back down into her chair. "Lucy's got the tact of a wart hog, and that's an insult to wart hogs. But try to understand." A chair appeared beside Maggie and Angela sat down, arranging her wings carefully behind her. "We couldn't let her remember you. She had come so far and missing you would have only depressed her. And she needed to remember all her changes as her own doing. It was the final step in her lessons."

"And after all," Lucy said, "how could she have explained you?"

"But . . ."

"Sweetie," Angela said, still patting Maggie's shoulder. "You really do understand."

Maggie sighed. "I guess I do. It just makes me sad." She sniffed and a lace hanky appeared in her hand.

"I know," Angela continued. "But she's doing so well now."

"Really? What's she doing?"

Lucy picked up the story. "She's got a boyfriend. Full time. They are thinking about moving in together. Barbara met him just after that evening with Walt. He's a banker and went to her boss about some legal matters. They met and hit it off immediately, both as friends and hot lovers. For a long while they dated, but continued to see other people. Now they've become exclusive and they're very happy."

"That's wonderful." Maggie wondered why she felt so empty. It was nice when Barbara needed her, looked to her for guidance, learned from her. Now her job was done and it was a letdown. She blew her nose.

"I know it's a letdown," Angela said, "but you can relish the fact that you did a super job."

"Would you like to see them, her and her boyfriend?" Lucy asked. "I can tune you in if you like."

"Not in the bedroom," Maggie said, curious to see the ending to Barbara's story. "I don't want to eavesdrop."

Lucy's fingers danced over the computer keyboard. "Not at all. They're out for the evening at a little place they frequent." She turned the monitor so Maggie could see.

In the picture, a couple danced, their bodies close. Barbara leaned against the man who held her, her mouth beside his ear. "I just love slow dancing," she whispered. "It's like making love standing up."

They turned so Maggie could see the man's face. "That's

Paul!" she cried. "That's the guy I was on the phone with that last night. That's my Paul."

"That's her Paul now, and they're blissfully happy," Angela said.

Maggie caught her breath. Paul. She had really loved him, she realized. She gazed at him for a while, getting pleasure from the obvious joy on his face. Maggie sighed and smiled. "We could never have been happy together," she said. "He was a banker and I was a prostitute. It would never have worked." She watched the screen.

Paul spoke into Barbara's ear. "You know, every time you talk about slow dancing, I remember a woman I once knew. Her name was Maggie and it was very long ago. I loved her."

"Do you still love her?" Barbara asked.

"She's been dead for a couple of years. I just remember her fondly. She always liked slow dancing."

"I vaguely remember someone named Maggie in my past, too. I don't remember when I knew her, but I get warm feelings when I think of her."

Paul pressed his hand into the small of Barbara's back, moving his body still closer to hers. "I like warm feelings. Let's go back to your place and feel warm all over."

As Lucy turned off the image on the computer screen, Maggie brushed a tear from her face. "I'm happy for them. I really am."

"I know you are, dear," Angela said, rising and circling the desk again. "But that still leaves us with the problem of what to do with you."

"Yes," Lucy said. "We're still confused."

"We had a bet about how this would end up."

"And we can't even decide who won."

Lucy leaned over and whispered animatedly to Angela. Although Maggie couldn't hear the words, it was obvious from the body language that the two women were arguing. Hands flew through the air, Lucy's tail swished, and at one point Angela's wings flapped and she rose several feet into the air.

Finally Lucy said, "That's the only answer."

"I think so."

"Well," Maggie said, realizing that her fate for the remainder of all time was being decided, "have you figured it all out?"

"Actually, no," Angela said. "But what about you? Where do you think you belong?"

"I don't know either. Heaven sounds real nice, I guess, but maybe a bit dull."

"Well, I have no complaints," Angela said, looking offended.

"I didn't mean to be insulting," Maggie said quickly. "I'm sure it's a lot of fun once you get used to it. But I'm not accustomed to sitting around all day discussing philosophy."

"See, I told you," Lucy said. "My place is much more interesting."

"Yes, I'm sure it is, but I'm not sure I want to associate with the people who go . . ." Maggie pointed her thumb downward.

"Shows you have good taste," Angela said. "And I think Lucy and I have arrived at a solution, at least for the short run."

"How would you like to be an operative for us?" Lucy continued. "You would just do more of what you did with Barbara. Fix up people's lives."

"Like Michael Landon in *Highway to Heaven*?"

Angela nodded. "Maybe, but on a more earthy level. You know, teaching people to love making love."

"Teaching people to love to fuck," Lucy said, turning to Angela, a mischievous grin on her face.

Angela hurumphed, and looked seriously at Maggie. "Would you do that? We've got a lot of cases like Barbara's waiting for someone like you."

Maggie swallowed her tears and thought about Barbara and Paul. Then she considered the offer for only a moment. "I think I'd like that."

"Good," Angela and Lucy said simultaneously.

"Okay. And this time, how about giving me some powers. You know, like *the stuff* Michael Landon had."

"We'll see as the situation arises," Angela said.

"Now, come over here. I want to show you a woman named Pam." Lucy's fingers flew over the keyboard. "She's a tough one."

Maggie swiped a tear from her cheek. The girls were right. Barbara and Paul would be so good together. But it was hard to grasp that that part of her life was over. Maggie circled the table and stood behind Lucy. "That's her?"

"That's Pam. She's almost forty, divorced and dumpy."

"She must weight over two fifty."

"Aren't you the one who believes that sensuality is as much a product of the look in the eyes as the body behind it?"

Maggie drummed her fingers on the back of Lucy's chair. "I hate hearing my own words thrown back at me," she said, "and you're right, of course. Anyone can be sensual."

"She really needs your kind of help," Angela said.

Maggie took a deep breath. "Okay, when do I start?"

Dear Reader,

Wouldn't you have loved to have someone like Maggie around when you needed help with your love life? I would have. But, like you, I muddled through and managed to have a lot of fun while doing so. If you enjoyed *Slow Dancing*, you might want to read my other erotic novels, *Black Satin*, and *The Pleasures of JessicaLynn*.

Please drop me a line and let me know which parts of the book you enjoyed most so I can include more of the same types of encounters in my next book. And please visit my web site at **http://www.JoanELloyd.com.** You can learn more about me, read more delicious erotica, and read some tips for enhancing your love life.

If you write to me, I will also put you on my mailing list so I can keep you informed about new books and other projects. E-mail or snail mail, I look forward to hearing from you at:

Joan Elizabeth Lloyd
P.O. Box 221
Yorktown Heights, NY 10598

JoanELloyd@AOL.com